For the Birds

For the Birds

a romance

Tara L. Roí

Bee

Bee Books
New Haven

FOR THE BIRDS. Copyright © 2018 by Tara L. Roí
All rights reserved. Printed in the United States of America
For information, visit BeeBooks.org

The Library of Congress Cataloging-in-Publication Data
is available upon request.

ISBN 978-1-7326187-7-0 (hardcover)
ISBN 978-1-7326187-6-3 (paperback)
ISBN 978-1-7326187-8-7 (e-book)

First edition: February 2020

Dedication

For the Beloved. And of course, for MacKenzie.

Chapter 1

Ocean Falls, Delaware

Teddy hopped from one foot to the other, his little voice squeaking in excitement. "Why do they call it graduate?"

"Ummm," Claire pulled her bike out from under the stairwell and lifted the flap for the bike trailer so her little boy could climb in. "Well…"

"Who is Grad, and why did you eat him?"

"What?" Claire laughed. "I didn't eat anyone. Silly!"

Teddy let out a happy giggle and settled himself into the trailer, wrapping his body in his superhero cape. "Get it? Grad. You. Ate. That was a good joke, huh, Mama?"

"They're getting better and better, Hon," she said, ruffling his curls. "Honey, sit back. I can't get the straps."

He was small for his five years. Still, Claire realized he probably wouldn't fit into the trailer much longer.

An image of the two of them riding around town on a tandem flashed through her mind.

"What will your job be after you graduate, Mama?"

The question stung. What *would* she do?

"Will you work at the gallery with me and Grandma?"

"Remember, Grandma's closing the gallery soon, Sweetheart?"

"Oh, yeah." Teddy's face fell. "Why does she want to get tired again?"

"Retired, honey." Claire made the final clicks on Teddy's harness straps, hopped onto her bike and pedaled away. *So many transitions; mom retiring, me graduating, Teddy starting kindergarten in the fall. Me starting my exciting career with wildlife, I hope.* Claire's thoughts shifted when she noticed the cottonwood trees budding along Main Street and the flowers on the ground. *Finally.* She pointed to the native blue-eyed grass they had planted in the curb-strips, and yelled over her shoulder, "Teddy, do you see how our flowers are growing?"

"Yay!"

The wisteria vines, Claire's favorite even though they were not indigenous, were starting to leaf out, too. She inhaled deeply, enjoying the mix of salt and sweet floral in the air. "Do you smell the trumpet honeysuckle we planted, Sweetheart?"

"Is that the hungry smell?"

"Yup," she laughed. *The hungry smell. So cute.*

At the corner, Claire turned left onto Beach Road/Route 13 East, the two-lane highway leading to their favorite spot.

"Mama, this is the wrong way!"

"We're going to the beach before graduation, remember? Are you excited to see the horseshoe crabs?" Claire needed to see the horseshoe crabs, breathe the ocean air, and maybe even try to meditate for a minute. She was, she told herself, excited about giving the speech at graduation — not scared, not stressed, excited. A strange tension gripped her body. If she was honest with herself, she was actually feeling stressed, but she had learned to reframe "Stress" as excitement. It felt better, more manageable that way. Excited. Yes. And she was so excited she just needed to relax for a few minutes before the big event. *Totally normal.* She took a deep yoga breath and let it out slowly, as much as that was possible while pedaling a bicycle with a trailer holding a thirty-five-pound kid.

The scent of saltwater and seaweed filled Claire's nostrils as she pulled her bike into the parking lot at the beach recreation area.

A bright orange jeep-thing sat in the usually empty lot. A gas guzzler; it had to be a guy who owned it.

Still panting slightly, Claire unhooked Teddy's straps, then reached into her pocket and interlaced her keys between her fingers, like she had learned in self-defense.

"Good morning."

A man's soft voice sent ripples up Claire's spine. *Stay calm,* she told herself, turning quickly toward the sound. He was tall, maybe six-one, with sandy blonde curls like Teddy's, dark brown eyes, and a trim build. Why was he wearing a flannel shirt and cargo pants in this heat? Claire nodded at him, her face expressionless, her body shielding Teddy, hoping the guy would get the hint, hoping that he wasn't some creep.

"Last day before this place closes for shorebird nesting," he said.

"Yup." Claire maintained her stance, ready for anything. *Can he see me shaking?*

"Well, enjoy!" He said and hopped into his gas guzzler.

Claire exhaled and shook out her body. Not off to a good start, but as the jeep-thing left the parking lot, Claire felt herself relax. She looked past the high shrubs and beach roses at the sand and saw several horseshoe crabs near piles of greenish, jelly-like eggs. Some of the crabs were slowly making their way to the water. Others were flipped onto their backs.

"Look, Sweetie, there they are!"

"Where?"

"Take my hand; I'll show you." Claire pointed at the crabs, and she and Teddy stepped onto the soft sand.

"Those greenish hats?"

"They do look like hats, don't they?"

"They don't look like dinosaurs," Teddy said, sounding confused.

"I know it, but they are the last living dinosaur on earth. Come on, you can help me flip them."

"How long are they visiting?"

"About a month to lay their eggs, then they'll go back into the ocean."

"Why?"

"Because that's what they do. Do you remember how we helped them last year, too?"

Teddy shook his head, no.

"Oh. Well, you were still only four, but you're a big boy now. Ready to help? Watch me first, please."

"Okay."

"See how I pick up the crab by its sides, not by its tail?"

Teddy nodded, his eyes wide.

"Good, and then I just gently turn her slowly, so she doesn't get nervous, and I lower her back onto the sand."

"She looks scary, Mama."

"I know, but guess what? Horseshoe crabs are actually very gentle creatures and do not bite."

"Really?"

"Really. Come on, here's a little one you can help." Claire led Teddy to a small crab lying on the sand. "Ready?"

Teddy stared at it. "How come they're upside down?"

"Sometimes, the waves are so forceful, they flip the crabs right over onto their backs."

Teddy looked at her for reassurance. She nodded, and he reached for the crab.

"That's it! One hand on each side. Good job, Honey. Lift her up. That's right, now slowly flip her over."

"Ahh, Mama."

"I know her legs are going everywhere, but it's okay. She's just scared. Are you okay?"

"Yeah."

"Okay. Good. Just lower her onto the sand. Yes. Good job! Yay! You saved your first horseshoe crab of the year, Super Teddy, Wildlife Hero!" Claire clapped. "Wanna come back tomorrow and do it again?"

Teddy jumped up and did his special superhero happy dance, flapping his cape around himself.

"Okay, then! Let's go home and get cleaned up for graduation. Remember, you get to sit in the front row with Grandma and Grandpa."

Claire trembled as she ascended the stairs. There was a time, years ago, when she gave presentations to investment groups, boards of directors, CEOs, and felt confident. Those occasions felt like another lifetime. Now, as she nodded to each of the faculty members on the outdoor stage, steadied herself against the podium, and turned to face the rest of her graduating class in the enormous quadrangle where all of the college's big functions occurred, Claire was almost overcome by nausea.

She inhaled deeply through her nostrils and exhaled slowly until her belly pressed against her spine. *Steady*, she told herself, thinking of tree pose. *Stable*. Claire scanned the front row until she saw her parents beaming proudly at her. Her mother's long teal skirt draped around her ankles; copper bracelets jangled as she lifted her hand to wave at Claire. At 63, Jane Dessalines always managed to look elegant, trim, and otherworldly, as if she'd stepped out of a Lippincott painting — a magical fairy, with a Tinkerbelle figure, purple died hair, artisan jewelry, and flowing garments of silk chiffon and crepe. Claire sometimes felt like an Amazon next to her tiny, gorgeous mother. Now, Jane brought her hands to her cheeks, the signal that she was excited by something — most likely the fact that Claire was about to give a speech. Next to Jane, Frank sat tall and robust, his blue eyes sparkling at her. He was Claire's hero, both literally and figuratively, and even now, Claire couldn't help wanting to impress her father. He winked at her and put his free arm around Teddy, who was waving happily, swinging his dangling feet in the air below the seat. Claire winked at her son, wiggled her first two fingers; he did the same — their unique signal for "I Love You."

The applause died down, and Claire began:

"As you enter the real world, most of you for the first time, I want you to ask yourself: How do you measure success? I always wanted to protect wildlife, but when I was younger, didn't have the courage to pursue my dreams. I took the safe route, earned my B.A. in finance, and went to work for one of the top investment firms in Boston. By many people's standards, I was a success — earning great money, making my clients happy, but the work turned my stomach. Despite my efforts to steer clients toward eco-friendly investment options, one after another wanted to take the safe bet and invest in fossil fuels. They made a killing — in every sense of the word. The cost to the planet, to wildlife, and to people in the most remote, environmentally intact areas was much steeper than the financial reward my clients got for their investments. Look at the polar bear, or at our local horseshoe crabs! Bill McKibben said if it's wrong to wreck the climate, it's wrong to profit from that wreckage. But try to tell someone making fifteen percent on their two-million-dollar investment that there's another way; a way that might earn them only eleven percent but won't be so destructive… Their measure for success is skewed. Don't let yours be."

She paused and let the applause wash over her. "Five years ago, I had the opportunity to reconsider my path. That led me here to earn a second dual bachelor's in Environmental Policy and Wildlife Biology. Along the way, I have been inspired by some amazing teachers and by many of you, and I've learned two important lessons."

"One: It's never too late to follow your dreams. I'm thirty-three and just finishing my B.A. To make the impact I want in the field of Wildlife Preservation and Rehabilitation, I'm going to need to earn my Ph.D., take some internships, and hopefully get a few paying jobs along the way. By the time I really start my career, I'll be forty."

She shuddered dramatically and got a laugh.

"My son will be a teenager then, maybe starting to think about his own career. Some of my friends from high school will be thinking about early retirement, and I'll just be getting my feet on the ground. But so, what? I'd rather work toward something meaningful than watch the clock until I retire. Wouldn't you?"

A murmur of assent rippled through the crowd. Claire continued to read, lifting her gaze to connect with different people in the audience. People looked stunned, but at least she wasn't putting them to sleep. One person seemed wide awake, fully engaged, maybe even fascinated. He was leaning against a tree. Was that who she thought it was? She scanned the crowd and inhaled deeply, preparing to launch into lesson two. Her eyes returned to the man standing against the tree. What was he doing here? Momentarily thrown, she stumbled over the next few words:

"I, uh, finally." She paused, took a deep breath to regain her composure, refocused on the page in front of her: "The web of life isn't some kumbaya hippie idea — it's scientific fact. We are at a tipping point in the history of the world! Whatever profession you're entering, you have the power to promote environmental harmony, and you must. This is the only action that will matter in the long run. If you and I don't act, we'll all be stuck on an overheated, overpopulated, miserable wasteland. We humans are interdependent with each other, with the millions of wildlife and plant species on the planet, and with the planet itself. Conquering nature was an old school measure of success that actually led to the biggest failure humanity has ever created — climate disruption and wildlife degradation. Today, and in the foreseeable future, real success is something we can only achieve together, each of us doing our part to stop climate disruption. If you haven't already started, begin today — empower yourself with knowledge and then act on it. It's not too late… yet."

Claire let the idea hang in the air, then bowed to the audience, said, "Thank you," and left the stage to a moment of stunned silence, followed by whooping and wild applause. Her legs wobbled as she made her way to her seat. Before she reached it, a hand gripped her shoulder. The Dean of Students beamed a smile at her, his eyes warm with affection. "Claire, come back up and take a bow. They're clapping for you."

Feeling awkward, she turned and followed the dean back to the dais. When she arrived on stage and looked out, she saw hundreds of people cheering and standing, at first one-by-one, then in a wave. Stunned, Claire spoke into the microphone.

"Thank you. And congratulations! Now it's time to go out and be the success the world needs you to be… but no pressure!"

Two hours later, when the ceremony had ended, and Claire was reunited with her family, she was still shaking. *Adrenaline,* she thought. Holding Teddy soothed her fragile nerves as she accepted praise and congratulations from her parents, friends, professors, and complete strangers. It was both overwhelming and comforting. On the one hand, Claire felt like her old self—comfortable in a crowd. In another sense, she felt vulnerable, exposed, exhausted, and eager to get away. That's when he appeared at her side.

"Strong words, Ms. Dessalines!" His voice reverberated through her body. She recognized him immediately, the guy she'd seen at the beach that morning and in the audience leaning against the tree.

"Umm. Thank you," she said, moving closer to her parents.

"You probably don't remember me. We ran into each other this morning."

"At the beach, yes. What are you doing here?"

"I teach here."

She raised an eyebrow. It was a small school; she'd never seen him on campus. Plus, all the professors had been on stage with her, in their graduation gowns and poufy hats.

"Well, I'll start teaching here in the fall," he said, his mouth curved into a smile. "Intro to Environmental Science."

"Huh. Really." Alarm bells were starting to ring in Claire's head. She was safe now, with her parents right there and hundreds of people around, but—

"Brian Melodus," he said, jutting out his hand. "I also work for Flora and Fauna."

Claire could feel her lips sliding into a disbelieving sneer. "Don't you people normally wear badges or something?"

"Uh…"

This man was way too friendly.

"Helloooo, Brian! What are you doing here?" Her father's deep voice boomed.

"You know each other?"

"Claire Bear, this is the guy I was telling you about. The one I helped rent Jake's place."

Claire Bear. Thanks, Dad. Claire scowled at her father, but he winked at her, his tanned face brightened by his smile and extra white teeth.

She forced a response, "Aha."

"I tell you what, Brian, this beautiful young woman is all work and no play. She needs to get out of the house if you know what I—"

Claire cleared her throat, felt her cheeks burn. "Okay, Dad. I can arrange my own social life, thank you."

"Did I overstep? Janie, did I overstep?"

"What?" Claire's mother shifted her attention from an old friend she'd run into to Claire's face, then turned and shot a playful scowl up at her husband. "What did you do now, Frank?"

Jane slid her hand onto Frank's rear end and tapped it. In public. They had no shame, those two. Had Brian seen it?

Claire lifted her eyes to his face. Brian met her gaze, eyes sparkling, fingers pressed to his lips as if he was stifling a laugh. Sure, the guy was cute. Beyond cute. He opened his mouth to speak, and, for the third time that day, she felt ripples running up her spine.

He was totally her type — the hair, the eyes, the lashes that would make any woman envious, the full lips. He had a trim build, and he wasn't too tall, just a few inches above her height, just tall enough to—

What the hell was she thinking? Granted, she'd gone years without sex. She hadn't even wanted it for a while, and... Anyway, single parenting was practically a vow of celibacy. What was she supposed to think? Was this guy safe or not? Sure, he was laughing silently with her, but all that meant was he had a sense of humor. Assholes laughed, too.

Knowing her father, he had vetted the guy, done a full search on him to make sure he'd pay the rent, didn't have any major outstanding debts or legal problems. Still, anyone could be a predator, even seemingly nice guys with credit scores above 760 and millions in the bank. Especially seemingly nice guys. *This man is too friendly, Claire. He's suspect, not someone to fantasize about.* His lips stopped moving. She hadn't heard a word he had said, and now he was looking at her expectantly.

"Mama, I'm hungry."

Claire shifted Teddy to her other hip. "Okay, Sweetheart. We'll go in a minute."

"Hey, uh, I'd love to speak with you about something I'm working on," Brian said.

"Oh?"

"I was impressed by your speech, and with what your dad tells me about your achievements... It's got me thinking: maybe you'd be perfect to help me prep for my fall class."

"How?"

"Can we discuss it over coffee next week?"

Claire lifted her eyebrow. Was this a come-on? *Coffee...* It sure seemed like one. On the other hand, if Brian were for real, then it would be a fantastic opportunity to help a professor working on environmental issues to prep for his class.

Brian reached into his wallet, a cool upcycled thing that seemed to be made from an old seatbelt, and pulled out a card.

"Massachusetts Flora and Fauna?" Claire asked.

"Just moved, as your dad mentioned. I should be getting my cards for the new job with Delaware Flora and Fauna soon. Meantime, my cell # is on this card, and that won't change. And you know where I live, so..." He let his voice trail off, then laughed awkwardly. "That came out wrong."

His face flushed, and he shook his head.

Hmmm, she thought.

Chapter 2

B rian struggled with the last box. What in the world had he put in it? Stephanie was right; he should have labeled the contents as well as the room. He stumbled over the stone threshold into the bungalow, stopped for breath, and lowered the box onto the kitchen table, still marveling at the deal. Thanks to Frank, he was renting a $500,000 solar-powered, geo-thermally heated three-bedroom beach house for less than he had paid to rent the one-bedroom oil-heated condo in Cape Cod. Two bedrooms downstairs, an updated kitchen and sun porch, plus a master bedroom upstairs, and a wraparound deck. Of course, he didn't need all that space. But maybe someday… The kicker was the setting — on a double lot with views of the wildlife refuge from the second-floor deck. The short walk to the beach would be great on those days when he didn't need to bring equipment. If only he had someone to enjoy this with. The phone rang. He fished it from his pocket, looked at the screen. Steph.

"Hey, Sis."

"Hey, Bro. How's the move?"

"Waylaid by some work stuff, but I'm about to start unpacking."

"You sound out of breath."

"I overpacked some of the boxes."

"I warned you."

"Yes, you did. Listen, this place is gorgeous and huge. Four bedrooms. You guys have to come visit."

"Delaware, huh?"

"It's on the beach."

"How romantic!"

"Sure is." Brian looked around the living room until he spied his bottle of water on the coffee table then collapsed onto the couch.

"Aww. I hear the loneliness in your voice, Brian."

"Yeah."

"You're in a new place with new faces. Why don't you start dating again?"

He sighed. They'd had this conversation too often in the last couple of years. "I will."

"I'm sorry. I shouldn't have brought it up. You'll know when the time is right." Steph made that clucking sound she always did with her tongue when expressing sympathy. "She was a good woman. You two were great together."

"She was," Brian said, feeling almost as if Adrienne were sitting next to him on the couch, her hand on his thigh, looking over his shoulder at the Ocean Falls welcome packet Frank had left behind. It used to annoy him sometimes, the way Adrienne read over his shoulder. The last three years, he would have given anything… and now… it was time to move on. He sighed again and lifted the brochure, so it caught the light from the window.

"Bring my little buddies up here. I can take them birding, maybe mini-golfing. The realtor left a welcome packet, and there's a coupon: two-for-one at Putt-n-Pup."

"That's cute."

"I miss you guys."

"We miss you, too. It was so easy to visit when you lived one state away."

"Delaware isn't that much farther from you than Massachusetts! Besides, it's healthy for the kids to see new places."

"Brian, Mom's off the rails again."

"What now?"

"I guess dementia affects depth perception, so she's been trying to walk around the center, but she keeps freaking out thinking she's going to fall off a cliff or something."

.

His chest tightened. "Oh, God. I'm sorry to leave you with that."

"Well, Dad's here, too. And Rob is always a great support."

"Thankfully."

"Anyway, someone needs to go out and save the world. And you're the only one of us who's qualified."

"Aww, shucks. Ain't nothin'." He said, quoting that old Western spoof they'd loved as kids.

"Ain't nothin'? Why my big brother's the hero we all been waitin' for."

"Alright, Sis. I'm gonna run. I'm not kidding. Talk to Rob. When do the kids get out of school?"

"Mid-June."

"Great. I'll see you then. Love you."

He hung up. Steph was right. *New place. New Start.*

Huh, Brian thought as he pulled into the parking lot of the rundown industrial park. *Can't say the state of Delaware is overspending on its environmental program.* He parked next to a beat-up Ford F-150 pickup and strode to the trailer with the broken sign marked "Delaware Flora and Fauna Serv. Field Office." Shadows stood in where the letters i-c-e had once been on the end of the word Service. The hinges on the door squeaked. Passing the empty cubicle marked Reception, he walked down the narrow aisle, noting a musty odor, and rapped on the entrance to Arthur Tetreault's cubicle.

A grunting sound rose from the floor. Brian looked down and saw Arthur wrapping duct tape around the leg of his wooden desk, getting his long gray ponytail caught in the tape.

"Am I early?"

"Oh, you caught me in the process of fixing my desk."

"With man's *real* best friend."

"Such is the state of affairs for Division of Flora and Fauna's Species Conservation and Research Program, Brian," Arthur said, as he pulled his hair away from the duct tape, and rubbed the end of the tape onto the leg of the desk. He stood, flashed

Brian a sardonic smile as he jutted out his hand. "Good to see you again. I hope what you've just witnessed doesn't send you running back to Massachusetts."

"Not a chance. Besides, up in Mass, we didn't even have money for duct tape. This is luxury."

Arthur laughed. "The move go okay?"

"Indeed."

"And when do you start teaching?"

"Early September."

"Great. Great. That's smart of you to take the teaching position as well as this — maybe you'll actually earn enough to buy groceries."

"My thoughts exactly, plus, you know, the whole *man on a mission* thing."

"My God, are you in the right place. We are a tad overwhelmed, what with managing nearly 50,000 acres of land providing habitat for—"

Brian's heart raced as he envisioned himself working in Delaware's wild areas, observing, cataloging, protecting over 800 species of wild plants, animals, fish, insects, and rare flora and fauna. He scanned the photos of some of Delaware's wild spaces lining one wall of Arthur's cubicle.

Arthur continued, "Somehow, we also managed to spearhead important wildlife and habitat conservation and education initiatives, including your new baby, the Wildlife Species Conservation and Research Program, and the Delaware Shorebird Project. I can't tell you how thrilled I am that you will be taking this over."

Brian smiled as energy coursed through his muscles. He could not wait to get into the field.

"We've had some big successes in the last ten years, and I was sad to see your predecessor move on, but you know — it's good to get fresh blood in once in a while, fresh ideas, fresh eyes. You know what I'm saying."

Brian nodded, letting his eyes scan the map on the wall next to him. *How many times have Arthur's eyes scanned this map, looking for the next area for restoration?*

"So, I expect you'll hit the ground running tomorrow. You already have the maps of our locations? Good. You've met with your key colleagues. You'll rarely see each other, but at least you know they're there. These will get you into the equipment buildings," he said, jingling the keys as he handed them over. "Take whatever you need, make sure you log it. If there's anything we don't have, you can put in a request form with the Receptionist, once we get one. Until then, you can just give it to me, and I'll lose it."

Brian laughed.

"But I'll make sure you get reimbursed."

"I know the drill."

"Great! How about lunch? There's a great little Mexican place down the street."

Brian stepped aside to let Arthur lead the way out.

"When do you want my action plan?" he asked, shielding his eyes from the sun.

"ASAP," Arthur said. "Of course, we already have our ten-year plan in place, so what I need from you is the detailed breakdown of how you intend to implement that. We've got all these citizen scientists mobilized right now, and it's a solid program, but you do need to keep an eye on them. There are rogues out there who think they're doing the world a service."

"They're everywhere, Arthur… Oh, the F-150 is yours."

"Like my desk, held together with duct tape. Is that Land Rover yours?"

"A gift from my dad."

"It's in mint condition!" Arthur followed Brian to the Rover and examined the body, then turned sheepishly toward Brian. "May I?"

Brian nodded. "My dad fixes and restores cars. Downside is, our front yard always looked like a junkyard. Upside is—"

Arthur opened the passenger door and ran his hand over the seatback. "Is this hemp upholstery?"

Brian nodded.

"And a wooden gearbox and console?"

"Reclaimed wood from a tree that fell in the Norwalk River."

Arthur let out a low whistle.

Brian let his hand rest on the hood, remembering the pride in his father's face when he lifted the hood and showed him the upgraded fuel filter he'd installed.

"Biodiesel all the way, huh Kid," he'd said.

"Aw, this is amazing, Dad!"

The afternoon sunlight made the Rover's orange paint glow. Outside the yoga studio, people stared. It was embarrassing. Brian would have preferred not to get so much attention for his vehicle. But he had never dreamed of trading it in. It wasn't just the sentimental value; he really loved the Rover. Was that nature or nurture? He didn't know, but a fascination with cars was something he and his father shared.

He grabbed his yoga mat bag from the passenger side, locked the Rover, and nodded at the people who had stopped to stare at it. Entering the yoga studio, Brian felt the discomfort of being the object of attention melt away. As his eyes adjusted to the shift in light, he saw it was empty, except for two women standing on the other side of the room, deep in conversation. One of them was Claire. Head tilted, leaning in, her attention fully focused on the other woman. He'd observed her presence with others at the graduation ceremony also. Most people were so easily distracted in conversation, but Claire really listened. His heartbeat increased.

"Look at this," The dread-locked, crystal laden woman showed Claire her cell phone. Claire wore only sweats and a sports bra with no jewelry. Perspiration glistened on her collarbone— unbelievably sexy. She pulled at the bun atop her head, and a mass of long, wavy, dark hair spilled over her shoulders. Brian took a deep breath and forced himself to look away.

"Aww. Greg, heart emoji? So cute!" Claire said.

"Just read it, though."

"Babe, something came up. Busy tonight. Guys night tomorrow. Saturday?" Claire shrugged at her friend. "So?"

Brian cleared his throat. The yoga teacher looked up, startled.

"Oh, hey. You're new here," she said, a smile spreading across her face.

"Is it that obvious?"

"Small town; we're all related." She laughed. "Not really, but it's not tourist season yet, so… Welcome!"

"Thanks," he extended his hand, "Brian."

"I'm Mazzie."

Brian smiled at Claire. "Nice to see you again."

She nodded. "Thanks."

Kind of an odd response, he thought.

Mazzie raised her eyebrows at Claire but quickly turned her attention to him. "Class doesn't start for a half-hour, but you're welcome to set up your mat, get settled in. Actually, I have a waiver for you to fill out."

She handed him a form and a pen and pointed toward the studio door. "There's water there if you need. Hydrate, hydrate, hydrate," she said a bit too cheerfully.

Brian took his mat and the form into the studio and settled in, grabbing cork blocks and a woven strap from the prop shelf in the corner. Even though they'd switched to speaking in low tones, the sound of the women's voices carried into the room.

"We were supposed to have dinner with my Aunt tonight. He knows how important this is to me. But now that we're getting close to commitment, he keeps finding reasons to run away."

"Oh, Mazzie."

"He's never gonna marry me."

"Did he say that?"

"It's that crazy Gemini wishy-washy energy."

Claire made a clucking sound with her tongue, reminding him of the noise his sister made when she was expressing sympathy. *Gemini wishy-washy energy?* He chuckled quietly.

Mazzie whined, "Your parents are the only couple I know who have that magical vibe."

"I know; they're nauseating."

Someone took a deep yoga breath. "Okay. Enough of that. Time to get ready for my vinyasa class. Hey, you did great, by the way, Hon."

"Thanks, Maz!"

"And it seems like your PTSD is easing, yeah?"

"I think so."

"Praise the Goddess!"

Someone giggled, low, sultry. Was that Claire?

Brian tried to return his focus to the registration form. PTSD. Claire didn't look like a soldier. Reflecting on her speech, though, he recalled her saying something about life giving her the chance to shift gears. What had happened to her? Had she lost someone, too? Maybe Teddy's father? Did they have that in common?

What was he doing listening to their conversation anyway? It was not his business. He knew better.

The bells above the door jingled, then Mazzie Swiffered her way into the studio. "Where're you from, Brian?"

"Connecticut, by way of Massachusetts and a bunch of other places. How long have you been here?"

"My whole life."

"Wow."

"Well, I went west for college, but Ocean Falls is just one of those places — hard to stay away for long. Claire lived in Boston for a while. Were you in Boston?"

"I try to steer clear of cities. What's the community like here?"

"Kind, mostly. People really care about each other. Look out for each other. And even though it's a small town we have a lot going on. We make our own fun, you know?"

"Nice."

"If you stop by the library and get on their mailing list, you'll know everything that's happening in town."

"Oh yeah?"

"And you'll get to meet everyone in town that way."

Brian felt a pang in his chest. Ocean Falls sounded like the kind of place he and Adrienne had always looked out for, a strong community to settle and have a family. He inhaled deeply and let it out slowly, hoping his emotion wasn't showing on his face. *New start. New life,* he reminded himself. *You got this, Man.*

Chapter 3

She knew the beach was closed, technically. And she understood why. Still, Claire thought it essential for Teddy to see the red knots. After all, their migration was so brief, and if they could just observe them from outside the brush… It was a solid plan. With another child, it would be too risky, but not Teddy. He was always so respectful.

"Now, you remember, we're not here to play, and we're not moving crabs today. We're just observing, and I brought goggles… um, not goggles, what are they called? Um…"

As they stood at the entrance to the beach, where someone had placed a "Beach closed" sign, she reached into her bag for the… what the heck was the word?

"Mama, look! Those birds are eating the crabs!"

Indeed, a flock of short-legged, reddish birds was eating the horseshoe crab eggs and snacking on the dead crabs.

"Yes! Those are the red knots! Isn't that great?"

"But those are the crabs we were saving the other day."

"Oh, well, that's true, but—"

Before Claire could even fish out the damn… binoculars, that was the word… Teddy had dashed onto the beach and was chasing the small birds, yelling at them, his little EnviroMan cape flapping behind him. *Shit*. The red knots took flight.

"Teddy!"

"Go away, mean birds!" He yelled, waving his little arms at them.

"Teddy, stop!" Claire ran after him, dodging crabs and piping plover nests. "Teddy!"

Just as she reached for him, he tripped and fell. "Ow! Mama!"

Brian crouched in the beach grass, observing the area's natural inhabitants through field glasses. *So far, so good on day one of the shorebird observation project.* He hoped it would provide officials with enough data to finally vote in permanent legislation to safeguard all the shorebirds that lived in or visited the state. It was ridiculous and frustrating that the process of protecting wildlife was so onerous and lengthy, that so many of the wildlife protection laws had built-in expiration dates, but there it was.

On the other hand, that lunacy kept him employed. Every aspect of the job was about education: collecting data, writing reports, meeting with government officials, gardening clubs, and other environmental enthusiasts. Education. He needed video. A permanent visual record to show the average person how the plovers, red knots, oystercatchers and other species engaged with the landscape. Plus, he'd have a way to review the data source. He'd need cameras hitting every angle at every hour. Was that too much? He needed a system. Once he hired an intern — *Oh, Shit!*

A little boy ran past the "Beach Closed" sign, yelling. The red knots took flight, a beautiful cloud of distressed birds sweeping over the bay. *Fuck.* They couldn't afford to expend energy escaping a little kid. The plovers nesting on the beach had started the per-weep sound of their alarm call. One, a day-old chick hurried toward its nest for safety. Meanwhile, a brooding female rushed toward the kid, feigning a broken wing to distract him. The boy yelled louder, then tripped and fell. The female dodged out of the way, but the kid fell onto the nest. The crying started immediately.

"Damn it."

A woman ran to the boy, who stood, smashed egg dripping from his hands, the downy plumage of the chick on his stomach and knees. The kid wailed even louder. The woman knelt by him, looking him over, touching his face, arms, legs. Brian couldn't see her face, but the woman seemed familiar.

FUCK! Get off the beach, woman! He wanted to yell, but if he did, he'd only startle the shorebirds more. *One stupid accident may have decimated the population of — ugh!* He felt sick to his stomach.

He trained his field glasses to the nest and saw three broken eggs. The chick that had rushed toward the nest for safety appeared to be dead. Only three nests remained on the beach. Now, the other three females rushed toward the child and his mother, sounding their alarm calls, feigning injury, trying to get the humans away from their nests.

Meanwhile, the red knots expended the energy they needed for their migration on this damn escape flight.

"Damn it." Brian rubbed his face. There were legal protections for these beautiful and delicate creatures. But what could he do? The laws had no teeth. He needed to educate this woman to prevent such an accident from ever happening again. One little kid had just wiped out nearly twenty-five percent of the season's plover population. *Unbelievable!* He needed to record what happened. Slinging the camera strap over his shoulder, he headed toward them.

"Are you okay, Sweetheart?" Claire asked, her heart pounding as she ran toward where her child lay face down.

Teddy pushed himself off the nest, stood, looked at himself, and wailed. Crushed eggshells and innards covered his hands and knees.

"Oh, Baby," Claire said as she reached him, touching his face, kissing his cheeks, and wiping his tears. "Are you hurt?"

Teddy sniffled and shook his head.

"Just surprised?"

He nodded.

She looked down and saw the nest Teddy had crushed. From what she could tell, there had been three eggs and a newly hatched chick, still covered in natal down. The tiny bird appeared to be dead. Was that a piping plover? Shit. The species was already endangered in Delaware. A wave of nausea passed through her. *He was not trying to kill the bird, Claire. Calm down. Breathe. Deep breath in. Slow exhalation. Yoga breath. Compassion. It was an accident.*

"Looks like you fell into a nest," she said, struggling to keep her voice even.

Teddy looked at the nest, "Did I hurt that bird, Mommy?"

"Ummm…" *Of course, you hurt that bird. It's dead.* Was five too young to understand such things? If she told him the truth, would it haunt him for the rest of his life, destroy him psychologically? Was it better to lie and say the bird was just sleeping? For all her reading of parenting books, Claire did not remember anything that covered this situation. There were no chapter headings like, "What to expect when your kid accidentally kills a baby bird on the state list of endangered species."

Fuck, fuck, fuck, fuck, fuck! Breathe, Claire.

"I think it's okay, Sweetheart. Let's go get you cleaned up."

"Okay."

"What were you doing, anyway?"

"Saving the crabs."

"Oh, honey! I told you today we were going to stay and observe." *Breathe.*

"What's observe?"

She sighed. How often she forgot he was just a little boy with few references for words and concepts. And now she had allowed him to cause the kind of environmental damage she was always fighting. Why? Because, once again, she hadn't followed the rules. The pain in her stomach worsened.

"Observe means to watch from a distance, like when you're at the playground with Fallon, and you want me to stay on the bench instead of playing with you."

"But those birds were hurting the crabs."

"Not the live ones. They were only eating the dead ones, Sweetie. Those are red knots. Remember your book about Moonbird?"

"Is Moonbird here, too?"

"Maybe. The last time anyone saw Moonbird was in 2015 at Mispillion Harbor."

"Miss who?"

She picked him up, carried him to the water, and helped him wash his hands and knees in the ocean. *Will he need some sort of tetanus shot after this? Do birds carry rabies? Could he get avian flu? Shit. Who would even know the answer to such a question?*

"You wanna go home and take a bath before going to the gallery, Sweetheart? Also, we might need to make another stop." She would call the doctor once Teddy was strapped safely inside his bike trailer, and she could make the call out of earshot.

Just as Claire was leaving the beach with Teddy in her arms, a tall, thin, man in a flannel shirt and work pants loped toward them. Brian. The sunlight behind him gave him a halo.

"Hey, Claire. Didn't recognize you from a distance." His voice sounded strained. "What are you doing?"

"I was saving the crabs," Teddy said, his voice dolcful.

Brian stopped short, disarmed by the child's sadness.

"Are you okay, little guy? I saw you fall."

Teddy sniffled. *Uh, oh.* Maybe he shouldn't have said anything. Wasn't this precisely what Stephanie was always telling him: don't bring up the thing that started the kid crying? It was bad enough to make his nephews cry; now, he was upsetting Claire's son, and he didn't know the kid. Then again, his nephews weren't running around killing animals. Animals that were a hairline away from being on the federal endangered list and were already on the state endangered list.

Focus, Brian. He took a deep breath and turned to Claire. "Umm… you saw the sign, right?"

She raised her eyes to meet his with a stare that would wither a redwood. She said nothing.

"Beach closed," he said. "Nesting season. You're, like, a big environmentalist, right? Didn't you just graduate with a dual degree in Policy and—?"

"I saw the sign," she said, her voice hard. "I brought binoculars so we could observe from outside the protected area. Unfortunately, I did not clearly communicate with my son, and he got carried away."

Claire sounded as mad as Brian felt. She was breathing forcefully as if she was in a yoga class.

He let his gaze travel over Claire's dark eyes, straight nose, and prominent cheekbones.   She had full, glossy lips, and a strong jawline.

"He ran into the protected area before I could catch him."

"You do understand—"

"Of course, I understand," she snapped.

"Good."

"We are leaving now. As devastating as this is, I have to ensure my son's safety."

"From???"

"Bacteria… pathogens… God only knows."

She gestured to the boy and the nest as if she didn't want to say more in front of the little guy. Brian recognized that closed-lipped gesture. A mom gesture, something he had seen his mother and sister make many times. Now, he saw the fear in Claire's eyes. Were those tears welling up? A pang of sympathy arose in his chest. He took a deep breath, exhaled, and his heartbeat slowed to a normal pace.

"Probably nothing to worry about," he said, attempting to make his voice soft, soothing.

"I hope you're right," Claire said, her voice edgy.

She turned and hurried away, child on one hip, backpack slung over her shoulder, tanned muscular legs glinting in the sunlight. She exuded both power and fear, a combination he found intriguing.

Chapter 4

Two hours later, satisfied by a phone call to the pediatrician that Teddy would not catch Avian Flu, rabies, or some other disease from falling onto the nest, Claire kissed him goodbye and watched him run to meet his best friend Fallon on the enormous wooden preschool playground. She thanked God for Messyland preschool and the nurturing teachers who Teddy couldn't wait to see each Monday, Wednesday, and Friday. She thanked God for Fallon and his family, who loved Teddy like their own son and gave Claire a break a few hours every week. She thanked God for her parents, and the apartment they offered at a reduced rent that, with the savings from her five years at Fidelity, had enabled her to get by since Teddy was born.

Now, it was time to find a new job, preferably in her field. Her savings were almost gone, she needed to save up for grad school, and her parents needed her rent to pay the mortgage on the building, especially with sales at the gallery as low as they had been the last few years. With her laptop, she could do her job search almost anywhere, but today, like so many days, she chose the library. The light was great, and her fond childhood memories of storytimes, playgroups, and volunteering there as a teen with Mazzie made the space felt like a second home. She found her favorite alcove and settled into the big comfy chair by the window, tucking her legs underneath her.

The scent of salt air wafted through the open window, and as Claire let it fill her, the morning's situation at the beach replayed in her mind. *You saw the sign, right? You're like a big environmentalist, right? Didn't you just graduate with…* Obnoxious man, throwing her mistake in her face. They were all the same, except her father. He would never. *Of course, I saw the sign. I just, for some stupid reason, thought I could… Oh, geez.* How could she let Teddy kill a piping plover chick and crush a clutch of eggs? *Let* was the wrong word; it was an accident. He would never do that on purpose, and she would never condone such behavior. Still, she had to be more careful, had to explain herself more clearly. She had to be more respectful of the rules she hoped to help create one day.

Actually, she had to open her laptop and get to work. *Right now. No more self-recrimination.*

After an hour of searching, she was rewarded with an interesting job opportunity: Endangered Species Review Assistant at Delaware Flora and Fauna. No, this was not her career goal. Still, the role would give her the chance to see the inner workings of the organization, like a paid internship. Hmmm. She clicked on the job description. It required passion and the ability to manage a complex database. She certainly had that. Passion for the environment — definitely. She'd learned all about database management in the financial world. Here, she would do a bunch of administrative tasks — *blech*. But she would also assist with reviews of proposed projects to determine the impacts to state-listed rare species. *That could be interesting.* She would help the Review Biologists to determine project mitigation, including permit follow-up. What did that mean? More time with Brian? She would also develop correspondence templates outlining regulations to provide various Division responses. *Ha! There's a fancy way of saying: write form letters.*

There was a tediousness to the job, for sure. And working with the man who had just scolded her was unappealing. Still, it was in her field. She doubted it would siphon her soul away like the finance world had. She might have the chance to meet the environmental movers and shakers in the state, too.

Claire wrote her cover letter, adjusted her resume to highlight the parts of her work life that fit the position more closely and clicked *apply*. Satisfied with herself, she stood up to stretch and look around. A chorus of little voices carried through the large hall, bouncing around the domed ceiling. Then a group of preschoolers, led by the librarian, paraded past Claire's little alcove. Claire thought Teddy might be among them, then realized these kids were younger than him. *That's right,* she thought. *Tomorrow is library day for the big kids.*

She returned to her seat and resumed her search. The process was getting to her. It had been months of looking and applying with not even a phone call from a prospective employer. Was she doing something wrong? Or was that just the job landscape these days?

But here was another listing with potential: Community Educator & Outreach Coordinator with the Ocean Falls Strawberry Jam-a-Rama. Of course, she had no experience in education. Nor had she ever worked in marketing — not technically. Sales was marketing in a sense, and being a financial advisor was definitely a sales position. She was a mom, so she was continually educating; did that count? And, actually, she'd been volunteering with school groups at the nature center for two years. Her work at the nature center was educational, just not classroom education. Maybe she was qualified after all. It was worth applying. Even if they didn't consider her for this role, they'd have her resume, and maybe another position would come up that was more aligned with her background.

She mentioned that in her cover letter: "Please consider me for this position or any other position where I may be of service." That demonstrated her flexibility, didn't it? Of course, it did. She was sure it did. She hoped it did. She'd find out eventually when she either did or didn't receive a phone call from someone at the Jam-a-Rama.

Claire shrugged, packed up her laptop and left the library. It was time for a break.

As she stepped outside, Claire heard the high-pitched squeak of the Downy Woodpecker, followed by its rapid drumming. She smiled. Without looking, she knew where the bird was: in the white oak tree on the grassy town common — drumming away, squeaking, drumming, and squeaking. She sauntered down the wide stone steps, appreciating that, for the first time in several years, she didn't feel the need to hurry.

As far as she was concerned, Ocean Falls had the most beautiful town common in Delaware — one that rivaled even those she had seen in the Boston area — and it felt so good to simply enjoy it.

She waved at the car that stopped for her and crossed Main Street West, stepping onto the sidewalk that bridged the common from Main Street West to Main Street East. The wildflowers she and Teddy had planted were in full bloom along the sides of the pavement: bluets, wild blue indigo, and Geranium *Maculatum* — low growing, self-seeding perennials that would flourish year after year. The *maculatum* was her favorite, not only because the flowers were beautiful, but because of its catapulting seed spreading system.

In the fall, she'd show Teddy how the plant shot its seeds as far as they could travel. He would love that. And next year, when little pockets of wild geranium started sprouting all over the common, Teddy would understand why, and he'd probably tell his friends, and they, too, would fall in love with plants and want to become little environmental superheroes like Teddy. If Claire had time, she would make capes for each of them, with kid-sized plant patches from the Flair shop.

"Well, what a lovely surprise," a voice behind her said as she reached the door to Book & Bean. Claire turned and hugged her mother.

"Fancy meeting you here at eleven a.m. on a weekday. Love your outfit, Mom. Is this new?" She fingered the paisley silk scarf Jane had tied around her waist.

"Your father's latest surprise." Jane smiled up at Frank.

"And how's my beautiful graduate? Enjoying a few moments of freedom from the tyranny of school and parenting a superhero-in-training," her father asked, holding the door open for them.

An overpowering scent of coffee and baked goods wafted through the doorway. "Just taking a break from the job search."

"Don't let it stress you out, now, Darling," her mother said, touching her arm as they walked up to the counter.

Claire stared at the baked goods.

"Getting stressed doesn't help," her mother added.

"I know, Mom."

She had learned from experience that melting into a panic attack at the start of every workday was a recipe for disaster. Sure, it had been a mistake to leave the job where she was thriving to follow her husband, *ex-husband*, to Denver. It had been the worst decision of her life, in fact. But she had to let that go. She took a deep breath and released it slowly.

The marriage had been a nightmare, and when it was over, discovering that the experience had killed her ability to stand the pressure of the financial industry was… well, she didn't even have words for it. Jim had destroyed her ability to handle conflict. When anyone yelled — be it a customer at the diner, or at the boutique, or her boss in the warehouse, or any of the other service jobs she'd lost in the year before going back to school — Claire either dissolved or flipped out. It was like Jim was yelling at her again, lifting his hand, ready to strike. The bruises had healed, but the emotional wounds were taking a very long time to close.

"Claire?"

She took a deep breath and looked into her mother's soft green eyes. Love. Support. Kindness. *This is where I am right now.* The mindfulness tools helped a lot. *Breathe in. Breathe out. I'm nowhere but here, in this moment.*

Going back to school had been the perfect choice. It had given her a sense that she had some control over her life, didn't have to be under anyone's thumb, whether a boss, a client, or a partner.

"Now that I'm looking for jobs in a field I care about, it's not so stressful. It's like, oh, I don't know, like I'm really going for something that matters, not just something to prove I can handle a job."

"That *is* what you're going for," her mother affirmed.

"And I think that'll make a difference when I'm working, too — really caring about the mission."

"Makes sense, Sweetheart." Claire's father handed her a hot chai with almond milk and honey.

She looked up at him over the steam.

"You go, Girlfriend," he added.

Claire grinned and leaned into her dad for just a minute, closing her eyes, feeling his strength and warmth. When she opened her eyes, she caught her mother's loving gaze.

"Wouldn't it be nice if you could find someone as thoughtful and attentive as your father?" Her mother asked.

Claire smiled. *Those men don't exist anymore, Mom.*

They settled at a table by the window. Her parents were holding hands. *What would it be like to be so close to someone? Is it possible for me?*

"B.T. Dub, Claire, what do you think of the new man in town?" her dad asked with a wink.

"B.T. Dub? Are you actually *speaking* in text speak now? Good Lord!"

"Hey, changing the subject does not change the fact that you need to get out, Miss Thing," her father said. "And don't roll your eyes at me. You do! You're a red-blooded American woman, and you need a date, for God's sake."

"Okay, Dad. This isn't 1648. I can find my own dates, thank you."

"And Brian is a hot, spicy young man, but more important, he's smart, like you, and kind, like you, and he's all earthy granola like you, *and* he's single."

"You do realize your clients pay you to look into the criminal and financial history of their possible tenants, not someone's Match.com profile, right?"

"He's just your type. And he's renting Jake's place for a song. You can't believe the deal I got him, but you know Jake doesn't need the money. So, here's this young man starting out in life, or restarting. I guess there's something about…"

"Brian made me an interesting business proposition, and I might just take him up on it. Okay?"

Frank pumped his fist in victory. "Good enough! Well, Janie, my work here is done, and now I shall romance you."

"Oh, Frank," she gushed, sliding her hand up his thigh.

Claire cleared her throat and stood.

"Alright, you two, have fun!"

Chapter 5

Claire's phone peeped as she stepped onto the sidewalk, and she realized she didn't have time to go back to the library. It was her day to volunteer at the nature center. *How could I forget that?* She race-walked down the block to the corner where her mother's art gallery stood, took the exterior stairs two at a time, fiddled with the lock, and dashed into her apartment. Ditching the laptop bag and grabbing her backpack, she filled it with a couple apples for the afternoon, her water bottle, and a small bag of nuts.

It was interesting the way the light had framed Brian from behind, the way it had given him a halo. Funny how, for a split second, she had trusted him because he looked like he was stepping out of the light onto the beach. There was a painting like that, but Claire couldn't remember the title or the artist. Someone contemporary, wasn't it? One of those new "painters of light"? Fossett? Engstrom? Wait, what was she doing thinking about him now? Her dad had planted the idea: that was the problem. Brian never would have crossed her mind, otherwise. She had too much else buzzing around her brain. Besides, he was a condescending jerk. *You're, like, a big environmentalist, right? Didn't you just graduate with a dual degree in policy and—*

Her phone beeped — a text from Mazzie. "Cute new guy at Vinyasa last night. Seems like your type."

Claire rolled her eyes. "Not you, too," she texted back, recalling her father's scheming.

"Think of the sex, though," and then, "Yogis are amazing in bed."

"LOL"

"Totally serious." Fire emoji.

"OMG. Off to Nature Center. L8R." Heart emoji. Kissy face emoji.

Out the door again, Claire ran down the stairs, unlocked her bicycle, and jetted down Main Street East onto Beach Road. She had to pace herself. On the one hand, she didn't want to be late. On the other hand, she didn't want to arrive a sweaty mess. There was a cooling breeze, at least, and she always had grooming essentials in her bag.

Before she even entered the building, Claire heard the cacophony. It's *going to be an exciting afternoon*, she thought, pausing to take in her surroundings. The nature center was set amid a salt-water marsh, which gave off a salty, earthy aroma. Claire inhaled deeply.

Today, Delaware environmental groups would have fought the placement of such a building in the middle of a marsh, but in the 1970s, the ecological groups just saw the location as inspiring. She flashed back to her own childhood visits here — the excitement she felt being surrounded by birds and marsh grasses, her parents pointing things out to her. Though they didn't understand what they were looking at, they appreciated the beauty. Her mother had taught Claire to draw on this very porch.

She opened the door to the octagonal building and was bowled over by the sound.

"Thank God you're here," Marian breathed.

In her fifties, heavyset, heavily made up, and teetering on kitten heels, Marian emerged from the middle of a group of loud school children.

"They arrived early, for some reason, and we were not prepared."

Claire smirked at Marian, then clapped her hands loudly.

"Okay! Settle down, settle down. Who's excited to be here today?"

A few kids raised their hands.

"Well, we are excited to have you here at the Ocean Falls Nature Center, and we have a great afternoon planned. Are you ready?"

"Yeah," a few kids mumbled.

"I can't hear you. I said, are you ready?" She raised her hands in the air.

"Yeah!" the group yelled.

"Alright! You can leave your bags here behind this round desk, and follow me to the art room. No, now no groaning. Art is fun, especially when the art is made of chocolate, am I right?"

"Yeah!"

Two hours later, Claire moved a pile of papers off the chair by Marian's overpopulated desk and fell into it with an exaggerated sigh. The Executive Director took her turn to smirk knowingly at Claire.

"I guess I was a little bit pompous when I walked in, wasn't I," Claire said. "Mea culpa. So, next week…"

"Next week will be the last week of the school program. Do you want to help with summer camp this year?"

"Maybe. The thing is, I'm looking for a job, so I don't know how much time I'll have to volunteer."

"Aha." There was a strange look on Marian's face.

"What's going on?"

"Nothing. Why do you ask?"

"You look… you have a strange…"

Marian shifted some papers on her desk. Claire caught sight of one that said *Development Coordinator*.

"Is that…." She pointed to the paper. "I mean, are you hiring? Are you hiring a new development coordinator?"

"Uhhh."

"Is Tony leaving?"

Marian took a deep breath and let it out slowly. "Something like that."

"Well, are you hiring someone to replace him? Do you have someone lined up already?"

"Well," Marian sounded guilty.

"Marian, I would love that job! And I think you know I'd be great at it."

"Maybe."

"Maybe?"

"You do have the background for it, and you've been great with the kids."

"Exactly! And I have three relevant degrees to back it up! I could do everything from budgeting to planning."

"After what Vinnie said, though…"

"Vinnie!" Her throat tightened and her voice came out in a squeak, "You talked to Vinnie about me?"

"He is my brother, Claire. We talk about everyone."

Claire dropped her head in her hands. When was the string of job disasters going to leave her alone?

"Marian, where else will you find someone with my experience? You do realize as a financial advisor in Boston, I worked with some of the most influential people in the state."

"Well, that's Boston."

"The skills carry over, Marian. And my dad's very well connected. I've known our state rep and senator since I was born!"

Marian took a deep breath, put her hand on Claire's soothingly, and said, "Claire, it sounds like you need more time before you're ready for a real job."

"Based on what? What happened at the diner four years ago?"

"We can't have our development coordinator flipping out on people."

"Oh, my God, Marian, have I ever flipped out with the kids? Or with the other volunteers? Or even with the parents?"

"There was that one time."

"He was yelling at me. And that was three years ago! I've done a lot of work on myself. I've been through therapy. I'm doing yoga… meditation… mindfulness training."

"We're posting the job tomorrow, Claire. If you want to apply, I can't stop you. But I certainly can't promise you anything either."

Claire closed her eyes, took a deep breath, and let it out slowly, then looked Marian directly in the eyes.

"I absolutely intend to apply, and I think you'll see with my education in environmental policy, my professional background… and I've been great with the school groups here."

"You have."

"Everyone makes mistakes, Marian. Everyone has tough times! For a position with this level of responsibility… Geez, I came back stronger than ever… more resilient than ever. And I'm, you know, I'm just more determined than ever to… nobody cares more about the environment."

Let her try to dismiss me now, Claire thought. The light in the room shifted to golden. Looking out the window, she saw the sun fighting its way toward the horizon.

The sun was sinking, and Brian was still irritated. How could he have spent any time being distracted by this woman who wasn't even with him in the field? She was beautiful; that was one reason. During her speech, he was wowed by her passion and intellect. And, in hindsight, on the beach with her son, she had been tender and — *Come off it, Brian. Foolish is what she was being.*

He had wanted her help, but after witnessing her judgment in action, he wondered if she would be as helpful as he had originally thought. He packed up his field equipment and loaded it into the Rover.

"Protected Wildlife Area signs posted every three feet. You didn't actually think you were doing the right thing, did you," he said aloud.

He knew he was talking to someone who wasn't actually there and knowing it meant he wasn't crazy. *Nope. I'm just weird,* he thought, then continued speaking to the imaginary Claire.

"There you were talking to your son about saving the horseshoe crabs. Meanwhile, you single-handedly brought the population of both the piping plover and the red knot to the brink of extinction. Okay, you're right, that's not fair. You didn't single-handedly; it's been a long time coming. And extinction is an exaggeration. Of course, the Governor won't care. He's probably just itching for a reason to cut our funding. The program could end before I've even gotten it started. Damn it; I was going to interview interns next week, too."

Brian came out of his furious trance and noticed that he was zooming down Beach Road. *Geez, when did I get into the car?* He slowed to take the right turn at Main Street East, kept his foot just lightly on the gas as he passed the quaint, tourist trap of a downtown. There was the brightly colored gallery with the "Art Gal" sign, the Yoga Studio and Meditation Center with its ubiquitous Tibetan prayer flags. He was getting the lay of the land pretty quickly.

"You're right, Claire. It's not the end of the program. I may end up with a pay cut and be unable to pay my rent, but who cares? I could get a raise and health insurance, but if the red knot dies out, what's it worth?"

He remembered Claire chasing after her son on the beach. She had been trying to help, he reminded himself. She had *not* been trying to flush the red knots off the beach and away from their food.

He flashed back to the day they met, when, as he was starting up the Rover, he saw her picking up a crab and flipping it onto its front so it could move across the sand and fertilize its eggs or get back to the water. There was something lovely and selfless in that act.

He remembered her rushing to her child this morning, the fear in her voice as she talked about pathogens. A single mom working so hard to do the right thing for her child and the environment.

"No, Claire, I see you were not trying to put these delicate species in further danger. You of all people must know that if this fucks up our harvest restrictions on the horseshoe crabs, fishermen will over-harvest them, and then the birds won't have enough to eat."

Claire's dad held the chrome door to Vin's Diner open and let her and her mother enter.

"What's going on, Claire Bear?" He asked. "Why are you shaking?"

"She's been very nervous today, Frank. She was shaking at the coffee shop this afternoon, too."

"Well, it's a big week for our little girl. Graduating college for the second time, that amazing speech, looking for work…"

"Oh, God, would you guys please stop," she said, irritated.

If she told them what Marian had said, they'd agree to eat somewhere else, but then they'd be even more worried about her than they already were. She couldn't have that. She'd just have to suck it up. She took a deep breath and let her eyes adjust to the interior light. It seemed more crowded today than usual. Louder. Claire started to sweat. Vinnie had been talking to Marian about her, had actually dissuaded Marian from considering her for a job that was in her field. She took another deep breath and let it out slowly.

"Claire!" Vinnie's voice boomed from the kitchen. "Good afternoon!"

"Good afternoon, Vin!" Claire yelled, turning to look at the overstuffed fifty-something man behind the order slips. He had his sister's narrow hazel eyes and prominent nose.

"Good to see you, Kid! Strawberry supreme on the house for you, Doll."

Claire forced a smile. At times, she loved living in a small town, where everyone was so connected, so interdependent, they had no choice but to forgive and forget. Then, there were the foolish few who chose to hold grudges and alienate almost everyone else, and apparently, Vinnie was one of them. Though now he was acting like he held nothing against her at all. WTF? *Oh, Lord, now I'm thinking in text — like father, like daughter.* Her parents chatted with Vinnie until the hostess, whose hair had changed color again, came and led them to a large booth. The decor was tacky as hell, but Claire still loved the purple and teal sparkly vinyl upholstery. It made her feel like a kid.

"Nice shade, Bel," Claire said, sliding into the seat across from her parents.

"Thanks," the hostess replied. "They call it Grecian column."

"It really brings out your eyes." Claire hoped the compliment would give Bel a little boost. She had been through a lot since high school, and Claire knew she could use all the encouragement and praise she could get. "Still looking into that certificate program?"

Bel sighed. "I gotta save up for it. You know how it is."

Claire nodded. "You can do it, though. You are going to be one awesome home inspector."

"I hope so!"

"Won't Bel be an awesome home inspector, Dad?"

"I believe she will!" Frank shot a thumbs up in Bel's direction.

"Hey, can you make sure Vinnie makes that strawberry supreme with soy milk instead of ice cream?"

"I'll send Terry over to take your order." Bel smiled and walked away.

Moments later, fortified by the vegan version of the strawberry milkshake she'd been getting since she was five, Claire sank into the upholstery and brought out the file full of info about environmental art. She had spent a month researching and was excited to share the idea with her parents, Jane, especially.

The old Airstream Trailer and attached 1950s-style chrome diner rose out of the landscape, just as Frank had described it. It was in such a remote area off Route 13 West; Brian never would have found it without Frank's instructions. Now, as he pulled the Rover into the parking lot, his mouth started to water. Intense emotions always made him hungry.

He hopped out of the vehicle and strolled into the diner. It was loud, some sort of party in the corner. Inside, a hefty server in a short pink dress and frilly white apron roller-skated from table to table. Brian nodded to the hostess, also in an extremely short dress. She pointed to a booth, "I'll send your waitress right over."

As Brian walked to the booth, he heard a man call his name. Scanning the room, he saw Frank standing and waving.

"Join us!"

Frank, his wife… what was her name? And Claire.

"You remember Jane and Claire."

Interesting emphasis on Claire's name. "Of course." He smiled. At least he hoped he was smiling. His heart pounded as he held out his hand to Frank's wife. "Nice to see you."

"And you!" Jane gushed. "As I recall, you had the most charming name."

"Brian?"

Jane giggled. "No, the last name, it sounds like Melodius."

She looked like a fairy straight out of a painting by Lippincott.

"Melodus." Brian chuckled, extracting his hand from Jane's.

As he touched Claire's hand, his arm went tingly. Was he having a heart attack? No, that would be the other arm, and he was only thirty-six. Why was his arm tingling? He rubbed it. Electricity, that's what it was. He hadn't felt this kind of electricity since Adrienne. *Betrayal* flashed through his mind. *I'm sorry, My Love.*

He stood at the end of the table, unsure what to do, until Frank gestured to the seat across from him. It just happened to be the seat next to Claire. He sat carefully, trying to keep a distance and knocked the silverware off the table. The back of his neck grew hot with embarrassment.

Claire hurriedly put away the magazine clippings and web page printouts. "I guess we're done here?"

She gestured to the file folder in her hand and looked pointedly at her father, then her mother.

They were both grinning at her like cats with mice in their jaws.

"For now, Dear. Let's enjoy dinner. Suddenly it's a party," her mother gushed. Why was she always gushing?

41

Her father nodded. "Claire, this is the young man I was telling you about. The one renting Jake's place."

The young man I was telling you about? Here we go. "We met at my graduation, Dad. Remember? You introduced us."

"Of course. That's right."

"We're always looking out for our daughter, Brian," Jane said. "You wouldn't believe what she's been through."

Claire cleared her throat loudly and glared at her mother. Why on earth would she tell this complete stranger about her abusive marriage? Her parents had no sense of boundaries. Of course, neither had she, until she learned about the concept in therapy. Growing up with no sense of boundaries was probably how she had wound up in the toxic relationship to begin with.

"Oh, I, uh, I'm sorry to hear that."

"No need to dredge up the past," she said, still glaring at her mother. "Anyway, I'm starting over."

Could Brian hear her voice shaking?

"Well, good for you."

"Good for me?"

"I, I mean, that's brave. You know? A lot of people just keep the status quo, then wonder why they're miserable."

Her chest tightened. She wanted to defend herself. Brian sounded like an asshole. On the other hand, no one had actually told him *what* she had gone through, so he didn't even really know what he was responding to.

"Yeah. Well, some people don't even realize they're a victim until it's too late," she said, then realized her statement made almost no sense. How could she steer the conversation in another direction? *Why is he here, anyway?*

"So, you went back to school, graduated top of your class, and now you're taking your new lease on life, huh?"

"Uh, huh," she said, relieved for something else to discuss.

"What are your plans?"

"Grad school, work. I believe it's important to keep educating my son about environmental stewardship."

"You can't start too young," Brian said, without a trace of irony. It was almost as if he agreed with her. Did he?

"Claire had a terrible time of it, Brian. You wouldn't believe how hard it is for single mothers to find a job where the boss understands their needs."

"Mom, really," she said, hoping to stop her mother in her tracks.

"My sister has two kids. She's happily married, but after she tried to go back to work with the first one, and that didn't go well, she and her husband just decided it would make more sense for her to stay home with the kids. They say it kind of balances out financially."

"Yes. And Claire was able to work it out for a while, and we helped," her mother gushed. She was always gushing, gushing about other people's business.

Claire sighed. "Well, enough about me. What about you, Brian?"

"Ummm, I just moved to town, as you know, from Massachusetts."

Was he staring at her again? *Ugh. How embarrassing.*

"I'm running the shorebird project for Delaware Flora and Fauna Service and hopefully figuring out new ways to protect the threatened and endangered species that rely on the natural resources here."

"I guess that's why we keep seeing you at the beach."

He smiled. "But I hope to NOT see you at the beach, at least not for the rest of the season. Your son is adorable, but…"

"Yes. I get it."

"The piping plover is threatened in the northeast, and the red knots are here to refuel, and—"

"I'm aware."

"And data collection is so important at this time, to keep our project going, and so easily skewed."

"Exactly," she said, trying to keep her voice even, yet firm. "You don't need to explain all this to me."

"Of course not." He paused awkwardly. "You know… actually, I have some reports to write tonight — boss wants me to come up with a plan of — oh, you don't want to hear about that. Anyway, I should go. You folks didn't come here to eat with me."

"Nonsense!" Frank said. "It's kismet that you arrived when you did."

Jesus. Kismet, Dad? Oh, my God. We should be doing another background check on this guy, not celebrating his spontaneous arrival and ability to mansplain the environment to me.

"Nah. I can see you were in the middle of a family thing. I do appreciate the recommendation to this place, though, Frank. It looks—"

I wonder if now is a good time to ask him about that job opening at FWS.

"Is everyone ready to order?" her dad asked, flagging down the waitress.

"I've been looking forward to the French fries and salad all day," she said. *Why did I say that?*

"Claire doesn't eat meat or dairy, Brian. She's a vegan."

"Huh, me too," Brian said. "How's the veggie burger, Claire?"

"Tasty," she said, trying to ignore her mother's pointed stare. *Yes, Mom, we're both vegans.* "But you have to make sure to order it without cheese, or they automatically put it on."

"Thanks for the tip. Oh, hey, Frank and Jane, I wanted to talk to you guys about the Partners Program. Has anyone approached you about that?"

Does he have any control over the hiring? Claire wondered.

"Sounds like some sort of pyramid scheme," Frank said.

"No, no!" Brian laughed. "Nothing like that. I think I mentioned it to you when we were signing the lease. Delaware has lost over fifty percent of its wetland acreage since European settlement in the past 300 years."

"Well, that's the cost of business, isn't it, Brian?" Frank asked.

Claire sighed. Her father was so frustrating sometimes. "Dad, that is too high a cost! I've been trying to tell him, Brian. Dad, our wetlands keep declining from invasive plant and

44

animal species. That's why Teddy and I plant native flowers along the main streets and open areas."

"Seriously, Claire? You planted the geranium maculatum and wild blue indigo?" Brian asked. "Usually, we have to coax people into action."

The question was: was Brian actually impressed, in which case this might be a great time to ask him about the job? Or was he hitting on her? If that was the case, she really didn't want to work with him, even if it was a great job opportunity.

"… Program in the first place," Brian continued.

"Which is what, again?" Jane asked.

"We focus on wetland restoration to help migratory birds and federally-listed threatened and endangered species. The Partners Program is a conservation program, where we work with homeowners in strategic locations. Riparian habitats—"

"Riparian?"

"Habitats along a river," Claire explained.

"Which have been nearly eliminated in many agricultural areas in rural Delaware."

"But we don't farm," Jane said. "We don't even live in an agrarian area."

"You don't have to, Mom. It's the reduction of riparian habitats in farming areas that has contributed to the decline in aquatic habitat quality in both the Delaware Bay and the coastal inland bays. See?"

"Ah, ha! Like the dragonfly effect!" Frank said.

"Butterfly effect, Dad, and not quite, but along those lines. Keep going, Brian."

"Endangered species like Delmarva fox squirrels—"

"What in hell is a fox squirrel?"

"They're squirrels, Dad."

She fished a pen from her bag and drew a map on her placemat to illustrate the point. She held it up for them to see.

As if on cue, Brian moved his finger along the drawing. "This species of squirrel keeps losing habitat due to the commercial forestry practices that convert native deciduous forests to more commercially valuable pine plantations."

Her heart was starting to pound, just listening to him. Maybe with Brian here, she could get her parents to take her seriously. She added buildings and stick figures to her drawing and held it up again. "With Urban sprawl, and increasing populations on the shoreline—"

Her father grinned. "So, what do you want us to do, Brian?"

"Well, you mentioned you live near Prime Hook Reserve. Could I come over and show you what I have in mind?"

It was a risk to even consider working with this guy. He seemed to be both interested in her and judging her at the same time. It was a risk, but she had to take it. This guy was clearly brilliant and had at least part of his heart in the right place. Besides, she'd never let herself get sucked into a romance with a coworker again like she had with Jim.

"Brian," Claire started, then saw the expectant look on her parents' faces. If she asked Brian about the job at Flora and Fauna in front of her parents, then they'd be hounding her for information all the way through the application and interview process. Torture. She'd have to find another time to ask. "Never mind. Some other time."

"Have you given any thought to my request?"

"Some."

"And?"

"I'm still thinking."

"You know, I'd love to have you all come to the observation station so I can show you what I'm working on."

Her parents looked mildly terrified. Claire would have been eager to go if someone else was making the offer. But Brian?

"Really?" she asked, testing.

"Yeah, I think once you see what I'm talking about, you'll understand I'm not just some crazy environmentalist with no scientific knowledge."

"Ha! I never thought that. I just thought you were some kind of stalker or something."

"Oh, good. That's so much better."

Chapter 6

Mazzie's text arrived with a plinking sound. "You know, you really should call him."

"Ugh. But he's just so nice."

"And that's a problem because?"

"He's seems TOO nice."

"???"

"That's how they start. They lure you with sugar, then bam!"

"Oh, Honey."

"His sweet shell is already cracking. The critic is showing through."

"R U sure about that?"

"Anyway, gotta focus on the job search now."

"Let's catch up in person. Walk tonight?"

The evening breeze brought the scent of salt and magnolia to the path that encircled the town center. Claire felt the dewy air on her skin; intoxicating.

"… call him," Mazzie finished, and cocked her head to the side, like she did when she was waiting for a response.

"Call who?" Teddy asked, pedaling his bicycle next to her, the training wheels catching his every wobble.

"No one, Sweetheart."

Claire looked at Mazzie and mimicked her expression: eyes extra wide, lips parted, nostrils just slightly flared. She called it Mazzie's hippie seduction face. Mazzie stuck her tongue out at her, another expression she'd been making at Claire since they were about three.

"I'm serious," Mazzie said. "It sounds like a great opportunity."

Teddy sped up.

"Not too fast, Sweetheart. Stop at the crosswalk," she yelled.

"You see that, right?" Mazzie asked.

"How are things with you and Greg?"

"Better," she smiled.

"Teddy, stop!" Claire ran to catch him before he crossed the street. "Stop! Now!"

He stopped, and Claire's heart slowed to its normal pace.

"I was stopping, Mama."

"Okay. What do you do before you cross?"

"Count to five. Look both ways for cars and people and bicycles."

"And????"

"Wait for you to catch up."

"That's right. You're too little to cross without me or another adult."

"I know, Silly Mama," he said, laughing.

She took a deep breath. "Of course, you do. Okay. Is it safe now?"

He looked both ways. *Yes!* He counted aloud to five and looked again. "It's safe, Mama."

She patted his back and walked next to him as he pedaled across the walkway, then watched as he zoomed away again. Would she ever get used to letting him go like that?

Mazzie caught up to them. "We're talking about having a baby."

"What??? Really???"

Mazzie smiled and nodded.

"But what about all his commitment issues?"

"His fourth chakra is open and he's letting our love energy flow freely!"

"I have no idea what you just said. Translate: are you getting married?"

"I don't know. We'll figure it out. Now, back to you."

"Nah."

"I want you to call this guy. You need a job, Claire, and if you help him prepare for his class, if you show him how useful and smart you are, maybe he can help you get an even better job. He's gotta know people."

"He's new to town, remember?"

"But he works in your field!"

"True."

"And he's a hot, spicy thing."

"Jesus, have you been talking to my dad? That's just what he said."

Mazzie laughed. It was infectious. Soon, Claire was laughing too, just like when they were teenagers. Her dad was always fun to impersonate. But Mazzie turned suddenly serious.

"Call him. Now. Get out your phone. Don't raise your eyebrows at me. That doesn't work with me."

"Come on!"

"I'm not kidding. You need to unblock your second chakra and this may be the guy to help you do it!" She reached into Claire's back pocket, pulled out the phone, and typed in Claire's password.

"You are so fucking obnoxious."

Mazzie scrolled through Claire's contacts, until she found Brian's info. Enough was enough. Claire grabbed the phone from Mazzie's hands and clicked dial. "That's the last time I give you my password!"

"Ha!"

"Hi, Brian? It's Claire Dessalines… TEDDY! STOP!"

She started running toward him, but Mazzie overtook her with her sprinter's legs, yelling so Claire didn't have to.

"Claire? Is everything okay?"

His phone voice made her entire body tingle. *Darn it.*

"Uh, yeah," she said catching her breath. "Sorry, we're just out walking. Listen, I can help you, maybe. I mean, you know, you can tell me about it."

"Awesome. Can you meet tomorrow?"

"Book and Bean?"

"Sure. I'll text you a few times, okay?"

"Great. See you soon."

She ended the call and ran to catch up with Mazzie and Teddy on the other side of the park.

Why had she put on mascara? Would he notice? If he did, he'd think she was trying to impress him. She shouldn't have worn any makeup. Claire fiddled with her skirt as she walked down the street. Jeans would have been better. *It's not a date, Claire. What were you thinking?* What she had been thinking, she guessed, was this was a quasi-professional meeting with a potential colleague. Still, at 6pm on a Wednesday, it also seemed kind of like a date. She didn't want a date. Did he want a date? She hoped not. The clock on her phone read 5:55. No time to go home and change. Hopefully, he wouldn't misread the signals. She should have insisted they meet during the day, when Teddy was at preschool, but Brian had said he couldn't get away from the field that early.

Brian sped down the beach road, trying to clean himself up as he drove. At the stop light, he reached for the deodorant in the glove compartment and applied it liberally. He should have given himself time to go home and shower, but Claire didn't want to meet too late. She had to put her son to bed. How was he going to work with her if she couldn't meet at night? Would weekends work? Lunch hour?

His heart raced as he stepped out of the Land Rover. In the distance he heard the excited whinnying call of the downy woodpecker. It soothed him, that familiarity, and his heart slowed just a bit. *Am I nervous? About meeting Claire?* It certainly felt that way. How annoying. Sure, she was beautiful, but come on, this was a business meeting. Wasn't it? It was happening in the evening at a café, rather than in his office at work or at the college. But this was just a 'getting to know you'. This was just seeing if they could work together, if she could be helpful to him. Right?

Sure, Brian. You tell yourself that, he heard Adrienne say in his mind. He felt a pang of guilt.

Now, don't go there, Brian, Adrienne said. *You know I want you to be happy.*

He stopped at the entrance to Book & Bean. He certainly wasn't going to walk into a business meeting, or a date, or whatever it was, with his dead wife talking in his head. He took a deep breath. Adrienne had been the one to get him to go to his first yoga class, like so many other things. Adrienne was the person always looking out for his health and hers, the one telling everyone who would listen about the health benefits of a plant-based diet and yoga, meditation, daily exercise. Sometimes, she had sounded like a broken record. She certainly had pissed off a lot of people. But then there was always that one unexpected person who would tell her how much what she had said had helped them. *Stupid disease.* Of all the people to die young, it was brutally ironic that it was the one person who took better care of herself than anybody else, who had no aches and pains, who seemed to have no illnesses. Cruel twist of fate that Adrienne would get a fatal diagnosis with a three-to-six-month prognosis. Genes could be such an unpredictable bitch. Her aunt and grandmother had both died young and suddenly. Her older brother had no genetic markers for the disease.

Four boxes of pregnancy tests. "All this puke. Total fatigue. What else could it be, Bri?" She had been glowing. Four boxes. "That one was expired. This one will work." She had been confused. Doctor. Specialist. Hospital. *Savor the time you have left together.* Thirteen weeks and four days, a second honeymoon.

Bri, don't go down that road now. We talked about this, remember? About you moving on after I passed. It's been three years.

"And two months and six days," he whispered.

It's time for you to let me go. Take a chance. Maybe Claire will be important in your life.

"You're not helping," he said aloud, just as an elderly couple passed by and looked at him, confused.

"Oh, sorry," he muttered, looking down.

You need to live again, Bri.

"The meeting with this woman is just professional, Adrienne. What you and I had—"

We'll never lose our soul connection, but your soul is big. Don't close yourself off, please.

Brian closed his eyes for a minute. Sometimes, shutting out visual stimuli helped him to re-center. Again, he heard the call of the downy woodpecker followed by rapid drumming on what had to be an oak tree somewhere. He opened his eyes, looked toward the direction of the sound, and saw Claire walking toward him. He felt his lips slide into an involuntary smile. She moved as if she was still on the bicycle — almost as if she was floating.

Whatever trauma she had been through, and he hadn't really been able to put that out of his mind ever since he overheard her conversation with Mazzie, it hadn't destroyed her. At least, not as far as he could tell.

"Hey," Claire said, arriving at his side. "You didn't have to wait for me. You could have gone in and gotten a table."

"Uh…" He didn't know what to say. "I, ah, I just got here. No big deal."   His stomach did a nervous dance. "Are you hungry, or…"

"Not really, but I'd love a chai. Jeet?"

"Huh?"

"Did you eat?"

"Oh, uh, no. Why? Are you hungry?"

"Not at all. But if you haven't been here yet, they make the best vegan chai and maple-sweetened oatmeal cookies!"

"Yum. Whenever I move someplace, I check out the bookstores. This was one of my first stops, but I haven't tried those cookies."

"I do the same thing. Not that I've moved that much. A few times. I also check out the libraries."

"Right on."

They reached for the door handle at the same time. Electricity shocked him as their fingertips grazed. He pulled his hand away, embarrassed, wondering whether Claire had felt the same thing. He snuck a glance at her face, observed an odd expression.

"Sorry," they said at the same time, then laughed nervously.

She stared at him, unsure what to do, coughed.

Brian stared into her eyes and spoke slowly, as if he wasn't sure how to say what he needed to say, "Are you. Going to. Uhhh?"

He gestured toward the door, "Open the door?"

"What?"

"The door. Did you want to go in?"

She looked down at her hand. She was in shock, she realized, from the jolt of something — what was that? A jolt of something had zipped up her arm when their hands touched. And now her hand was frozen on the old-fashioned door knob. Door knob. The door. The door! *Oh, God, what an idiot.* She laughed and pulled on the door handle.

"Great minds think alike," she said, laughing half-heartedly. *That was worse than one of Dad's jokes, Claire. Geez.*

"Yes. Reaching for the door at the same time. Clearly, there's a level of brilliance here that transcends what most people experience on a day-to-day basis," Brian said. She heard the playful tone in his voice, and turned back to see his lips sliding up into a smirk. Deep dimples framed his mouth. His eyes shone. She followed his gesture into the café.

At the counter, she ordered a chai with agave and hemp milk and pulled out her wallet.

"No, no, I've got this," he said.

"But—"

"No, really. I can write it off; it's a business expense."

How was she supposed to take that?

"If you'd like to go find us a table," Brian started.

"Sure," she said, walking away.

He was just too darn nice. He was sure to turn on her at some point.

A moment later, he slid her chai latte next to her hand. "So, this guy in line just ordered a half-cap, decaf, caramelized matcha cocoa with charcoal."

"Charcoal. Eew," she said, sticking her tongue out reflexively, then pulling it back into her mouth, embarrassed. *For God's sake, how old are you, Claire?*

"Right? And what's with all the add-ons and stand-ins? I mean, what's the guy drinking? I think you reach a point where you may as well just drink vomit. He's got all these ingredients; that's what it's gonna taste like."

She smirked. "Do you cook?"

"I know my way around the kitchen. You?"

"There're two ways to be vegan—the bread and tofu way, or the cooking from scratch way. I chose the latter."

"Nice," Brian said. "Have you tried egg replacer yet?"

"Awful."

"I once tried to make a quiche from it."

"From egg replacer?" She tried to imagine the consistency; what she saw in her head was goop.

"And fake cheese," Brian added. "Yup, that face you're making is pretty much how it tasted."

She giggled, and he didn't seem to mind her laughing at him. He was laughing with her. It felt really good to laugh like that with someone, like they were old friends.

"But you know life's too short to eat the same thing every day," Brian said. "You gotta go out on a limb sometimes."

"Absolutely. I've been experimenting with vegan French toast."

"And?"

"Eh. I'm still experimenting."

"Does your kid mind?"

"Teddy's been eating vegan since birth, except for breast milk, of course. Unfortunately, once my parents were able to give him solid food, they started filling him with beef and cheese and eggs."

Brian shook his head. "My sister's had so many arguments with my parents and her husband's parents about what to feed my nephews."

"How many do you have?"

"Two, ages four and six. My little buddies. They're junior environmentalists, like your little guy. Anyway, I guess we should get down to business. That's why we're meeting after all, right?"

"Of course," she was still chuckling. "How is it you think I can help you?"

"What I'd like to do is go over the syllabus with you and get your input. Because, you know, I've never written a syllabus, and I don't really know how to do it. If you could just tell me what you think would be interesting, or not."

"I can do that in a couple hours probably, maybe one hour. But off the top of my head—"

"The real work starts when I plan each class. I need to think about the lectures and the reading materials."

"Have you read *Essentials of Environmental Science*?"

Brian thought for a moment, then opened a journal, scrawled a heading READING FOR CLASS, and jotted the name of the book underneath. "Authors?"

"Uh… Friedland and something-or-other. Reyes? Raymond? Ray-something, I think."

"Ray Ban?"

She giggled.

"Rein deer?" He smirked, eliciting more laughter from her. His eyes shone with mischief.

She googled the book title. "Relyea."

"Well, YAY! I was close," he said, eliciting another laugh from her.

"Well, Yay. Relyea. Well done, Busta Rhymes," she said with a smirk.

Brian laughed and held his hand up for a high five. She obliged. Was that a spark again? No. It was a sting from how hard she had just hit his hand.

He took a deep breath, "Okay. Business. Focus, Brian. I can get access to the classroom now. I'd like to meet there and read the lectures to you. Even if you don't say anything, it will help me to see where you seem really engaged and where you seem inattentive."

"Got it. Keep you off Sleepy Hollow road. The thing is though, I'm looking for a job, so I don't know how much time I can devote to this."

"You know I'm paying you, right? It's not a full-time job, but, maybe three hours a week…" Brian named a price that sounded fair to her. She thought about negotiating something higher, but that didn't seem like it would be in the spirit of goodwill. She didn't want the guy to think she was going to take him for all she could. They agreed and set a date, and he stood to leave.

"Brian, one other thing. I applied for a job at Flora and Fauna."

"No kidding. The Review Assistant job or the field internship?"

"I didn't see the field internship. Does it pay?"

"Less than minimum wage."

"Ugh."

"So, you applied to the admin job."

"The thing is," she said, unsure whether to proceed. "I wonder, do you know anything about it that might help me get a leg up? Would it have… It said something about full benefits and—"

"You'd get everything. Health insurance for you and your son, which is ironic because field workers like me actually are considered consultants and don't get benefits. And where are you going to grad school? If it's a state university, you'd get free tuition."

Claire's jaw dropped.

"The thing is, and Delaware might be different, but in my experience working with other state organizations, they move really slowly on the paying positions. It could be six months or more before they hire you."

"Oh, really?" Claire felt her hopes deflate.

"So, if you need to work sooner than that and you're trying to save up money and stuff… I mean, keep that it your back pocket, but you really might wanna—"

"I get it."

"Have you applied for any fellowships?"

"I looked at a few, but none seemed promising."

"Look up: A.R.M. Fellowship."

"Arm?" She Googled it. Were those numbers right? At first glance, this looked like a fellowship that could pay her way through grad school. "Thanks, Brian. I'll read this later."

"I guess you should think about your career, too, and what you really want because sometimes people get stuck in jobs like that. And I don't see you being happy as a Review Assistant. It seems, from the little bit that I know you, that you have a lot more to offer the environmental field and wildlife restoration than shuffling papers around a desk."

She smiled at him. When was the last time a man had said something like that to her, had seen her potential? Her dad always had. Aside from him, she couldn't think of a guy who had been so encouraging and really seen what she had to offer.

Then again, this was a business meeting — a fun meeting, one that had almost seemed to be veering into date territory for a bit, but… No, Brian was fun, but clearly focused on work, as it should be. Yes, that was exactly as it should be. *So,* she wondered, *why do I feel so disappointed?*

Chapter 7

Claire wiped the sweat from her brow. The mommy-and-me yoga class was getting more and more challenging as Teddy was getting bigger. Holding chair pose with her 35-pound son in her lap… Doing Goddess squats with Teddy in her arms… For the first time, she noticed herself actually relishing corpse pose rather than wanting to jump up and get to the next item on the to-do list. There was something especially sweet about having her baby lying on her stomach, his little head nestled into her collar bone. He'd be too big for Mommy-and-Me yoga next year, maybe even next month the way he was sprouting up lately. Distressing, the thought of her baby growing up so fast. She allowed the thought to pass like a cloud in the sky, as Mazzie was always reminding her.

"Begin to deepen your breath," Mazzie said, her voice airy and soothing. "Wiggle your fingers and toes. Bigger kids, gently, quietly roll like a caterpillar off your mommy and onto the floor. Moms with babies, cradle your baby as you roll onto your right side. Take another deep inhalation and on the exhalation, come to a seated position for final Oms."

She chanted the sound "Om" with the group, held her hand to her heart in gratitude for the class, and said Namaste to honor the light in everyone and in Mazzie.

Brian stood in the doorway and let his eyes adjust. The sun glared outside, but in Mazzie's yoga studio, a soft glow of sunlight filtered through gauzy curtains, creating an otherworldly atmosphere. The door to the practice room opened, and a familiar little boy bopped out, followed by his mother. Svelte legs hugged at the thighs by tight yoga shorts, bare lean stomach with a touch of softness around the belly button, definition around the ribs, and a hot pink yoga top that wove a web over the collarbone. She definitely had the sexiest collarbone he had ever seen. He'd never even thought of that body part as attractive until he had seen Claire's. She followed her son to a cubicle, crouched down to help him put on his shoes and tie them. Clearly, she hadn't spotted him, which gave him an excuse to admire her for just a moment before approaching.

He sidled up next to her, careful to keep a healthy, respectful distance. She was now bent over from the waist, the vertebrae of her spine flowing gracefully toward the floor. He looked away, composed himself, glanced down, subtly adjusted himself, took a deep breath, and spoke.

"Hey," Claire heard behind her as she bent down to slip her foot into her hiking sandal. The voice sent electricity up her spine.

"Hey." She stayed low, pretending to fiddle with her shoe while attempting to smooth her eyebrows with her knee. They were always going haywire, like an old man's eyebrows, and looked especially insane after any type of exercise. She had to do something about that. *Not that it matters. Of course, it doesn't matter. Eyebrows. Ridiculous.*

"Uhhh, I brought you—"

She rolled up, hoping to appear graceful. "The syllabus? Great!"

"Here it is."

"Great!"

"And the photocopies of the first reading."

"I'll read it tonight and get back to you. Email okay?"

"Or we can just discuss it tomorrow."

"Great!"

"Great. Three p.m., right?"

"I'll be dropping the kid off at my parents, and then I'll pedal on over to campus."

"I can pick you up."

"Thanks; I prefer to ride." *Why do I sound so breathy all of a sudden? What's wrong with me?* "CO2 in the atmosphere and all that."

"Integrity. I like it."

She smiled, then cocked her head, confused. "But you drive that big jeep-thing."

"The Land Rover? Looks like a gas guzzler, I know."

"Isn't it?"

"My Dad converted it to biodiesel, made it totally fuel-efficient, hemp upholstery, LED lights, all that jazz."

"Sounds cool," she said, her voice going from breathy to squeaky. "But the eco-friendliest vehicle is one without an engine."

Brian cleared his throat, "For a car, it's eco-friendly, and with my job… Heck, every field job with Flora and Fauna involves lots of driving."

He looked at her the way Teddy did when he was seeking her approval — big eyes, a certain twist of the mouth. She smiled her approval, then wondered why. Why pat him on the back? Not just because his facial expression felt familiar. Was she starting to trust him? Or was it the surreal sense of relaxation she always felt after yoga class? It had to be the yoga glow.

Chapter 8

Mindset was such a funny thing, Claire realized as she locked her bike to the metal rack in front of the almost unbelievably ugly building where she had taken most of her environmental science classes. Normally, the thought of entering a building this industrial looking, with so few windows and so many cinderblocks, would have given her the hives. But now, as she looked at the hideousness of Granden Hall's architecture and construction, the familiar desire to leap out of her skin with excitement returned. True, not every class had been scintillating, but she was a woman on a mission to promote environmental harmony. And what she had learned in this building had prepared her to follow her calling.

Now, she would be helping Brian to inspire even more students; at least she hoped she would be helping. Mazzie was right — it was all about mindset! After two years, she was actually learning something in yoga besides poses.

The air was sticky and humid, and she was slick with sweat from the ride, but she did not care. Okay, she kind of cared. She didn't want her body odor to precede her, not because she was interested in Brian. She couldn't be interested in him, at least not romantically. Maybe as a friend, not that she needed new friends, especially not new male friends. She dug into her bag for the washcloth and lavender oil, swiped it over her face, neck, and arms, and paid extra attention to her underarms.

"Hey!"

Oh. My. God. The familiar electricity ran up her spine at the same time as embarrassment flooded her cheeks with warmth and brought even more sweat to her underarms. She turned slowly, hoping he hadn't seen her wiping her armpits in the middle of the parking lot. Why, oh, why hadn't she waited to get to the restroom? She folded the washcloth around the essential oil bottle and slipped both into the mesh bag attached to her backpack.

"Hi, there." Did she appear casual?

"Have a nice ride over here? It's a hot one."

"Haha," she chuckled, then bit her lip. "Mmm."

She fell into step with him, and they entered Granden Hall, her heart pounding as they walked down the hallway. Why? Why was her heart pounding? In that moment, she was walking down a hallway she had walked many times before. So, what? Her only plan was to listen to a lecture and give Brian some feedback. What was the big deal? *Get a grip, Claire.*

When they reached the classroom, Brian held the door for her. She inhaled slowly and deeply, reminded herself that she could choose her mindset — calm, focused. She entered the classroom and felt her heart do a happy dance. Being in this lecture hall was like reuniting with an old friend. She hadn't had any classes in Granden 108 since her junior year. After that, it had been all labs and small workgroups. The room was set up like an amphitheater, much larger than the other classrooms. At the front, two long fake wood tables flanked a podium with a microphone.

She sat in her favorite seat in the front row and reviewed the syllabus again. She was excited to see Friedland and Relyea's text, as well as E.O. Wilson's *The Creation* listed as required reading. She had finished Wilson's book in two sittings.

"Good evening."

Her head snapped to attention.

"I'm Professor Melodus, pronounced mel-OH-dus, but I'm not into titles, so, please, just call me Brian."

She smirked. It was kind of a cute way to start the class, but also kind of corny. Should she tell him that? She didn't want to hurt his feelings. She made a note in her notebook.

"I have worked as a wildlife biologist for ten years…"

Claire wrote in her notebook: "Skip the intro – always seems pompous."

"I started as an intern at Flora and Fauna Service, earned my BA at Dartmouth, worked around the country, then completed my MA/Ph.D. at the University of Massachusetts."

Also, she needed to tell him that the intro felt like a Match.com date. Then again, did she just have dating on the brain? She started sweating again, then snorted to herself. *This is not some sort of date. Be professional, Claire.* Brian stopped the lecture and stared at her. She tilted her head up at him and smiled self-consciously. The look on his face was questioning. He paused until she nodded at him, then cleared his throat and resumed.

"My research into the symbiotic relationship between the Red Knot and the Horseshoe Crab led me to Canada, Argentina, and finally here, where I am leading a project at the Flora and Fauna Service. I've started teaching in addition to doing fieldwork, because I'm on a mission to create enviro-harmony, and I'd like you to join me."

This, she realized, was why she was helping him, why she wanted to work with him, and at least partly why (embarrassingly enough) she had a crush on him. *No, you don't, Claire. That's ridiculous.*

"Also, because fieldwork pays next to nothing and doesn't provide health insurance."

She giggled. He was so funny.

Two hours later, she had filled fifteen pages in her notebook with ideas and diagrams, both his and her own. She continued writing furiously, trying to keep up with the professor. He spoke a mile a minute, wrote as quickly, and had been introducing new concepts left and right. No, they were not new concepts to her, but she wanted to be able to comment on everything he presented. It was exciting to keep up with his pace.

"To those of you who are still with us, I present this challenge…" Brian wrote *Challenge: red knot* on the board. "Figure out why the population of the red knot is dying out, despite all efforts by FWS to increase it."

She piped up, "Professor, you expect us to solve a problem that professionals haven't been able to?"

"Just research the factors contributing to the problem and brainstorm ways to mitigate these circumstances. Okay? It'll take a few hours, tops." Brian looked at her as if she was his real student, not his pretend student, then turned his focus back to the imaginary students in the empty room. "See you next time. Oh, uh, if any of you want extra credit, research the American Oyster Catcher, another one of Delaware's threatened shorebirds."

Brian felt the tension leave his shoulders as soon as he closed his laptop. A sigh of relief escaped, and he felt heat rise to his cheeks. Claire clapped, which made him blush even more. He hoped he wouldn't blush like this in front of his students. That would be embarrassing. Should he sit with her now? Then she might notice his hands shaking. He maintained his grip on the podium.

"Thank you, thank you," he said and bowed his head. "Now, really, what did you think?"

Her lips curved into a smile as she looked into his eyes. "Inspiring."

"And…?"

"I love that you're pushing your students from day one,"

"And?"

Claire took a deep breath and released the words in a rush of air, "*And* I'm not sure if it isn't too much too soon? These are frosh, remember. Eighteen-year-old kids. Babies, really."

"Hmmm."

"Also, did you look into Kolbert's *The Sixth Extinction* as a text? Have you read it?"

"Good call!"

"I like your casual style, the no title thing. I think that will go over well, but be careful, too. I saw that backfire with some professors who tried to be buddy-buddy with the students."

"How so?"

"The kids didn't seem to respect them for very long. They took advantage. They're just kids, after all."

He nodded.

"I feel like there was a nice balance of slides, but some you moved through too rapidly."

"Which ones?"

She flipped through her notes for what seemed like an inordinately long time, then finally spoke without looking up.

"The part where you transitioned from the basics of what makes an environment to how humans affect their environment. This is the intro class, and some of these kids are really unaware of how everyone's choices impact the world around them."

"Interesting."

"I mean, I think they'll get it with you teaching them," she said, looking up.

As her eyes met his, he felt his breath catch in his chest.

"…need a little more handholding than you imagine," she finished.

He had noticed her eyes before, of course — a deep chocolate brown that made him hungry. What caught him tonight, though, was the intensity, coupled with respect, admiration, and perhaps even caring. Yes, he thought he saw caring in her gaze, and it stirred him.

He would have to stand behind the podium a while longer. *Five times five is… Too simple. 105 times 200 is… still too simple, Brian. Birds. Dead birds. The piping plover. It was an accident. Poor kid looked so sad. Claire trying so hard to be a good mom, to show her son—She's staring at you. Say something. Say something before—*

"Hey, ah, on another note, would you and your son be interested in giving me a tour of the bike paths around here?"

"You have a bike?"

"I haven't taken it out yet; I'm still unpacking and stuff, but…"

"That's right, you just moved here."

"It feels like I've been here my whole life in a way."

"I know," she sighed. "It's hard to find time…"

"Just thinking I'd like to drive less, whenever I can, learn the safe routes. Maybe if you two are out anyway, I can just tag along—"

Way to sound desperate, Man.

"Sure. I mean, hmm, maybe."

Claire bit her lip. Why was she biting her lip? Was including him on a bike ride that much of a conundrum?

"Not that you… I mean, of course, I don't want to trouble you," he said.

"No, no."

"Look, I get it. You've got a kid, you're looking for a job, and now you're spending free time helping this young professor prepare for his first class," he smiled but wondered if she really was too busy or if she just didn't want to spend the time with him.

"And I'm helping my mom with her final art show before she closes the gallery."

"No kidding. What kind of art?"

"Not sure yet. I have an idea I want to run by her."

"You *are* busy." It had felt like they were beginning to develop a friendship. In reality, maybe the only reason she was spending time with him was that he was paying her.

Chapter 9

The next morning, Claire and Teddy huddled at the entrance to the beach in a tattered quilt, watching the pink light of pre-dawn on the ocean. They were well away from any nests; Claire had made sure of that. She could not imagine being more at peace than she was at this moment, holding her sweet little boy (who was quiet for the time being), feeling the sand under her and the sea breeze around her, the moist air caressing her face. The beauty of the light seemed indescribable to her, and she wished she could paint it. Although she had talent, she had never really wanted to be an artist. Still, at moments like this, she understood the desire to capture the beauty of creation.

She inhaled deeply, wanting to fill every cell of her body with the ocean air. It dawned on her that this was yoga breathing, deep inhalations that filled the lungs and deep exhalations that expelled the stale air. She wanted to laugh, thinking about how complicated it seemed to do this on the yoga mat, but how simple it truly was. She closed her eyes, listened to the gulls in the distance, the gentle lap of the waves on the shore. Her reverie was interrupted by the sound of a motor. She tensed.

"What's that, Mommy?"

"Sounds like a boat," she whispered.

"When's the sun gonna rise?"

"Shhh."

A light scanned the beach in front of Claire and Teddy, missing them by a foot. Claire knew what this was, and she had to do something.

"Stay here, Sweetheart. Don't make a sound."

"Why?"

"Shhh. Promise."

A fishing boat dropped anchor a few yards from shore. Two fishermen got out and waded to the sand with a plastic tub.

Claire stood and stepped into the light. "Hey! What are you doing?"

One of the fishermen looked up, surprised. "What's it to you?"

The other fisherman grabbed horseshoe crabs and threw them into the tub. Claire cringed.

"Those crabs are protected."

"By who?" The second fisherman laughed. "You?"

"Don't worry, Sweetheart, we know what we're doing."

Both fishermen laughed and continued collecting crabs. *Sweetheart. Ick. Typical condescending men!* Claire was incensed. Realizing there was nothing she could do at the moment angered her further. These ignorant jerks were taking her beautiful crabs, a near-threatened species, and would sell them to the highest bidder. And if she pressed them on it, they'd say they had mouths to feed or whatever. Of course, in a way, she couldn't blame them for doing what they knew how to do to pay the bills. Still, it infuriated her. They had to know they were breaking the law, and they obviously didn't care.

She stepped out of the light and returned to Teddy. She couldn't stop them now, but she could observe them. They apparently didn't see her as a threat, as they were continuing their nefarious work. She would watch what they were doing and how they were doing it so she could tell Brian so maybe he could do something about it. She whispered into Teddy's ear, "Stay silent, okay? It's really important. No sounds. We're going undercover like spies. Nod if you understand."

Teddy nodded.

Claire slid her smartphone from her pocket, turned it to silent, made sure the flash was off, and snapped photos of the fishermen. She could only hope the images would come out in the pre-dawn light.

As the sun started to rise over the horizon, Claire slipped her phone back into her jacket and pretended to close her eyes. If the fishermen did look her way again, she wanted them to think she was meditating, not watching them. But they didn't. They collected the last of the crabs, hi-fived each other on the great haul, then climbed back into the boat and motored away. Claire took a picture of the boat as they sailed into the sunlight, but it was backlit, and as far as she could tell, there was no identifying information on the boat anyway. She sighed.

"That, my child, is what we call observing."

"You mean when we watcheded the men like spies?"

"Watched, Sweetheart, not watcheded. Watched. And we didn't say a peep, we didn't move, we just watched, or observed."

"Well, you said a peep, Mama. You stood up and said a peep."

"True, but then I sat with you and observed. Great job observing, Super Ted!"

"Do I get a new cape for that?"

"Hmmm. Maybe. You are amassing quite a collection of Superhero capes!"

"Cuz I am a super-duper superhero!" Teddy jumped up. This time, Claire grabbed him before he could do any damage, lifted him high in the air, and flew him in a circle.

"You certainly are Mama's super-duper superhero!"

She lowered him gently to the ground and hugged him tightly. "Now, we're going to slowly and carefully pack our blanket, and Mama's going to carry you to the bicycle."

"Fly me!"

"I will fly you when we get home."

And after flying her son, she would make a phone call. Brian would know what to do about this, and he would want to know this had occurred. With luck, she had captured some useful evidence for him.

Chapter 10

B rian was driving down Main Street, enjoying the breeze through the windows. Glancing toward the sidewalk, he saw familiar tan, muscular, feminine legs. Little white dress. Dark hair flowing in waves down her back. Claire. Brian slowed to get a better look, but he couldn't stop in the middle of the road. In his rearview mirror, he saw Claire enter the book store. Perfect. He was going there anyway.

Moments later, he saw Claire perusing art magazines. Interesting. He wondered whether to approach her. She wasn't always friendly. Yet he felt so drawn to her. He watched as she flipped through an *Art Forum,* then an *Art News* and *International Artist.* She wandered away from the magazine section into the Nature books, scanned the shelves, and finally picked up E.O. Wilson's classic, *The Creation* plus a newer book, *Half-Earth.*

"That's a good one," he said, coming up alongside her.

Claire gasped and turned slowly to face him.

"Read any of Wilson's other stuff?"

Claire nodded her head and walked away. He followed.

"There's another book you might like. Hold on…"

He ran back to the Nature section, scanned the shelves until he found the book.

"*Last Child in the Woods,*" he said, but she hadn't followed him. "Claire?"

She reappeared with her fingers over her lips. "Shhh."

He smirked. "It's not a library."

"People are reading."

Claire had looked adorable walking down the street, and up close, Brian could see she looked absolutely stunning. "Always dress up to buy books?"

"Why not?" Claire blushed. "My mother always says: dress for a party."

"Hey, uh, can I buy you a cup of tea?"

Claire looked at him without saying anything. *Was it a mistake to ask her? She was so friendly in the classroom. What happened?* But then her dark eyes were searching his, and he saw something there beyond the anger she so often presented. Fear. Sadness. Softness. Kindness.

"Sure," she said. "Let me just pay for my things."

A few minutes later, they stood side-by-side in the line at the cafe.

"Their vegan no-bake cookies are the best," Claire said, thumbing through *Half-Earth*. "Hey, listen to this: The only proven way to halt the destabilization of the living world is to protect the largest possible reserves and the native biodiversity surviving within them."

"Human beings are not exempt from the iron law of species interdependency," he jumped in, excited to share one of the most moving passages he had ever read. He practically had the book memorized. "The biosphere does not belong to us; we belong to it."

"Wow." Claire shook her head and looked into his eyes again.

His heart pounded faster. "I know; he's brilliant."

Claire held up *Last Child in the Woods*. "This looks great, too. Thanks for the suggestion."

He nodded and looked into her eyes. "If I ever have kids, I'm gonna base my parenting heavily on that book. Richard Louv is…"

She cast her eyes down as if she was embarrassed.

"Uh, oh. Did I insult you? I, I'm not trying to tell you how to parent."

"Huh? No. It's just—"

"Actually, from what I've seen, I think you're probably doing… Anyway, it's not a parenting book. It's theoretical."

She nodded. The woman confounded him. He took a deep breath and smelled a soft feminine scent, maybe perfume, or just shampoo. Whatever it was, it was—

"Brian," she said suddenly, "Are fishermen supposed to be taking crabs right now?"

"No! Why?"

"I wanted to stop them, but Teddy was with me, and—"

"Shit. How many did they get?"

"A whole boat-load. They were fast; they came right before sunrise and left right after. I took a picture of their boat with my phone, but it didn't come out. Plus, there was no identifying information on the boat that I could see."

Suddenly, it felt like his head might explode. He inhaled sharply and focused on the wall menu, not that he could read when he was this upset; the letters swam in front of his eyes.

"Hi there," a familiar female voice said. There was a touch on his arm, but not Claire's touch. He looked up and saw Tilly. She hugged him.

"Oh, hey. This is a surprise. You two know each other from yoga, right?"

"I don't think so," Claire said, suddenly prickly again. "Well, catch ya later."

"What?"

Claire walked toward the door.

"Claire."

She ignored him. He hurried after her. "Where are you going? I thought we—"

"Oh, I can see you're busy. I'll just grab something down the street. I really want to start reading this book."

"But, uh…"

"See you around." She touched his arm, and he felt a zing run straight through him.

"No. Wait."

"Brian, what do you want?" Tilly yelled from her place at the counter.

"Claire," he touched Claire's shoulder. Zing. He didn't want to let go, and she wasn't pulling away. "Hey, stay off the beach for a while, okay? Those creeps could be dangerous."

"Thanks."

"Seriously. Let me handle this. Please."

Claire nodded.

"Good, well, maybe we'll bump into each other again."

Claire smiled with her lips, but her eyes looked disappointed. As he watched her leave, he hoped she would turn around and look for him. Instead, she just strolled down the street. He returned to Tilly.

"I ordered you a soy cappuccino," Tilly said.

"Thanks." Brian hated cappuccino.

Chapter 11

The phone rang early, just as Claire was stretching her way out of bed and wondering what Teddy might want for breakfast. Who called anyone at seven a.m.? She didn't recognize the number, but something told her to answer it anyway.

"Hello?"

"Claire Dessalines?" The voice was husky and soft, like an elderly woman's voice. "This is Veronica Meery, from the Ocean Falls Strawberry Jam-a-Rama. You applied for a job here as our Community Educator and Outreach Coordinator.

"Mrs. Meery? Bill's mom?"

"The very same."

"Hi, I'm happy to hear from you."

"I hope it's not too early. It's just that we're in a time crunch, and I'm anxious to get this position filled."

"The Jam-a-Rama's happening in a few days."

"That's right. You wouldn't be working on this year's Jam-a-Rama, but we start planning for next year as soon as this one is over, so we really need to have this position filled by the end of next week."

Perfect, she thought.

"We'd love to bring you in for an interview."

"Okay, great! When?"

It was Tuesday. They scheduled the interview for Friday afternoon. It seemed crazy to Claire that they would want to meet her on the first day of their big event, but Mrs. Meery had practically insisted they meet at the Jam-a-Rama. She had also insisted Claire bring Teddy.

"I haven't seen you, but in passing, since you were his age! I think it would be just delightful to see you both."

"Thank you so much, Mrs. Meery."

"Veronica, please."

"I look forward to seeing you, Veronica."

When Friday rolled around, Claire's typical sense of excitement about the Ocean Falls Strawberry Jam-a-Rama had been replaced with a mild sense of dread. She always stressed out about job interviews, but there was something extra aggravating about this particular one, and she really couldn't put her finger on it. Teddy had been a little grumpy all morning, and Claire couldn't figure out why. He was usually so excited about festivals and fairs.

Normally, they would meet her parents at the start of the Jam-a-Rama, but because she had the job interview, she didn't want to do that. The last thing she needed was her parents fawning all over her while she was trying to look professional. Never mind that they probably knew at least one of the organizers and would insist on "putting in a good word" in the most inappropriate fashion. She told them the soonest they could meet would be at four o'clock. At one o'clock, she and Teddy stepped out of their apartment and into the fray.

The smell of fried foods and sugar filled the air. Claire watched her son take in the sight of the normally quiet town common, now alive with colorful decorations and festivities.

"What should we do first?" She asked.

Teddy smiled and pointed to a tent with a larger-than-life sculpted puppet at the entrance.

Moments later, as they neared the tent, they heard familiar voices.

"Oh! Sam, Liza, what a surprise," Claire said, as she popped her head inside.

Fallon's parents generally favored sports over the arts. She couldn't imagine what had compelled them to bring their son to an artsy-craftsy activity.

"Fallon really wanted to come," Liza said. The whiny quality voice always grated on Claire's ears, but she was a nice person. A few years older than Claire, Liza had moved with a different crowd in high school, neither bullying her like some of the preppy kids nor fawning over her like the artsy crowd. Sam had graduated before Claire even started high school.

"He knew Teddy would be here, and he hasn't yet realized how b-a-d we are at a-r-t," Liza added.

"We're trying to make a football puppet, but we're struggling with this chicken-wire," Sam laughed.

She flashed the couple a knowing smile.

Mrs. Quinone, the ancient high school art teacher, rolled her eyes. "If you had come to even one of my classes, Sam, this wouldn't be such a struggle for you."

Liza and Claire exchanged a smirk.

"Now, here's a quick study," Mrs. Quinone said, pointing to a man in the corner. He turned around.

"Brian?" Claire said.

"Didn't know I'd see you here," he smiled.

Claire's heart did a little flutter, and her stomach balled up in knots.

"Who's that, Mama?"

"This is Brian Melodus. Do you remember meeting him at my graduation?"

Teddy shook his head.

Claire shrugged apologetically at Brian.

Brian wiped his hands onto his jeans and extended his hand to Teddy. "We also met at the beach."

She felt her breath catch in her throat. Where was he going with this?

"You were being a real hero, trying to save some crabs," Brian said.

"Oh yeah," Teddy said, looking down and shuffling his feet. "I did it wrong."

"But you really tried," Brian said.

Claire looked at him, noticed his focus on her son. His eyes radiated kindness and appreciation. She felt her body relax, and her heart open a crack. He wasn't bringing up the subject to blame the boy, but rather, it appeared, to praise him for his efforts.

"We need more heroes like you," Brian said, then smiled at Claire. "We oughta have an environmental hero school for Teddy and his friend here."

"You know, I've been thinking the same thing," Claire said.

"We'll have to talk about that," Brian said. "Hmm, that just gave me an idea for one of my classes. Anyway, guess I'd better get back to my puppet. What are you guys making?"

"We haven't figured that out yet."

"Mama, we're making a horseshoe crab, of course!"

Claire laughed. "Of course."

"Right on," Brian said.

"What are you making?" she asked.

"See for yourself," he gestured.

She walked to the side to get a better view. There stood a chicken-wire sculpture in the shape of a bird. "What species?"

"I bet you can guess."

"Well, I don't really know your artistic ability, but going by the shape, I would guess one of the Rufa species… perhaps a red knot."

"You'll just have to wait and see," he winked.

"Mama, when can we start?" Teddy asked.

"Mrs. Quinone, are you ready for us?"

"I sure am," she said, handing them some chicken-wire. "You remember how to do this, don't you, Claire."

"I think so."

Mrs. Quinone smiled at her.

Claire took a large piece of poster board and a marker and drew a footprint of a horseshoe crab. Then she explained to Teddy how they had to make the bottom of the wire sculpture match that footprint, and they might need several layers of chicken wire.

They started, slowly, building the sculpture from the ground up using the wire.

"Well done, Brian!" Mrs. Quinone said when Claire and Teddy were on their last layer of wire. She looked over and saw layers of fabric covering Brian's chicken wire structure.

He smiled. "I guess I need to let this hot glue set for a bit. You guys want some help? I don't know what I'll do with myself otherwise."

Claire opened her mouth to decline, but then Teddy nodded so earnestly, and so eagerly, she felt there was no alternative but to accept Brian's offer. She couldn't let Teddy down, especially not on Jam-a-Rama day.

"Hey, Teddy," Brian said as he came over and joined them in working on the wire sculpture. "How do oceans say, hello?"

"I don't know. How?"

"They wave."

Teddy laughed. "Fallon, did you hear that one? How do oceans say, hello? They wave! Get it?"

The two boys giggled.

"Brian, what do you call a bald eagle? I mean. No. Mama, what is it?"

She leaned over and whispered in Teddy's ear. "What animal needs to wear a wig?"

Teddy repeated the question to Brian, who feigned confusion.

"A bald eagle!" Teddy shouted and did a little dance of excitement.

Brian laughed. "Good one! What's brown and sticky?"

"Ummm," Teddy tapped the side of his head, as he did when trying to sort out a difficult problem. "I don't know."

"A stick."

"A stick," Teddy doubled over with laughter. "A stick! Mama, a stick is brown and sticky!"

She laughed at his cute little laugh, then suddenly found herself doubled over. *A stick. That is hysterical. Wait. Really? These jokes are inane. Why am I laughing?*

Usually, silly jokes drove her a little bit crazy.

"Ooh, look at that!" She stepped back from the sculpture. In front of her was a five-foot wire replica of a horseshoe crab.

78

"Teddy. Come stand here and look with me. Look what we made!"

Teddy came, and Brian followed. The three stared at the sculpture for a moment.

"Wow!" Teddy said. "Can we put on the fabric now?"

They bent over a box of fabric scraps and pulled out all the pieces that were army green, olive green, drab, and generally horseshoe crab colored. They even pulled out a few pieces of camouflage fleece. Brian made jokes as he helped them glue the squares and strips of fabric to the wire. He had Teddy in stitches.

She couldn't believe how comfortable she felt around Brian at that moment. Now it seemed her son also did. Could he really be as nice as he appeared, or was she missing something? She recalled his caustic words at the beach. *Aren't you some sort of environmentalist?*

She studied him as he made jokes, noting his warm, open body language. His eyes seemed sincere. His smile was wide and looked genuine. Was she a fool to begin trusting him?

He and Teddy were laughing again. Fallon ran over to join them, leaving his parents to struggle with their attempt at art. Their football-shaped puppet looked more like a crushed egg. How could someone who had been so adept on the sports field, so coordinated and graceful, lack any coordination when it came to putting some materials together into a basic shape?

Her phone beeped, and she looked at the time. "Oh, my goodness," she said. "I have to meet Ms. Meery in five minutes. Teddy, honey, we have to go."

"Oh, no, Mama, we're just getting started."

"I know, Sweetheart, it would be great if we could stay, but we'll come back."

"No, Mama." Teddy sat on the ground.

"Sweetheart," she said, putting the warning tone in her voice.

"Mama," he whined, looking down at his lap.

Why is he fighting me? It's so unlike him.

"Hey, I wouldn't mind if he stayed with me. We could work on your sculpture until you get back," Brian said.

"Oh, that's awfully kind of you."

Liza piped up, "And Sam and I will be here for a while, I think." She gestured to their artistic disaster.

"Are you sure, Liza?" she asked.

Brian seemed nice, but what did she really know about him? Liza and Sam were like Teddy's second family. If they would stay, then she could feel safe.

"How long will you be?" Liza asked. "An hour?"

"Probably about that. I'm not really sure, but I could check in. I do have to go. It's a job interview."

Sam and Liza assured Claire they would stay there until she returned. Brian told her he was happy to entertain Teddy. And Teddy placed his soft little hands on her low back and pushed her gently out of the tent.

"I won't go anywhere, Mama. I promise."

"Alright. Behave yourself, please."

Claire exchanged her secret two-finger wave with Teddy, then strode to the information tent on the other side of the town common. There, she found an elderly woman with fluffy mouse-brown hair and a sweatshirt embroidered with strawberries. As only women of her generation did, she was wearing a blazer over the sweatshirt, despite the heat.

"My goodness, Claire," the woman said, extending her hand. "You look just the same, but all grown up."

"Hello, Veronica, it's a pleasure to see you."

"Where's your son?"

"He is fully engaged in puppet making, and luckily there are friends here doing the activity with him."

Veronica introduced Claire to the other people at the information tent, then guided her around the event, stopping at every tent and booth, asking her to comment on each of the activities. She wanted Claire's assessment of the quality of each activity as well as its apparent success based on the attendance at each site. Claire didn't have many criticisms to offer, but she did note a few things she thought could be done better.

"Did you see any of our ads this year, Claire? Or any of our social media posts? You know we're on all of the social media channels?" Mrs. Meery puffed up her chest as she said this and whipped out her smartphone to show Claire the Facebook page, the YouTube channel, and the Instagram and Twitter feeds.

"You're really up to date. It seems to me that for an event of this size, you could get more followers than you have, though. And I mean, I don't know much about marketing myself, but I wonder, have you engaged anybody to coach you on how to boost your social media marketing?"

"You know, we haven't," Mrs. Meery said, stopping at the fried dough booth and ordering one for herself and Claire, who accepted gratefully. Maybe it was nerves, or just smelling the festival treats for hours, but her stomach was rumbling with hunger. Knowing fried dough was vegan, she slathered a piece with strawberry jam and bit into the sweet, greasy fluffy crispness.

They continued their stroll around the town common. Mrs. Meery said they weren't interviewing many people for the job and that Claire was an impressive candidate. "Not that I can promise you anything."

"Of course not. Of course not. But I'm glad to know. What's the next step?"

They made their way back to the puppet tent and stood outside so Claire wouldn't be distracted by Teddy.

"I'd like to bring you into our office on Monday," Veronica said. "Here's my card. Please let me know if you have any thoughts about what we discussed or any particular salary or scheduling requirements."

Veronica and Claire shook hands, and Claire entered the tent. *Thoughts about what we discussed. Salary requirements! Yes, Mrs. Meery, I know the protocol for thank you notes, and I will write mine tomorrow morning when my mind is fresh, and Teddy is sound asleep.* She looked back and saw Veronica peeking in. She gave a little wave then turned to see her son fully engaged in gluing fabric and buttons and other decorative things onto the crab sculpture. During the hour Claire was in her interview, Teddy and Brian had made progress. On the other hand, Fallon and his family hadn't gotten far at all.

"Look at this! You made the whole horseshoe crab! You even put the tail on it and the compound eyes and- whoa! Is that the lateral ridge?"

Teddy nodded vigorously.

"That is astounding!

"And we finished Birdman's red knot," Teddy boasted.

"Birdman?"

Brian shrugged. "Guess I've joined the environmental superhero ranks. All I need is a cape."

Claire raised her eyebrows.

"Mama can make you one," Teddy said.

"Can she?"

"She makes the goodest capes. See how good mines is?" Teddy spun around to show off his Eco-Boy cape.

"Hey," Claire said, wanting to change the subject, "How did you guys make the feathers on the red knot look so real?"

"Magic," Brian said. "Wanna help us finish the crab?"

"Why not. Hey, Sam, Liza, do you guys want help, too? This new guy's kind of an expert," Claire winked.

"Nah," Sam said. "We're good. Right, buddy?" He asked Fallon.

Fallon looked at the odd football shape. "It's a spaceship!"

"I see it, Fallon," Claire enthused. "That's so creative!"

She, Brian, and Teddy set to work, adding finishing details to the crab. When it was done, Claire stepped back, took in the sight, and breathed a sigh of satisfaction.

"Tomorrow," said Mrs. Quinone, "We can put these on poles, and you can walk your horseshoe crab in the parade around the town common."

"Really? Mama, can I?"

"Of course! Oh, hey, it's time to go meet Gramma and Grampa."

Her parents waited arm in arm in front of the Ferris wheel. Jane gazed up at Frank, and he looked down at her. It was, Claire thought, as if they were just falling in love. She could not remember a day when they had not looked at each other like this. Oh, sure, there had been arguments, but they always came back together stronger and seemingly more in love than ever.

When they saw Teddy and Claire, Frank bent down and opened his arms wide. Teddy ran into them, and Frank lifted Teddy high into the air. "Should we go on the ride first or get cotton candy first?"

"Cotton candy!"

"Not too much, please," Claire warned.

"Oh, don't worry. We won't spoil him any more than we spoiled you," her father promised.

Of course, they did indulge her child. Teddy had not one, but two cotton candies, plus French fries, plus fried dough. Claire could not imagine how he could fit so much food into his tiny stomach. *No sense fretting about that now*, she thought, as she tucked him into bed and listened to him recount the excitements of the day.

Indeed, the day had turned out to be quite extraordinary. *Things are about to get much better,* she thought, as she kissed her son goodnight. "Sweet dreams, Teddy Bear. I love you."

"I love you, too, Mama Bear."

Her mind jumped forward to the brighter future she envisioned as she left the door to Teddy's room open a crack and entered the bathroom. She turned on the shower, then recalled the thank you notes in her nightstand. *First thing tomorrow morning,* she thought.

Chapter 12

It was still dark when Claire heard Teddy's cry, then the shuffle of his slippers in the hall. Then he was at her bedside, his little face next to hers.

Before he could even get the words, "I don't," out of his mouth, he spewed all over Claire's bed.

Claire sprang up, wiped the vomit from her cheek, lifted Teddy into her arms, and rushed him to the bathroom. "Oh, sweetheart. I'm sorry you're not feeling well. Are you okay?"

"No."

"You'll be alright. It's alright."

He continued heaving into the trash can. Didn't that just figure. Her parents had spoiled him, and she was left to deal with the aftermath. She cursed herself for letting them give him all that junk food, but it was too late now.

When Teddy finished vomiting, she wiped his face, ears, and neck with a warm washcloth, slipped a new pajama top over his head, and carried him back to his own bed. She sang softly to him and rubbed his back until he fell asleep.

In her room, she ripped the sheets from her bed and threw them into the laundry basket. Oh, how she wished they had a washer and dryer. She would have to bring the sheets to her parents' house during the day.

Saturday, Teddy was still ill. That surprised Claire. He couldn't possibly have gotten food poisoning from the fair food. Cotton candy didn't go bad, did it? Fried dough? French fries? Didn't it need to be an animal product? No, when she thought about it, that wasn't the case. Any food could spoil or become contaminated with bacteria.

Anyway, what did it matter? Her kid was puking; that was indisputable. She had never seen so much vomit in her life. He was sweating and feverish. Claire put him into a cool bath, then called her parents.

When Jane's voicemail message ended, Claire said, "Mom, Teddy's sick. I really need you. I'm running out of sheets, and he's vomiting everywhere. I don't dare put him in the bike trailer like this. But we need to get to your house to do the wash, or I need you to come take it."

A few minutes later, the phone rang, and Jane's face popped up on the screen.

"Where are you guys?"

"Dear, we're at the airport. Don't you remember we're leaving for the Azores today?"

"Oh, you're kidding me."

"I'm not kidding you. We just boarded the plane. We'll be gone for three weeks."

"Your timing is terrible. And you guys gave him too much junk food."

"Dear, I don't think junk food has this kind of effect. How much is he vomiting?"

Claire described what had occurred in the kind of gory detail her mother actually enjoyed. Jane clucked her tongue on the other end of the line, then Claire heard Jane's muffled voice as she recounted the story to Frank. His sympathetic sounds came through the line. But there was nothing they could do. They weren't about to cancel their trip for the repercussions of a little binge eating. Besides, at this point, they had already settled into their seats.

"You'll get through it, dear. Trust me, I went through similar situations with you many times."

Claire sighed. Of course, she would get through it. And she thanked God the weather was warm enough that she could open the windows. The odor of vomit was starting to overpower the apartment, and Claire was fighting nausea herself, as a result.

She woke with a start. After another night of very little sleep, the sounds of Teddy retching again carried into her room. *Two days vomiting is unusual for an overconsumption of junk food, isn't it?* She ran to his room, where he was vomiting into the paper bag she had left by his bed in the middle of the night. Sitting on the bed next to him, Claire rubbed her little boy's back, placed her other palm on his forehead: hot.

"Mama, I don't feel good."

"I know, sweetheart, I'm sorry."

"It's too bright in here."

"Too bright?" The morning light filtered through the curtains. "You normally love bright light."

"But my eyes hurt, and my head hurts."

"Let me get you some water, darling."

"Don't leave, Mama."

"I'll be right back. I just wanna get you some water, okay?"

She heard him crying as she turned on the tap. She filled a water bottle with water. A glass would be too hard to handle in his weakened state.

"Okay, sweetheart, have a sip of this." She wiped his mouth. The stench was awful. He looked pale, but his cheeks were bright red. What was going on?

Teddy took a few sips of the water.

"How does that feel on your throat?"

"Good." He kept drinking.

"How about I run you a bath?"

"I'm cold, Mama."

"I think a bath will make you feel better." She ran to the bathroom, gave the tub a quick scrubbing, and filled it with warm water, went back to the kitchen, and got the ginger syrup.

In his room, Teddy lay on his side, moaning. Teddy never moaned. He rarely even whined. She had never seen him like this. He accepted the teaspoon of ginger syrup, something he always liked and sometimes asked for just as a treat. If anything would settle his stomach, this would.

Once Teddy was in the bath, Claire looked at his body for little red bullseyes, a possible sign that a tick had bitten him.

Seeing none, she ran her hands through his hair, feeling for bumps that might be a tick embedded in his scalp and looked for the bullseye under his hair. Nothing. That was a relief. Lyme disease was a bitch.

"Have any of the kids at school been sick?"

Teddy shook his head side to side.

Claire was puzzled. He had a mysterious fever, no tick bites, was vomiting non-stop and couldn't stand light.

"Do I have a fever?"

"You do."

"Is that bad?"

"Sometimes it's good. Sometimes a fever burns off any little buggies that are trying to make you sick."

"But I am sick."

"That seems to be true. So, I'm just going to make you comfortable, okay, and we'll see how it goes?"

Her phone beeped.

A text message from her mom. "How's our boy feeling today?"

"Not good, Mom. He has a fever now. I don't think this is all the junk food you guys fed him."

"Are you taking him to the pediatrician's Saturday hours?"

"Letting the fever do its work. If he doesn't get better soon, I'll call the doctor. You know how he hates doctors."

"He's as stubborn as his mother." Mule emoji.

"Thanks." Frowny face emoji.

The next text was a photo of a mountain retreat. Claire knew her mother wasn't intentionally trying to rub in the fact that they were in paradise while she was in a vomitous hell.

On Sunday, Teddy's fever was 104 degrees. He complained of pains in his body and insisted on wearing sunglasses to shield his eyes from the light. She wished she had brought him to the pediatrician on Saturday morning. A call to Dr. Samuelson's answering service confirmed what she already suspected: she had no choice but to bring him to the emergency room now.

She texted Mazzie, "Help! Parents in Portugal. Teddy violently ill and high fever. Need to get Boy to E.R. ASAP"

"Shit! OMG You know I would help, but Greg and I are in New England," Mazzie responded immediately.

"You're missing the strawberry Jam-a-Rama?"

"Romantic getaway. So sorry!"

"OK. Gotta go."

Her next text message was to Fallon's mom.

Liza's reply was also immediate. "Oh, sweets," sad face emoji, "you know we would help you, but we can't risk making Fallon sick if this is a big thing + Sam has really important mtgs all week. We just have to keep our own health." Rainbow emoji. Heart emoji.

Fucking emojis. Like those made the situation better. It was unbelievable, actually. Her support network was all missing-in-action. If she still lived in Denver, she'd call a taxi or get an Uber. *Fucking small town, pristine lifestyle bullshit.* Claire racked her brain to think of someone else she could rely on. The only person who sprang to mind was Brian. That was ridiculous. She barely knew him.

On the other hand, he was kind, and Teddy liked him. He had a car.

And she knew how to reach him.

If not Brian, she'd have to call an ambulance. She'd call one if she had to, but...

She took a deep breath and sent Brian a text message. "So sorry. You are my last hope. I need to get Teddy to the Emergency Room."

"Ambulance?"

"You are my last hope before ambulance. Don't want to freak Teddy out more than necessary."

"Got it. On the way."

Claire scrambled out of her pajamas and into some jeans and a clean t-shirt.

Thank God, Brian is coming, she thought. *We couldn't stand a repeat of...* she tried to put the scene out of her mind before it lodged there, but it came in flashes.

Jim in the doorway.

She ran a warm washcloth over her face and neck. The stench of vomit remained in her nostrils.

Three-year-old Teddy cowering in the corner.

She brought a warm cloth to Teddy's face then sponged his body down before covering him with a clean t-shirt and a pair of sweatpants. He moaned and put the sunglasses back on his face.

"Warm enough, honey?"

Her baby screaming.

He shook his head. She put his hoodie on over the t-shirt, kissed his forehead, and reassured him that he would feel better soon.

Blood puddled beneath her feet.

Her phone peeped. "Above the gallery, right? I'm here."

"Come on up," she texted back.

Flashing lights.

"Baby, our friend Brian is here. We're going to ride in his car."

Inside the ambulance. Teddy shaking in her arms.

"Why?"

"Can you stand up?"

Teddy tried standing but sank to the floor. Claire's heart thudded. She lifted him. He slumped over her, like a sack of potatoes.

"Okay, Sweetheart. You're okay. We're going to get help."

The sound of the front door opening, followed by Brian's gentle voice and soft footsteps, was a welcome relief.

"Claire?" He called.

She went into the kitchen to greet him. "Thank God."

"You look tired."

Brian put a hand on Teddy's hair. "Hey, buddy, can I carry you? Is that alright?"

"Mama." Teddy buried his face into Claire's neck.

Claire shook her head and stroked Teddy's back. "He's never like this."

"Have you eaten or anything?"

"He's just been vomiting, and I've been trying to clean up after it, but we don't have a washer or dryer, and we really need to go. The fever is getting higher, and ibuprofen didn't touch it."

"But have you eaten today, Claire? You seem, uh..."

"I think I ate something yesterday."

Brian nodded, took a deep breath, and swept Claire off her feet, literally, holding her with one strong arm beneath her upper back and the other cradling her knees. In another situation, Claire might have felt excited or terrified. As it was now, she felt relieved. She had not realized how exhausted she was until she found herself in Brian's arms. Although it went against everything she believed in, Claire allowed her cheek to rest against his chest.

"Car seat?" Brian asked.

"It's in my parent's car, at the airport."

"Got it."

Brian carried Claire and Teddy out the door and down the stairs. The next thing she knew, she was strapped into the back seat of Brian's Land Rover, with Teddy strapped in next to her.

"What do you need, Claire? Do you have your phone and your wallet?"

"Upstairs"

"Where?"

"I don't remember. The bathroom?"

"And your wallet? You never carry a purse."

"My phone case is a wallet. Hurry, Brian." She was trying not to whine but was feeling more frantic about Teddy, more helpless, and completely exhausted.

"Shhh, shhh," he soothed. "I'll be right back."

Claire watched Brian through the window. *You never carry a purse. What a strange thing to notice.*

He took the stairs two at a time and dashed into her house. He moved very differently than Jim — lighter, easier, freer.

A moment later, he bounded down the stairs with one of her small canvas totes. He handed it to her, closed the car doors, and jumped into his seat and zoomed away.

Claire looked inside the bag and saw her phone, plus one of Teddy's books, two apples, a jar of peanut butter, some rice cakes, and her two reusable water bottles. He had even packed a butter knife. She hadn't realized how hungry she was. She was probably dehydrated as well, and now she had everything she needed for the moment, thanks to Brian. Waves of gratitude and remorse washed over her. She hadn't trusted him, had kept him at a distance, a new person in town just trying to connect, and now here he was saving the day. Jim would have blamed, screamed, hit, made things worse.

She took a long sip of water, felt the coolness on her parched throat.

Jim is in prison. We are safe now. We are very safe.

Chapter 13

B y the time they reached the hospital, Teddy was asleep. Brian lifted the boy from the back seat. He was light, despite the listlessness of his body.

"I'll take him, Brian."

He shook his head as he helped Claire out of the car and nodded toward the seat. "Do you have your bag?"

"Thank you; I almost forgot."

He could feel the relief in her voice.

"I'll take him now," she said.

He looked at the dark circles under her eyes, heard the tremble of exhaustion in her voice.

"Look, let me just carry him inside for you, okay?"

"But if he wakes—"

"If he wakes, you'll rub his back and tell him you're with him. You're wiped out, Claire. I can see it. Just take whatever rest you can get while you can get it. It might be a long haul in here."

"Mmm. You're right." She looked up at him with what seemed like gratitude. "Brian, I—" Claire's voice trailed off as they approached the building.

"Yes, Claire?" He looked down at her. Were those tears in her eyes? "Aww. It's okay. He'll be okay."

She nodded. "Thank you. For everything. I—"

"Don't think about it. That's what friends are for."

He regretted saying it the moment it escaped his lips. *That's what friends are for.* It was cheesy, for one thing, and they barely knew each other, for another.

"I guess we are becoming friends, aren't we," she said.

"I hope so." He smiled at her as the electronic doors to the emergency room slid open, and they passed through.

Inside, as he had suspected, the emergency room was a whir of activity. At the registration desk, he stood holding Teddy while Claire collapsed into the chair and filled out the paperwork. The boy's soft breath felt hot and wet on his neck. He was glad the kid was breathing, given how lifeless his body appeared.

When Claire finished filling out the paperwork, an aide brought them into the exam room. Brian expected them to kick him out any minute, but no one did, not even Claire. It was only when the doctor arrived that Teddy stirred and asked for his mother.

"Where am I?"

"You're in the hospital, Honey," Claire said, taking him. Her voice was soft and soothing, but Teddy started panicking.

"I wanna go home now."

"It's okay, Sweetheart. The doctor's going to make you feel better."

"I wanna go home, Mama. Please."

"Sweetie, try to calm down. You're okay."

"Please, Mommy," he cried.

A pained expression crossed Claire's face. "He might be having flashbacks," she whispered.

"Flashbacks?" he whispered back.

Claire nodded.

"Mommy, please can we go home NOW?"

"Heyyyyy there," a booming voice came from the other side of the curtain, and a doctor appeared and scanned Teddy's chart. "Teddy! Hey there, Teddy! What's going on today?"

Teddy started crying and whimpering and tried to bury his face in Claire's neck. Claire told the doctor what had occurred in the last few days, that she had thought it was a simple case of overeating junk food, then maybe food poisoning, and now she wasn't sure. The doctor gave her a condescending look; it irked Brian. Who was this guy, discounting the maternal instinct?

"Sounds like we might have the flu, here. I'm gonna put this funny thing in your ear real quick, Teddy." The doctor inserted a thermometer into Teddy's ear canal with one hand, while holding the boy's wrist with the other, nodded, looked at the readout on the thermometer. "You might feel a little cold on your back. It's just my stethoscope. You know what that is, Teddy?"

Teddy nodded.

The doctor listened to his heartbeat, then looked at Brian.

"I think what we have here, Dad, is the flu."

"Oh, I'm not—"

"So, we wanna bring that fever down."

"I've been giving him ibuprofen and cool baths," Claire said.

"Great job, Mom! Keep up the baths. Forget the ibuprofen. Let's use good old-fashioned Tylenol to get that fever down. You can treat the sinuses with a humidifier or just run a hot shower to get the bathroom nice and steamy, then sit in there with him. He's listless, so don't leave him alone in the bathroom."

"I would never, ever."

"Glad to hear it. He should be able to keep down clear liquids and Jell-O. A bone broth or vegetable broth will be fine. The fever should be down by nightfall, but if it's not, make a trip to your pediatrician in the morning. Okey dokey?"

"Thank you," they said in unison. Why had he said thank you? Did Claire notice? Shit. He hoped she wouldn't think he was overstepping his boundaries. Anyway, what did it matter? He was just being polite, and the important thing was that Teddy would be okay with some rest and soup stock and Tylenol. *What did Claire mean about Teddy having flashbacks? The kid's five.*

Thirty minutes later, they walked into the apartment. The stench hit like a wrecking ball. Claire paused in front of him, coughed, and turned back toward the door.

"A little fresh air," she gasped.

94

He moved aside to let her pass. "Where are the dirty sheets, Claire?"

"What?"

"The dirty sheets. I'm taking them to the laundry for you."

"Oh, no, you're not."

"Is the laundry basket in the bathroom," he asked, walking down the short hallway.

"Brian, I'm serious," she called after him.

"Claire, let me help you."

Normally, he wouldn't just saunter around someone's home. Usually, with permission, he'd pause to get the lay of the land, get a feel for his new friend's vibe. Peruse their bookshelves. Not right now. He peered into the bathroom: empty. Peered into the bedrooms at the end of the hallway and spotted a small basket filled with puke-covered sheets and pajamas in Teddy's room, and another small basket filled with vomit-covered sheets and towels in Claire's room. No wonder she hadn't had time to tend to her own needs; she'd been dealing with a hell of a lot of puke. The sheets on each bed were clean. He took both laundry baskets to the kitchen, dumped the contents into a large trash bag, grabbed a bottle labeled "vinegar + water + tea tree" from under the sink and sprayed each basket down before returning them to the end of the hallway.

When he finished, he found Claire sitting in a chair by the kitchen door, Teddy asleep in her arms. She stroked her son's hair and looked up to meet Brian's gaze.

"Hi," she said.

"Hi."

"You gathered my laundry."

"I hope you don't mind; I just thought—"

"No one has ever done such a thing for me."

"Have you had the need?"

She released a quiet, stilted laugh.

"Do you make a habit of getting your kid to puke everywhere so you can see whether people will jump to your aid?"

"Ha. Ha."

"Just wondering."

"Thank you."

"My pleasure."

"Your pleasure," she said, giggling.

"Where's the laundromat?"

She shook her head.

"Why are you shaking your head?"

"The nearest place is about a 30-minute drive."

"Conveniently, my laundromat is only about ten minutes from here."

"Your laundromat? Oh." A look of understanding swept across her face. "You mean the washer and dryer at your house. Oh, no. No way. That's not fair to you. It's gross. Who wants to deal—"

"I do. I want to do this, Claire. Period. Thank you for letting me help you. What else can I do before I go?"

"I… uh…"

"So, I'm going to go start this laundry and clean out my car. I'll see you tomorrow."

"Oh, I don't think I'll be up for a lecture—"

"When I return the sheets. Okay?"

Claire smiled. Brian ruffled her hair and left.

Was that condescending? God, he was as bad as that pompous emergency room doctor. He couldn't stand himself sometimes. Ruffling her hair. *What a jerk.* He'd better not tell Stephanie about this episode. She'd gag.

Chapter 14

Monday morning, Claire woke to the sound of Teddy wheezing in her arms. Was that wheezing? It was a raspy breathing sound coming from Teddy's throat. Actually, it sounded deeper than that — as if it originated in his chest. Claire guessed that meant the sound was actually coming from his lungs. Why was he wheezing? This wasn't good. She had thought a solid night's rest in his mama's arms would bring Teddy over the hump, but he appeared to be in worse shape than before.

She lifted her phone from the nightstand to look at the time—8:30 AM. They never slept that late; clearly, they'd both been exhausted. Clearly, he still was. Teddy was sound asleep. Claire took the opportunity to slip out of bed to get the thermometer and pop it into her son's ear.

"Mama," he groaned.

Claire stroked his hair. "How're you feeling, Baby?"

"My legs hurt."

"Your legs?"

"And my ankles and knees and elbows."

"Really?"

"My neck hurts."

"Wow. It sounds like everything hurts. How about your hips?"

"Mm hm," Teddy whimpered. He was not the kind of kid who whimpered. She was going to have to call Dr. Samuelson. How would she get out of earshot of Teddy when he was feeling so poorly?

"Do you need to go potty?"

"No. My throat hurts."

"I'll get you some water, Love," she said, springing up and dialing the pediatrician as she left the room.

The pediatric nurse advised Claire to bring Teddy in as soon as she could get him out of the house. Claire brought the water to Teddy and changed into clean clothes while he drank. He looked a little dehydrated. A quick squeeze of the skin on his forearm confirmed it; the skin didn't spring back into place immediately. She monitored his sips. He wasn't drinking enough.

She returned to the kitchen to start her tea water and look for something breakfast-y, then popped a few oranges and snack items into her backpack. As she was pulling clean clothes from Teddy's dresser, it dawned on her that they needed a ride to the pediatrician once again. Then again, did they really? It was only a half-mile down the street. She could carry him that far, even in her exhausted state. She felt more energetic than she had the day before.

"Sweetheart, can you eat anything?"

Teddy shook his head.

"Can you put on this warm sweater? Lift your arms, Honey."

Teddy groaned, "Ow, my shoulders."

"Seriously?"

"Mama," he cried.

"Oh, dear," she said, wrapping him in her arms. "Mama's sorry you're feeling so bad."

Had the ER doctor really tested for Lyme? Or was he just placating her yesterday? *Don't be paranoid, Claire. Why wouldn't he run the test?*

An hour later, in a waiting room surrounded by sniffling, coughing, pallid kids, Claire listened to the mothers talking. Kai's mom said one of the vendors at the Jam-a-Rama had caused a bout of food poisoning. *The Jam-a-Rama. Shit.* She hadn't called Mrs. Meery. Veronica and her team had wanted to set up an interview at their offices for today. She had never sent the thank you note or even an email. Everything had been a whirlwind. *What am I going to do?* She wondered if it was too late to call them. Had they filled the position already? She had planned to follow up immediately.

How long would they sit in the waiting room? Did she have time to call Veronica Meery now? She had to try. Then again, with children screaming and crying and laughing all over the room, Veronica would probably not be able to hear a thing. Plus, Teddy was in rough shape, and she didn't want to leave his side even for a moment. Nor could she. It was hard enough to step away when he was sick at home. Here, he would fall apart emotionally.

Ninety minutes later, the doctor opened the door and called Teddy's name. Teddy lay across Claire's legs, half asleep. She picked him up gently and stood.

Doctor Samuelson smiled, "We have to stop meeting like this, Claire," he said with a wink.

It was an old joke he used with everyone. He had said the same thing to her mother whenever she had brought Claire in for broken bones, earaches, cases of strep throat... His hairstyle had changed over the decades - from long and ponytailed in the 70s to mulleted in the 80s, cropped and thinning in the 90s, and now monkish and graying, but his smile had always been wide and welcoming.

"So, the Lyme tests came back negative," he said before they were fully in the room. "How are you feeling, Buddy?"

Teddy moaned, and Claire recounted the events of the past forty-eight hours. The doctor nodded solemnly. Unlike the ER doctor, Teddy's pediatrician really listened. He touched each of Teddy's sore spots, examined him thoroughly for tick bites while acknowledging and praising Claire for doing the same thing the other day. He pulled a large text from his bookshelf.

"Psitti... Ah there it is," Dr. Samuelson said, then read silently while she stared off into space.

"Claire, do you remember when you called me a week or so ago?"

"Sure."

He mouthed the next sentence silently, "Teddy had fallen into a nest."

Claire nodded, appreciation for the doctor's sensitivity welling up inside her chest.

"I'm going to order blood and sputum cultures, an antibody titer test from the lab, and a chest X-ray. You remember where the lab is?"

"Just around the corner, right? Shore Point Avenue?"

"They'll take excellent care of your boy there, and you'll be done in no time."

"What are you testing for?"

"Bacteria. Pathogens."

"That's exactly what I was afraid of that day!" *Shit! Why wasn't I more careful?*

"A mother always knows! Teddy, you've been so brave today. Would you like a lollipop?"

Teddy shook his head.

"Really? No? It's okay, Honey. Dr. Sam says it's okay."

"Tummy hurts."

"How about some ginger syrup?"

Teddy nodded.

She pulled the bottle from her backpack and gave him a spoonful. Doctor Samuelson placed a gentle hand on her shoulder, and she felt reassured, even though she also felt like the worst mother in the world.

Thanks to the friendly, speedy lab staff, she and Teddy made it home in time to call Veronica Meery before the lunch hour — a relief. It was the first time in a few days Claire got to do something normal. She savored the experience of sitting at the kitchen table and talking on the phone, a steaming cup of tea warming her hand.

"Why that's terrible, Claire," Mrs. Meery said in her papery voice. "What an ordeal."

Claire sighed, "It has been."

"I wondered why we hadn't heard from you, and now it all makes sense. Are you free tomorrow?"

Claire wished she could confirm tomorrow, but how could she when everything with Teddy was so uncertain? "Mrs. Meery, I apologize. I have to take things day by day until I know what we're dealing with here. We should have the tests back in two days. May I call you Wednesday? Will that be too late?"

"Of course, we had wanted to start someone by then, but we have a few other people to interview. I suppose—no, I don't suppose—I *know* we can work around your needs in this very extenuating circumstance. I'm sure things like this don't happen to you all the time."

"Definitely not."

"Then we'll just have to be a little patient."

"Thank you!"

"I have a good sense about you, Claire. I enjoyed meeting you on Friday; it seems like you have a lot to offer. Again, that's no guarantee. We are considering, as I said, a few candidates, and they're all quite good."

"Of course. Mrs. Meery, thank you! Thank you so much. I will call you once I have the lab results back and know what we're—Oh, dear. Teddy?!? I have to go. Sorry."

The retching sound, coupled with wheezing, carried down the short hallway. She ran toward it and into her son's room. He stooped on the floor, his head in a paper bag. How many times was this now? Was he choking on his own vomit? She ran to his side, knelt beside him and rubbed his back. He was dry heaving, thank God. Not even bile was coming up.

"Mommy, who's talking?" Teddy managed between heaves.

"What do you mean, who's talking?"

"The voices."

"Ummmm. I don't hear any voices. Where do you hear them?"

"In my ears."

Was he hearing things? It certainly seemed so. What did that mean? Claire slid her phone from her pocket and googled "hearing voices." The results were terrifying or laughable. She was pretty sure her kid didn't have schizophrenia or any other mental illness. On WebMD, she located a more extensive list. No, he wasn't using alcohol. He didn't have dementia. Brain tumors: doubtful. Epilepsy: he wasn't having seizures, so… Hearing loss: probably not. High fevers and infections. That had to be it. "Some infections, like encephalitis and meningitis, can make you hear things, along with the other symptoms. The same is true for high fevers," it read.

That had to be it. High fever. She felt his forehead again. At the ER, his temp had been 105. At Dr. Sam's, it had been 103. He still felt hot. She grabbed the thermometer from his nightstand and popped it into his ear again.

"Ow. Mama."

"I know, Honey. I'm sorry." 102.5. The Tylenol wasn't doing a whole heck of a lot. But Dr. Samuelson had said she could give it every few… well, right about now, he was due. Plus, he had probably puked more of it up than he had assimilated.

"Alright, kiddo. Time for more Tylenol and ginger syrup.

She was pulling the ginger syrup out of the fridge when she heard the knock on the door. She turned and looked through the window in the door. Brian.

"I come bearing sheets," he said, as she opened the door. "How's my little friend?"

"The same. Lab results in two days, and somehow I feel like life will be back to normal after that."

"Maybe sooner. Where do you want these?"

"That chair is fine. Hey, Brian?"

"Hey, Claire?"

"Thank you. Really. I owe you big time."

He bowed low, like some Shakespearean hero or something, and said, "At your service, m' lady."

She allowed her lips to slide into a smile. "I don't even know what to say to that."

"You already did, and now, I shall take my leave."

"Did you recently watch one of those old movies about knights and princesses or something?"

"No, I'm just a nerd."

She laughed. "Good to know. Thanks for making me laugh. I needed that."

Brian bowed low again, tipping an imaginary hat.

She smirked. "Okay, time to go give my kid his medicine."

"Make sure you eat," he said, leaving something on the counter and ducking out the door.

After giving Teddy his ginger syrup, she returned to the kitchen. She loved surprises, and Brian had left her a little tea cake wrapped in tin foil. The handwritten label read, "Brian's Magic Marble Bread: bananas, oat flour, cocoa powder, egg replacer, almond milk, maple syrup, vanilla."

"Did you make this?" She asked as if he were still there.

She unwrapped the bread, pulled off a hunk, and tasted it. Perfectly moist, and the marbles of banana bread with chocolate cake made her taste buds dance. She took another bite. The texture was off, rubbery, and on the third bite, she realized the sweetness was overpowering. Still, she was hungry, and she was too tired to make anything else. She finished the tea cake. If there was a silver lining to this whole crummy situation, this was it. She fired off a quick text to Brian: banana emoji, bread emoji, smiley face, "Thank you! That was so thoughtful and kind!"

Chapter 15

Two days later, the antibody titer test results arrived. When Dr. Samuelson cleared space in his calendar to see Teddy, Claire knew they were in trouble. He ushered them into his office rather than the examination room.

"We have to stop meeting like this, Claire."

Claire forced a smile.

"Teddy, what are you watching these days? Do you still love Kratt's Creatures?" The doctor said, wrapping an iPad in a protective film and handing it to her son. "It's all loaded up, kiddo."

Yet another reason to worry. Doctor Samuelson only brought out the distractions when he didn't want the child to hear the adult conversation. Teddy took the iPad, nestled into Claire's lap, and watched the Kratt brothers begin a wildlife adventure.

She looked at Doctor Sam, wide-eyed. "So…"

"The test shows the presence of antibodies to the bacteria that causes Psittacosis."

"Antibodies?"

"Antibodies are proteins the immune system produces when it detects a foreign, harmful substance such as bacteria or a parasite."

"Right, right. I think we learned that in Bio. And sitta—what is it?"

Doctor Sam printed the word in capital letters on a prescription pad. It looked much different than it sounded out loud. Then he wrote, "a.k.a. Parrot Fever."

"What is that?"

"It's a form of pneumonia that occurs when humans touch the plumage of infected…"

"Got it," she said, taking a sharp breath in, hoping Teddy hadn't heard and wouldn't understand what the doctor had just said. Falling on the nest, putting his little hands on the downy feathers of the dead chick — who must have been infected with the illness — Teddy had contracted the same illness.

"But why didn't we see something sooner?"

"The incubation period is up to fourteen days."

"He's been at school, with my parents, at the Strawberry Jam-A-Rama. Is this c-o-n-t-a-g-i-o-u-s?"

"Human to human — rarely. Very rarely. Have you or anyone in your circle been experiencing similar symptoms?"

"My stomach is fine."

"Wheezing, sensitivity to light…"

She thought of Teddy insisting on darkening the room and wearing his sunglasses inside.

"Muscle pain. Chills. Weakness."

"No. I haven't. No one else has said anything. I think everyone's fine."

"Claire, did you also handle the—"

"No, I don't think so. I just helped w-a-s-h the h-a-n-d-s and… you know."

"Watch yourself and alert contacts, but I seriously doubt we will see any spread of the d-i-s-e-a-s-e."

Disease. That sounded so formal, so scary.

"So, my dear, I'd like to admit our friend to…" He mouthed, "the hospital."

Claire's jaw dropped. She knew Dr. Sam would never send Teddy to the hospital unless there were no alternatives. "For how long?"

"Five days to start."

"To start?" Five days in the hospital seemed like a very long time.

"I'll order treatments with azithromycin and nebulizer. We're going to watch his progress. Occasionally, this can cause inflammation of the lining to various organs."

"Which means…"

"It can be incredibly serious. I'm optimistic in this case. Various factors — age, overall health, excellent diet. Still, we can't be too careful, my dear. Five days to start, possibly longer. I've been reading up on this. The f-e-v-e-r can last three weeks or more."

For Teddy's sake, Claire tried not to react. She needed to stay calm. Doctor Sam's demeanor made that easier. She took a long, deep breath and let it out slowly. "And you'll be there to check in?"

"Saint Mary's is my second home, outside this office. Now, how are we going to get you there? I can call an—one of our special vehicles, but that's expensive, and we both know how our friend reacts to those things. Are your parents—"

"Traveling."

"Aha. Where's Frack these days?"

"Let me text her."

She pulled out her phone and typed, "Maz, are you home yet? Need to admit T to hospital now. Serious."

"Where are you?"

"Dr. Sam's"

"Meet at your place in ten."

"THX!"

"By the look on your face, I'd say you reached her, and you have a ride. Tell that girl I said hello, would you? Of course, I hate to see anyone in my office, unless it's routine. Still, I have such fond memories of you two spraining ankles together and coming in crying together, holding hands until you were all patched up. Frick and frack."

She felt her mouth curve into a smile. In some ways, she and Mazzie were still very much joined at the hip.

"Thanks so much, Dr. S."

He nodded, gesturing with his chin at her son.

His eyelids were closed. "Teddy," she whispered. Not a stir. She gently pried the iPad from his hands and handed it to the doctor.

Chapter 16

The fact that Teddy had a private room instead of a shared room with only a thin curtain separating him from another ill person was utterly lost on the child. But Claire was relieved. The situation would have been much worse with a stranger sharing the room. She hated hospitals: the constant beeping of machinery, the bland walls, and fake art. The drone of TVs and patients moaning coming from every other room. The worst thing was the smell.

She hadn't stayed in a hospital since she gave birth to Teddy. An awful experience, except, of course, for the outcome. If she ever had another child (if she could ever even find a trustworthy man again), she would absolutely do the earth-mama thing that Mazzie had encouraged her to do from the start: have the baby at home.

Being in the infectious diseases ward was so much worse than giving birth in the maternity ward. This was, in fact, the worst hospital scenario she could have imagined for her boy. The "negative flow/negative pressure" room was sealed to prevent Teddy's infection from spreading through the air ducts. Special filtered vents carried a steady exchange of air to and from the room but gave the air quality a canned feel, like being on an airplane.

To make matters worse, she and anyone else who approached her son was forced to wear a virtual hazmat suit. That included sterile gloves, a clear plastic mask that covered their entire face, all the way up to the hair, paper booties over their shoes, and a dressing gown.

Nothing soothed Teddy like her touch, but when she tried to caress his face, he pulled away, whining, "cold."

She knew it was not just the temperature, but also the rubbery sensation of the glove against his skin. When she tried to stroke his hair, the glove stuck to it, causing him to cry out in pain.

She thought she might scream if she had to explain one more time that he couldn't go home for several days. She wanted so badly to take him home, for him to pull through, for the nightmare to be over.

Doctor Sam had said not to bring any toys that could not be sterilized. Any coloring books Teddy used in the hospital would have to be incinerated.

This all seemed overly precautious. After all, he had said not to worry that Teddy had infected his classmates, teachers, or even her parents, who cuddled him as often as they could.

But the doctor reminded her that people in the hospital were in a state of decreased immune function. In fact, Teddy was now in a state of decreased immune function, and he would be for weeks. That was why Claire was supposed to sterilize everything when she got home. Doctor Sam actually encouraged her to use bleach on the sheets, towels, and bathroom and kitchen surfaces, knowing full well her aversion to such toxic chemicals.

She did agree it would be worth it just this once. Per his instructions, she would also use rubbing alcohol on all the doorknobs and other surfaces bleach might ruin. Tea tree oil would probably do the trick, but she would not be taking a risk on "probably."

Which reminded her that Brian had handled their soiled bed linens, had even carried Teddy. He was tough, but she had to warn him. And Mazzie had transported them to the hospital. She should at least wipe her car down with rubbing alcohol. Claire fired a quick text to Mazzie, then sent one to Brian.

Mazzie responded with a thumbs-up emoji. "Will do, Mama."

Brian's response was more surprising. "What room? Can I come?"

"Brian, I'm telling you to sterilize your car, etc. Make sure you don't get sick."

"Got it. But when can I come? What can I bring you?"

She didn't know how to respond.

"Sorry. Don't mean to intrude, just concerned."

"No, it's lovely," she texted back. "I'm sure Teddy will appreciate a visit from his new superhero."

Bird emoji. Superhero emoji. "Bird Man, at your service."

Chapter 17

T he lap of the waves at low tide was gentle and peaceful. Brian loved this part of the day. The sun was just beginning to warm the sand. The air was fresh. He was in communion with nature.

Since it had been quiet on the beach this morning, he had been able to collect samples in peace. He labeled a plastic zip bag filled with feathers, writing the date, time, and location where the specimen was collected. Later, he would collect samples of hermit crab shells and shell fragments. Now, he grabbed a plastic vial from his toolbox and walked to the water. As he filled the vial with water, he heard a commotion behind him and looked up. People bounced down the boardwalk on the other side of the Restricted Area sign.

He closed the vial, labeled it, then walked across the beach to the recreation area. As he got closer, he saw teenagers setting up a picnic spot in the intertidal zone like it was just a regular beach and any other beach day. *Like they didn't just blow past a huge sign telling them to stay the fuck out. No respect for nature.* He hoped none of the beach chairs was actually sitting on top of a crab egg nest, mangling the eggs. With wet sand covering the nest, it would be hard to tell.

"Hey," he said, keeping his voice low, so he wouldn't frighten the nesting birds.

They ignored him. Oh, this was going to be fun.

"Kids," he said firmly. "You are trespassing on protected property."

"What's it to you?" One of them slurred, standing up to his full height. He had a good four inches on Brian. *Great. Big and drunk.*

"You are violating about ten different laws just by being here, never mind what you're doing here."

"We're having a picnic. Is that against the law now?"

"It is at this site. And at your age, your picnic ingredients are illegal."

The kid and his friends started laughing.

"Here," one of the girls said, tossing a crushed beer can at Brian's feet. "I'm done with this one."

The kids roared with laughter. "Yeah, pick it up, Mister Clean," one of them yelled.

The birds were getting nervous.

"I'm asking you once more to leave."

"Or what?"

"Or I call the police."

"How about I throw your phone in the ocean, while it's still in your pocket, asshole?" The kid stood and stumbled toward Brian.

Brian pulled out his cell phone and dialed 9-1-1 as he walked away.

"9-1-1. What's your emergency?" The nasal voice came over the wire.

"I've got a group of drunk and belligerent teenagers at the restricted site at Shelter Beach. I'm with Delaware Flora and Fauna doing fieldwork here, and they're not only breaking the law with underage drinking, they're breaking state law by being at a restricted site during nesting season."

"Oooh, nesting season," the tall one cooed.

"Hear 'em?"

"We'll send a squad car over."

What made kids turn out like this? Had these obnoxious teens started out sweet and silly like Teddy? Like Stephanie's boys? Like he had been? Had they been neglected or traumatized at some point? Sure, kids drank. He had experimented in high school, like so many kids, but he didn't remember ever being so rude and callous. He hoped Teddy would remain caring and kind. *You really seem to have the right idea, Claire, showing your son how to help wildlife, making it cool for Teddy to do the right thing, tapping into every boy's desire to be a superhero. Right on, Claire. Right on!*

Thinking of Teddy reminded him—the boy was seriously ill. Not that he had forgotten Teddy was in the hospital, but focusing on his work had forced the issue to the back of his mind. Now that it was front and center again, he felt his chest tighten. Why was it always the good ones who got sick? Like Adrienne. *No. Not like Adrienne. This is just an infection. A bird disease. Ironic, but not life-threatening. No, it is life-threatening, Brian. It is. It has the potential to be. It won't be deadly. He's going to recover.*

A siren chirped close by. Car doors slammed. He inhaled and exhaled slowly to calm himself. The trespassing issue was about to be resolved. Next, he could assess and document the damage left by the little punks, then get back to collecting his samples, and finally, at the end of the day, go see his little buddy... and Claire.

Chapter 18

C laire lay curled around her son's sleeping body, the hazmat mask slid above her face, so she could kiss her baby's head. She felt the rattle in his chest through his hospital gown. It tugged at her heart. She inhaled deeply, trying for the thousandth time to meditate herself into a state of calm, but the smell of his illness brought more anxiety. A knock sounded on the door. She opened her eyes. How long had she been lying there? Early evening sun shone through the window, casting a pleasant warm glow on the otherwise stark room. The knock sounded again, and the nurse walked in, her shoes squeaking on the linoleum, her vivid uniform bringing color into the space.

"Is our little guy up for visitors?"

"He's asleep," Claire whispered, wondering why that wasn't obvious. Did the woman need a nursing degree to recognize the difference between waking and sleeping states? "Who's here?"

"Your friend Brian."

She smiled, extracted her arm from around Teddy's torso, sat up, and ran her fingers through her hair. Tangles. Did she have a hair tie? She felt for the band around her wrist, retrieved it and wound her hair into a top knot. Her tongue felt fuzzy. How long had she been lying there in her half meditative, half asleep state?

"One second. Let me just brush my teeth."

The nurse smiled conspiratorially as she strode to the monitors at the head of Teddy's bed. "Well, the O2 Sat's improving!"

O2 Sat, Claire had learned, was the amount of oxygen saturating Teddy's lungs. They wanted the number to be above 90 before he could come off the oxygen mask. He hated wearing the mask. She found herself praying hourly that his O2 Sat would improve, because if it didn't, he'd probably end up with neurological damage, or organ failure, or... Tears welled in her eyes again. She took a deep breath to calm herself. *He'll be fine. The O2 Sat's improving.*

The nurse prattled on loudly (why were nurses always so loud?) as Claire ducked into their tiny private bathroom, peed, splashed some water on her face, and finally brushed her teeth. None of this mattered, she realized, as she slid the hazmat mask back over her face. Still, she appreciated being clean, or somewhat clean. She tried to remember when she had last showered. Was it before the visit to Doctor Sam yesterday? Or the day before that?

"Sweetheart," she whispered, back at his bedside. "You have a visitor."

She slipped the mask off her face just long enough to kiss his forehead. "Baby."

His eyelids fluttered. *I wonder what he's dreaming about.*

"Doctor Samuelson will be doing rounds shortly," the nurse said on her way out.

Claire could hear her explaining the safety protocol to Brian: the mask, the gloves, the hospital gown.

A moment later, he tiptoed into the room. "Hey," he said softly. He looked like an astronaut.

She held up a hand in greeting.

"Quite a setup you have here."

"Anything to impress my friends," she smirked.

"How's he holding up?"

"His O2 Sat's improving, apparently."

Brian nodded, as if he knew what that meant.

"That means—"

"I know what it means."

"Oh?"

"Adrienne."

"Who?

His face visibly tightened. "My wife. It became a problem at the end."

He was married. The end. Her death? Claire didn't know what to say. "I'm sorry."

"How are you holding up?" Brian asked, touching her arm. "Have you slept?"

"A little. There's not much to do here besides watch TV." She stuck out her tongue.

Television bored her. It wasn't active enough and she hated being marketed to constantly, having her son marketed to constantly. He got enough of it visiting friends.

Brian slid the tote bag off his shoulder. "Have you eaten?"

"Umm…"

"Since you liked the banana marble bread, I brought you some more."

"Thank you!" She smiled and clapped her hands together softly. *Maybe the second batch will be better.*

"And my special vegan molé enchiladas."

"You're kidding."

"I am not kidding."

"Molé is my favorite, but you can never find it vegan. How did you do this?"

"Magic. You hungry?"

She was now. Brian pulled a blue and white checkered cloth from the tote bag. "Where should I put this?"

She smoothed the sheets on the extra bed and lay the tablecloth over it.

"We could probably eat directly off the floors here," he said, sitting on the bed, "but this is more fun."

She laughed, watching him extract a glowing electric tea light in a glass candle holder from his bag and place it in the center of the picnic blanket. Following that, he lay some fresh picked purple fringed gentian and pink wild geranium flowers near the fake candle.

"You're like Mary Poppins. What else is in that bag?"

There was a small set of bamboo dishware, a wrapped present for Teddy, and finally, the food, in covered Pyrex containers.

"Uh, oh. What do we do about the masks?" Brian asked.

She ran through the rationale for the safety protocol in her head.

"I think it's okay," she said. "Teddy has been around both of us all this time. We're sitting several feet from him at the moment."

"True."

"We'll put the masks on as soon as we finish eating. This is probably all overkill, anyway."

She slid the mask off her face and took a forkful of enchilada.

The veggies were overcooked and the corn tortillas were the texture of baby food, but the flavor was good. The first bite was a savory mix of spice and salt, of fresh zucchini, spinach, onion, and— "Is that sweet potato?"

He nodded, smiling. His dimples deepened. She really, really liked his dimples. She wished that she really, really liked his food. How much could she eat without insulting him?

"Brian, this is something! Where did you get this recipe?"

"Online."

She took another bite. The molé sauce... There was something positive she could focus on. "This molé is smooth, but not too rich. You know how it can be sometimes? It's like… a perfect sauce. It's actually perfect."

"Aw shucks, ain't nothin'."

She laughed, recognizing the hero's famous line from that ridiculous series of Western spoofs she and her dad had watched together so many times.

"Why you're the hero we all been waitin' fer," she said.

Just then, his eyes caught hers, and her heart stopped. What was that radiating from him? They had started out sharing a silly joke, but now there was something deeper in his eyes. It was as if he wanted to be her hero. Their hero. He had rescued them and brought them to the ER. He had done their vomitrocious laundry. He was now making sure, for the second time, that she was nourished so that she could tend to her son. If they were in a different place, or a different time, she might lean over and kiss him. She might. Or maybe he would lean over and kiss her.

It almost felt like they were somewhere else, somewhere beautiful, magical, and romantic, not sterile, stark and colorless. It almost felt that way.

He placed his hand, palm up on the picnic blanket near her plate. She looked into his palm, then into his eyes, and placed her hand in his. He held her gaze, and she felt the tension drain away. Electricity zipped up her arm and suddenly her whole body felt vibrant.

"Mama?" Teddy squeaked.

Her head snapped to attention. "Yes, Love. Mama's here."

She slipped the mask back over her face and rose to greet her child.

Chapter 19

B rian's first thought upon waking was of Teddy lying in the hospital bed, and his mother, his *beautiful mother* by his side. Now, Brian stretched his body long, until the tightness in his muscles released, then settled back into the firm mattress. The visit Thursday night had been so delightful, so unexpectedly romantic. He hadn't consciously been trying to create that mood. He'd just wanted to see Claire smile, to cheer her during a stressful time. Yet, romance had arisen, without warning, over conversation about enchiladas with molé sauce. Was it the candlelight? The flower petals?

Claire knew the old Westerns. She had quipped her line on cue, as if she, not his sister, had been the one with whom he had played that old bit for decades. She was in on their inside joke. Those were cult classics, not popular Westerns. It was a particular person who appreciated the silliness. She had given him that look, that melty look that made his heart race. Her eyes, that deep rich shade of brown, like chocolate, full of so much unspoken emotion. He'd almost forgotten they were sitting in a hospital room, until Teddy had said, "Mama."

He opened his eyes, took in the morning sunlight sparkling on the water in the salt marsh, then turned his vision inward again. *Claire snapped to attention when Teddy called her. His voice was barely audible, but Claire heard it and sprang into action.* She was a mother. A *mother.* A natural caretaker and guide who knew her child, tended to his needs, and gently showed him how to move in the world. That was incredibly sexy.

He and Adrienne had dreamed of having children, but it wasn't meant to be. Actually, he had wanted to be a parent more than Adrienne. He had always wanted kids. He had envisioned himself to be the kind of father his own father had been: just attentive enough, not smothering, not demanding or overbearing. His father had given him and Stephanie the freedom to explore the world, whether it was the world of their back yard, or the beach down the street, or college. *Dad was always excited to hear what we discovered.*

If he got to the hospital early enough, he might catch Teddy awake. After Claire had texted him the photo of Teddy coloring in the Wild Birds of America coloring book, he had gone out and bought another present. It would be fun to play with the Legos together. True, they were plastic. But, since Lego was now using sugarcane-based plastic, instead of petroleum-based plastic, in some of their building elements, Brian did not need to feel quite as guilty. *Thank God for ingenuity!*

He hoped that Claire would either play with them — that would be so fun — or use the opportunity to take a break from the sterility of the hospital. He envisioned her stepping outside, inhaling the fresh air and reveling in it. She deserved a moment of rejuvenation. If they were a couple, he would give her a shoulder massage in the hospital. Then, when they were out of the hospital, he would send her to a spa for a day, or a yoga retreat, whatever she wanted. He'd put it on a credit card if he had to. Those things could be expensive, but she deserved it. *Okay, you're getting ahead of yourself, Brian. Way ahead of yourself. If we were a couple? Please. You haven't even been on a date. Make her a fresh green juice this morning. See how that goes.* He debated whether to make a kale juice or a chia berry smoothie. Perhaps both. Remembering when she described her experimentation with chia French toast, he exhaled.

"Just make the smoothie, Man," he said aloud.

It was noon when he arrived at the hospital with the green juice. Brian suited up, placing the plastic mask over his face, the Johnny gown over his body, the booties over his shoes, and the latex gloves over his hands. He entered the hospital room. Claire

119

sat in a chair between the window and Teddy's bedside, with her hand on his arm. The boy's light snores rose over the beeping monitors. Claire appeared to be absorbed in reading *Last Child in the Woods*, the book he had recommended. The sunlight framed her face beautifully. Despite the ridiculous plastic mask, he could see the radiance of her skin.

She looked up and smiled at him. "Fancy meeting you here."

"I was just in the neighborhood."

"Oh, really. You hang out in hospitals?"

"When people I care about are in them, I do."

He held the juice out to her.

She read his handwritten note and smiled. "Aww."

He extended his other hand and gave her the second wrapped gift for Teddy. "I hope you don't mind me bringing another little treat to cheer him up."

"Normally, I would say you're spoiling him, but under the circumstances, I think he deserves a little spoiling. I really, deeply appreciate it. Thank you."

She stood and gave him a gentle, awkward hug. *Damn hazmat suit*, he thought. Still, he felt a zing of electricity, even through all the paper and plastic.

"How are you, Claire?"

"Hanging in there."

"It's beautiful out. If you wanna get out of here for ten minutes, half an hour, even a couple of hours, I've got some time."

"Oh, Brian, I can't leave him."

"I thought you'd say that, but maybe when he wakes up, if he wants to play with me, you'll reconsider, huh? It'd do you some good."

"I know you're right. I just… I can't. But thank you."

He nodded, wanting to take her into his arms again, to stroke her back. Instead, he said, "You're a devoted mommy. I admire that."

She smiled, her chocolate brown eyes crinkling at the edges. He liked those little crinkles, loved seeing her smile, liked knowing that his words had made her smile. "Hey, whatever happened with the Jam-A-Rama job? Did you hear anything?"

Claire inhaled sharply. "Oh. My. God. Oh. My. God. Oh, My God, Oh my God, oh my God!"

Damnit, why did you bring that up, Brian? What is your problem?

"Brian, I was supposed to call them or email them and set up a meeting, and I completely forgot with everything that's been going on, and it's been — I don't know — what day is it?"

"Saturday."

"Oh, God! It's been over a week. I did nothing. Oh, this is horrible. And it's Saturday. They're not even gonna be there if I call."

"You never know. They might be."

"You think?"

"It's worth a try."

Claire was shaking. "It's all too much, Brian." Tears filled her eyes.

"Hey," he said, putting a hand on her arm. "It'll be okay. I'm sure they'll understand."

"They were in such a hurry to get someone, though. And they were already holding off for me. This is just, this is just too much."

His heart sank. He had brought her from joy to despair in less than a minute; all he had wanted was to help her through this scary time. He knew what it felt like to sit at the bedside of your most important person, to hope beyond hope they would be okay. He, too, had planted himself inside a hospital room for fear that if he left, his most important person might wake up to a sterile, empty space. She was hyperventilating now, walking around in circles.

"Hey, Claire," he said, reaching for her hand. "Breathe with me."

He modeled a deep inhalation and exhalation.

"This is so embarrassing," she moaned, coming to stillness by his side.

"No, please. I'd be freaking out, too, but it's really gonna be okay. Breathe with me, please."

He caught her eye, then exaggerated deep inhalation and exhalation again, moving his free hand up and down in front of his torso with every breath. She joined him, slowing her breathing, moving her free hand up and down in front of her body.

"You've got so much going for you, Claire. You'll end up with a great job."

"You think so?"

"You're a great catch, Claire. It'll all work out."

You're a great catch, Claire? Jesus, Brian. She's looking for a job, not a man.

"Mama? Why are you crying?" Teddy croaked.

"What, Honey?" Claire snapped to attention and went to Teddy's bedside. "How are you feeling, Sweetheart?"

"I heard you crying."

"Me? What? Oh, hey, look who's here to visit you again!"

"Hey, Super Teddy!" *I guess she's just going to pretend everything's okay.* "Hey, do you like building stuff?"

Teddy nodded.

"Because I have a pretty cool surprise for superheroes who like building stuff." He held out the gift.

"Can I, Mama?"

"Of course," Claire said, lifting the mask just long enough to wipe her eyes. "What do you say?"

"Thank you, Bird Man!"

"Open it up. We can play if you want."

Watching Teddy open the gift gave Brian the same warm feeling he got watching little Paul and Jared open presents. The delight that spread across Teddy's pale face when he discovered the Legos with superheroes made him feel like a kid himself. "What do you think?"

"Let's play," he half-whispered half-croaked. Teddy was smiling, but his exhaustion was palpable.

"Claire, do you want to play with us after you make that phone call?"

She looked at him, quizzically, at first, like she couldn't figure out his motivation for making the suggestion. He smiled and held her gaze until the fear in her eyes softened.

"Thanks, Brian. I think I will. Teddy, Mama will be right back, okay?"

"Where're you going?"

"Just into the hallway for a minute. Will you be okay with Brian?"

"Oh, sure, we'll be fine, Mama."

Her eyes lit up at her son's casual reply. Brian stifled a chuckle. *Oh, sure, we'll be fine. Too cute.*

By the time Claire returned from making her call, and presumably pulling herself together, he and Teddy had removed all the building components and laid them out on the bed.

"That goes there, Bird Man," Teddy said, moving a plastic tree into a corner. "All the trees go in the corner, so it's like a little forest."

"Got it! Hey, why didn't the tree answer your question?"

"Hmmm. I don't know."

"Because it was stumped. Get it?"

Teddy looked confused. "What's stumped?"

"Oh, a stump is what's left when you cut a tree. Have you ever seen that kind of flat thing in the ground where a tree used to be?"

"Oh, yeah! And it has those rings inside it!"

"That's right! That's called a stump. And do you know what another meaning of the word stump is?"

Teddy shook his head.

"It means confused. See? So, the tree was stumped — it was confused."

"And it was cut down to the rings!" Teddy giggled. "Stumped!"

He was still giggling when Claire walked in and smiled. "Looks like you two are having fun."

"Mama, why didn't the tree answer your question?"

"Tell me."

"Because it was stumped!" He giggled again, then launched into a coughing fit.

Claire rushed to his side and rubbed his back. "Good one!"

Brian tried to read her face. Was she more relaxed? He didn't want to ask the question out loud, didn't want to risk her breaking down again, especially not in front of Teddy. He caught her eye and hoped she could read the question in his eyes. She nodded, a faint smile on her lips, but the stress showed in the tension around her mouth.

"V-o-i-c-e-m-a-i-l," she said.

He nodded. "We built a forest while you were gone. Care to join us? Your son is quite an urban planner."

A genuine smile spread across Claire's face, and he felt himself relax. *She's okay. She'll be okay.*

Chapter 20

A deep voice intoned from behind the curtain, "Teddy, Teddy, Teddy, we have to stop meeting like this."

"Hi, Doctor Sam," Teddy said, sounding forlorn.

Claire smiled, "Hey, Doctor Sam."

The doctor winked at her, then focused on her son. "Why so glum, old chum? Have you had enough of this place?"

Teddy nodded.

"Then I have excellent news for you," Doctor Samuelson said, looking from Teddy to Claire.

"We get to go home today?"

"There's that old superhero smile. Yes, Teddy, and as a special parting gift, I present to you the first and only Super Patient cape ever bestowed by this hospital."

He withdrew it from behind his back with a flourish. "Now, this is important. You get to go home today, but you and your mom need to CHILL OUT for ten more days. You know how many that is?"

Teddy counted on his fingers.

"Correct! Brilliant! So, you will have to save your rescuing activities for June 11th. I'm going to send you home with some medicine to make you better. You must take it twice a day to regain full superhero strength, but on June 11th, no more meds. Got it?"

Teddy nodded.

"Now, let's find you a ride home."

Brian locked the Rover and walked toward the field. He estimated he was looking at two hundred cars and even more proud EV and BioDiesel car owners. The familiar smell of diesel fuel burning filled his nostrils. He sighed. *It'd be great to share this with Dad.* Moving toward the first row of vehicles, which looked like all BioDiesel conversions, he pulled out his phone and started recording. He could share it with his father via email.

"Dad, check this out. I'm at the Delaware Eco-Friendly Auto Show; it's a semi-annual thing down here. Maybe you can come next—"

His phone rang, stopping the video recording. *Crap.* It rang again. He looked at the screen. Claire.

He answered, "Hey. How are you? How's Teddy?"

"Are you busy today?"

"Why? What's up? Everything okay?"

"We're going home, and I was wondering if you have time to pick us up. Mazzie's teaching back to back until evening."

"Of course. I'm at a car show," he started to say, then stopped mid-sentence. Claire was so anti-car. How could he explain the emotional connection he felt to his dad when he looked at a refurbished vehicle? He'd figure that out later. For now, he said, "I'm forty-five-minutes away. Alright?"

"Thank you so much! Take your time."

They hung up.

Take your time. She surely didn't mean that. From what he knew about Claire, she was: one — not patient, and two — eager as hell to get out of that hospital.

He started a new video, panning across the field of vehicles.

"Dad, what you're looking at is the Delaware Eco-Friendly Auto Show. And this is as close as either one of us is getting to it this weekend. I've got a friend in need who just texted me for help, so I'm skipping this today. Hope to get back here next weekend. Pretty sure it runs both weekends. It'd be great if you could come down. Miss you, Dad."

He clicked the send button, heard the whooshing sound that meant the video was on its way and loped back to the Rover. *Feels good to be needed.*

Chapter 21

Her muscles ached from the exertion. Claire had been swimming for hours with Teddy on her back. The pathogens followed close behind, growling and screeching. Another wave of terror rippled through her, as her legs threatened to stop moving.

The phone rang, rousing her from the nightmare. *Aching muscles: a sign of Psittacosis. Should I be concerned?* Were her muscles really aching, or was that just the dream? She did a quick body scan: feet, legs, hips, arms, shoulders, back — all felt fine. She took a deep breath and reached for the phone. Just as she looked at the screen, the ringing stopped. The number was unfamiliar anyway, probably a telemarketer. Who else called at seven-thirty a.m.? The voicemail tone bleeped, and Claire lifted the phone to her ear to listen.

"Claire, it's Veronica Meery. I just heard your message from Saturday, and I wanted to get back to you immediately. You were such a solid candidate, and I apologize that we are not able to offer you the position. The truth is, we hired someone equally qualified who was available immediately. So, you see, it truly was a simple matter of timing. I'm so sorry, Claire, but you know I'd be happy to stay in touch, and if I hear of anything… Actually, I did just learn the Ocean Falls Nature Center is hiring a Development Coordinator. Wouldn't that be perfect for you?"

Yes, if Marian wasn't already dead set against hiring me.

"— the absolute best and truly, please stay in touch. Bye for now."

Bye for now.

She dropped the phone, took a deep breath, buried her face in her pillow, and screamed.

The sound of Teddy screaming in delight soothed Claire's nerves.

"Okay. One more time," she yelled, then chased him around the play structure.

Teddy squealed as she caught him in her arms and scooped him into the air, then flew him around the playground.

"Hey," she heard from across the playground. Her body tingled at the sound of his voice. *Brian.*

"Is this a superhero convention?"

"Birdman!" Teddy wriggled from Claire's arms and ran to Brian, stopping mid-way to catch his breath.

Her heart sank. Four days into his recovery, Teddy was still wheezing.

Brian looked at her with concern as he lifted Teddy into his arms. "Hey, Little Buddy! I mean, Super…" he looked at the cape, "Snail?"

"Slow and steady wins the race, Brian," she explained, hoping he would catch her meaning. Making the Super Snail cape had been her way of encouraging Teddy to slow down during his recovery period.

"Aha! How ya feeling, Super Snail?"

"Good," Teddy said, coughing.

"Yeah?"

"I can run around the playground again."

"Just for a little while," Claire reminded her son. She smiled at Brian, noting how well his jeans fit him. "What are you doing here?"

"I was on my way into the library when I saw you. So, what are we playing now?"

"Ummm," Teddy started.

"I have an idea. Why don't we all fly on the swings?"

"Wow, Claire, that's a great activity for superheroes in training. Get those flying muscles in shape."

"Exactly," she winked at him.

"Birdman, can you push me?"

Brian deposited Teddy onto a swing. "How high do you want to go?"

"As high as the sky!"

"You got it," he said, pulling Teddy's swing back and releasing it. "Pump those legs, Super Snail."

"Mommy, I'm flying!"

"Yes, you are!" She beamed at her son, then at their friend.

"Would you like a push, too, Claire?"

Was he flirting with her? She blushed and sat on the swing next to Teddy's. "Fly me as high as the sky, too, please."

"You got it."

His hands gripped the chains on either side of her hips. It had been years since a man's hands had been anywhere near her hips. The heat made her feel jumpy. He pulled the swing back, let go, and she flew through the air. Automatically, she pumped her legs as if she were a child again. Suddenly, she felt as if she didn't have a care in the world. *The magic of play,* she thought. Then she felt his hand on her low back, giving her a little push. Her breath caught in her throat. She wanted more of his hand on her back.

"Hey, Brian?"

"Hey, Claire?"

"You wanna come over for dinner tonight?"

"Love to! What can I bring?"

"Yourself."

"And… how about a vegan veggie pizza with cashew cheeze?"

"Sounds delicious, but I invited you, which means I cook."

"Unless it's a potluck, and since you guys are still recovering, why not let me do the heavy lifting?"

She smiled and stopped pumping her legs. He grabbed the chains, slowing her swing to a halt.

"You're sweet," she said, looking into his eyes, then at his full lips.

"Don't worry," he said, dimples deepening. "I'll leave the dishes for you."

Of course, Brian could not leave the dishes for Claire. It just didn't feel right, when she was clearly still exhausted from the events of the previous ten days. He had agreed to let her make tea after dinner. Now, he snuck a peek at her as she moved around the table, setting out an assortment of teas, sweeteners, and jars of homemade almond milk and hemp milk.

She was beautiful, both strong and delicate, and he found her graceful movements entrancing. She hummed quietly as she worked. An image of her unbuttoning her shirt flashed through his mind. He turned back to the sink quickly so she wouldn't see him getting aroused.

"Dinner was lovely, Brian," she said softly, coming to stand beside him at the sink. "You're so kind. Thank you."

"My pleasure," he said, kissing the top of her head.

She looked up at him and smiled. Was this a good time to kiss her?

"You wouldn't believe what she's been through, Brian," he heard Claire's mother say in his head. Then Mazzie's voice, "The PTSD's getting better."

No. Not the right time. Whatever had happened to her, it seemed clear that she wasn't ready for a relationship. And he could not risk opening his heart to someone who couldn't risk opening hers. It was not the right time. It might never be the right time. She might not be the right woman.

Dear God, Brian, all these 'might nots.' Sounds like you're still holding on to us, even though we agreed you'd move on.

He sighed. *Adrienne, do you have to do this now?*

Me? Man, you're the one hanging back from the possibility of love that's staring you in the face.

"Is everything alright, Brian?"

"What? Yes. Fine. I just was thinking…" It was safe to face her now without shaming himself. He turned toward her. "How's the search going?"

"Ugh! Jam-a-Rama hired someone else."

"What?" He said. "They're crazy."

"Thanks for saying that. Listen to this message she left Monday."

Claire cued up the voicemail and handed Brian her phone. He listened. "Geez, that's the best rejection I've ever heard. She wants to help you!"

"I guess that's something to be grateful for."

"Sure is. But you know, I've been thinking: why don't you just forget the job and go to school? Why defer your admission?"

"Moola, my friend."

"Did you look up that fellowship? Could pay your whole ride."

She sighed again, "I missed the deadline. Anyway, I doubt I qualify."

"Hmmm," he said. He'd have to reach out to Nick.

Chapter 22

She locked her bike to the rack. Teddy unbuckled himself and climbed out of his trailer. "Ta-da!"

Claire clapped, "You did it!"

"Well, look who's feeling better! Hey, big guy!"

Teddy beamed at Brian and put a finger to his lips.

"This is one of Ocean Fall's greatest superheroes, Brian." She pointed to the letters on Teddy's chest, "S. Super. S. Silent. M. Man."

Teddy jumped in the air, a big smile on his face, then ran around the bike rack, his purple cape flapping behind him, big cloth ears flopping atop his head.

"Hey, hey, hey, Sweetheart, chill, remember? Doctor Sam said—"

"Doctor Sam said when I have full superhero strength, I can run around again."

Brian smiled — *those dimples* — and fell into step with her. "Looks like Super Silent Man has full superhero strength," he said.

"Teddy," she said, pointing to the building. Teddy ran to the door, tried to open it, then discovered the blue button for wheelchair access, pushed it, and clapped as the door opened on its own.

"Only because he slept all day," she told Brian. "He's still up and down."

"Sorry to hear that. You sure you wanna do this now?"

Inside, she took Teddy's hand, as much to center herself as to calm him.

How could I let you down after all you've done for us?

"We both really needed to get out of the house, and this is pretty low-key."

She led Teddy to a seat in the front row, perfect in case he might want to lay a blanket on the floor and fall asleep.

As she pulled out her notebook, pen, and syllabus, Teddy unpacked his small menagerie of quiet toys, books, and coloring implements.

Brian cleared his throat, smiled as she looked up at him, and began:

"At this point in our history, it is impossible to separate climate change from biodiversity. As Wilson so deftly elucidates in *Half-Earth*, the removal of one species from its native habitat has unexpected ripple effects. For example, a decline in the wolf population at Yellowstone National Park resulted in a sharp decrease in aspen trees, since without wolves, elk had no predators and the increase in—"

"Mommy!" Teddy whispered loudly, "I'm hungry!"

She whispered in his ear. "Shhh, Honey. Shhh."

She pulled an almond butter sandwich from her backpack and unwrapped it for him.

"Thirsty, Mama."

She handed him his water bottle, then pointed to the acronym on his costume. "You're Super Silent Man. Remember?"

Teddy looked down dejectedly until Brian came over and ruffled his hair.

Claire smiled, surprised by her own reaction. She was sweating and nervous and smiling at the attention he was giving her son? What was this? This was a professional meeting, not some sort of romantic encounter.

"Now," Brian continued, "some have suggested that extinctions can be balanced out by the introduction of alien species into new ecosystems or that extinct species might be brought back through cloning. Let's look at that idea."

She soon found herself engrossed.

Brian finished his lecture just as his timer beeped. *Yes! Right on time!* He assigned homework to his "class" of two and asked if there were any questions. A small snore arose from the floor. He looked at Claire, then at her son, who lay on the floor clutching a stuffed turtle. The family resemblance was strong, except for the hair. They both had cherubic faces and lean builds. Teddy's eyelids fluttered as he dreamed.

"I think that's our cue. Does this time work next week?"

She nodded.

"Sweetheart, time to go," Claire said as she packed Teddy's stuff. She strapped her backpack on, then tried to lift Teddy from the floor. Apparently, Claire had not considered the possibility that she might not be able to wake him if he fell asleep.

"Teddy, honey."

Brian slung his bag over his shoulder and offered his hand to help her stand, then lifted Teddy and his blanket and headed for the door. She followed, silent. Claire was so quiet that he looked back to make sure she was still there. Had she been staring at him? There was an odd look on her face, a dreamy smile, and when she noticed he was looking at her, she blushed and looked at the ground. Claire hurried around him and held the door open.

"Hey, Claire? Now that things are somewhat back to normal, what do you think about that bike tour?"

"Oh, um…"

"To sweeten the deal, how about I make you guys dinner after?"

"Seriously?"

"I'm a veritable vegan gourmet," he said, putting on a French accent.

"And modest, too," she giggled.

"And I would love to cook for you, a lovely meal in a lovely setting," he said, continuing the bit, remembering the joy on Claire's face as she tasted his molé enchiladas in the hospital.

"A wee bourguignon de jackfruit meat substitute."

"Oh, my goodness. Even in faux-French, you rhyme!"

"I am, as they say, a po-et."

"And you don't even know-et," Claire said, putting on her own faux French accent.

They were both giggling as they reached her bicycle. As they faced each other, his heart tingled, noticing she still had that dreamy look on her face. A warm breeze passed between them. Teddy stirred in his arms.

Claire sighed, then broke his gaze and opened the flap to the bicycle trailer.

He asked, "I don't suppose you'd let me drive you guys home, would you, since it's dark out?"

Claire reached across her handlebars and flicked a switch. White light glowed from the handlebars, and three flashing red lights shone on the back seat and both sides of the bike trailer.

The idea of them riding a bicycle home in the dark made him queasy, but he'd learned to allow people the dignity of their own path. She'd probably done it many times, and both she and her son were still alive.

"Will you ride one of those safe paths now?" He couldn't help asking.

"At night, I think it's actually safer to be on the main road where there are a few street lights and people."

Brian lowered Teddy into the bicycle trailer and strapped him in. "Did I do it right?"

Claire inspected the harness and nodded. "So, you want someone to show you the bike trails?"

"Yes, please."

"Oh, I wasn't volunteering!"

"What? Oh."

Claire laughed and tapped him on the arm playfully. Her eyes shone in the moonlight. "Just kidding. Just kidding. Of course, I'll show you."

Was she flirting with him? First the arm tap, then—

"I'd be happy to show you. I mean, I'm practically the Ocean Falls Bicycling Ambassador!"

"Be nice if you got paid for that, huh?"

"No, kidding." She inhaled deeply and let it out with a sigh.

She's sighing now. Damn it. Why did you have to remind her about the job search, Man? You know how stressed out she is about it!

"So, call me, and we'll see what we can arrange."

She forced a smile, climbed onto her seat, strapped on her helmet and waved goodbye.

As Brian watched her ride away, he felt an odd sensation in his chest, as if something was being torn from his body. Should he follow them home, just to make sure they were safe? Would that be creepy? *Adrienne, what would you do?*

Follow your heart.

Seriously? That old line?

There's a reason people say it all the time, Brian. It's the best advice.

He sighed, got into his Land Rover, turned on the flashers, and drove until he caught up with Claire. When he reached her, he rolled down the window and yelled, "Is it okay if I follow you, just to give you some extra light?"

"It's really not necessary."

"But is it okay?"

"I guess," she said, keeping her pace.

At the first stop sign, she knocked on the side of the Rover, and yelled, "It's a little creepy, actually."

"Will you text me when you get home, then, so I know you're safe? Please?"

"As long as you don't follow me."

He saluted her, rolled up the window, and drove around her and toward home.

He was just getting into bed when the text message came in.

"Made it. Thanks for caring and respecting my boundaries."

Wow. What was he supposed to do with that?

"Glad to know it. May I call you tomorrow?"

"Anytime. Goodnight."

Brian turned off the phone and pulled out his journal. Ideas for the class were starting to formulate in his head, but they were still in that pre-verbal stage. White Multiflora rose flowers. Vines wrapping around a crab apple tree, choking it. Invasive species. Hundreds of thousands of seeds.

He doodled the images that arose until his eyelids drooped, then he snapped off the light and drifted into sleep.

Chapter 23

S unlight and a warm breeze filtered through the kitchen window. Normally, Claire would be planning an attack on Multiflora rose: organizing other activists and digging up invasive plants on roadsides, in yards, and on bike trails. It felt odd to be indoors on a beautiful day, but a relief to be out of the hospital tending to her son's needs at home. Besides, it wasn't terrible for her to have extra time trolling the job sites. In fact, she felt more relaxed than she had in weeks and found herself humming as she scrolled through listings on idealist.org.

The sound of frantic footsteps ascending the stairway outside jarred her from her almost meditative state. She recognized the rhythm of the steps. A moment later, she smiled as her father burst through the door

"Where is that little boy?" He boomed.

Her mother followed close behind him, "Where's my Teddy? My little Teddy Bear?"

She seemed on the verge of tears as she hugged Claire quickly, "I just can't believe we missed this entire ordeal!"

"It's okay, Mom. Who could've known this would happen," she said, then added, "Of course you could've come home."

"3,000 miles?" Jane shot her look.

Claire shrugged. "I'm just saying if you were that distressed…"

At times like this, she was glad to be an adult who could no longer be punished. Instead, she suffered her mother's withering glare.

"We knew he'd be alright," her father said, settling the matter.

Her parents bounded down the hallway toward Teddy's room. She could hear them clucking over him, showering him with kisses, cooing over his quiet response. He certainly didn't have the energy yet to respond with his typical boundless energy.

She returned her attention to the screen, only to be interrupted a moment later by Frank reemerging into the kitchen, his face white.

"My God," he whispered. "He's dropped weight. He's down to nothing."

She felt her heart thud. Had she not noticed? Of course, she had. She had observed it somewhere in the back of her mind. But being with him day-to-day, the changes had not been quite so obvious. Her parents hadn't seen him in three weeks. Of course, the difference would be dramatic to them. The fact that her father was detecting Teddy's weight-loss meant nothing about her goodness as a parent. She was a perfectly fine mother. Her child had not gotten sick because of anything that she could've done or prevented. True, she could've not brought him to the beach that day. She could've explained more clearly that he was not to run around or chase after birds. She could've defined the term 'observe' explicitly. But the fact that she made the choices she had on that day didn't make her a bad mother. Did it? She fought the urge to say something defensive back to her father. He's *not trying to attack me*. She resisted the urge to cry. Her father looked down at her and then sat in the chair next to her and patted her hand.

"How are you holding up, Sweetheart?"

The tears started flowing immediately. As she sobbed, she recounted every stressful incident of the last three weeks. She told him how Brian had come to the rescue and had been so kind, and that, in fact, maybe Frank had been right about the guy after all. Maybe Brian was a really decent human being who deserved a friend in his new community.

Frank smiled. "I guess there's a silver lining to this after all then. And I don't see how you could've done anything different than you did, Claire Bear."

She sniffled. He took her chin in his hand and tilted her face up, so she was forced to look into his eyes. "I'm not just saying that. Now, your mother and I are here. We want some time with our grandson, and we, quite frankly, don't want you in the way. So, get out."

Claire opened her eyes wide.

"I said, get out. Go do something. Get a manicure, call Mazzie, take a yoga class, take a walk whatever. You're not looking so hot yourself, Kiddo."

"Gee, thanks, Dad."

"You know what I mean. You need a little Claire time, and we need a little Teddy time, so it just works out. We'll see you this evening."

"It's only ten a.m."

"I'll call you if he needs anything we can't handle."

"Promise?" she asked

"Pinky swear."

Chapter 24

H e had made too many waffles again. He always did that, always cooked for a crowd even when it was just himself. Adrienne had teased him about the habit.

There was no way that he could eat all of them right now. He would freeze them. They wouldn't be as perfect as fresh from the waffle iron, but on a busy day, they would do. The phone rang. Looking at the number that popped up on the screen, his heart did a little dance.

"Good morning, Claire."

"Hi! Are you busy?"

"I was just fixing up a feast of waffles. Can I feed you?"

"Umm… I… Sure. And I have some free time, and I thought I could give you that bicycle tour if you like."

"Do you want to come here for waffles and then take me on a quick tour?"

"See you in fifteen minutes!"

The kitchen was amazing. Because it had a convection oven with the warming feature, he actually *could* keep the waffles warm for fifteen minutes, and they wouldn't get all soggy like they did when he just covered them with tin foil. *I love this house!*

A warm breeze came through the screen door, cooling his bare skin, reminding him that he should probably get dressed before Claire arrived. *Although it would be fun to greet her in my birthday suit, someday. Hopefully, sooner rather than later. Right. Given her skittishness, it could be a long while before she wants to see me au naturel.* Why was she so wary? He hoped it had nothing to do with him. Initially, he had wondered whether to take it personally. But after the connection they had made in the hospital and at the play park and in her kitchen, he knew she felt it too. *So why is she so edgy?* Something was going on with her that had nothing to do with him at all. What was it? *Should I ask?*

He dashed upstairs, threw on a pair of bicycle shorts and a T-shirt and looked in the mirror. *With these skin-tight biking shorts, who needs clothes? Wrong message. We aren't going for some hard-core twenty-mile ride. I don't need bicycle shorts.* He slipped out of them and put on a comfortable pair of cargo shorts. *Hey, Claire, I was wondering: why are you so skittish?*

His next move was to set the table. It was a perfect day to sit on the patio. With Claire coming, he would make sure that there were real dishes there and a little jar with flowers. *Candles would probably be overdoing it.* He wondered whether to make a smoothie. Did he always have to make her smoothies? Did she even like smoothies all the time? *Dude, you invited her over for waffles. You don't need to have an entire brunch laid out. She's not gonna expect anything with fifteen minutes' notice. You set the table and put flowers on it. But it would be so lovely to please her. It would be so nice to make her feel extra special. Smoothies is probably overdoing it. What about fresh orange juice?* He stopped his ruminating, got out a half dozen oranges and the old-fashioned orange press and squeezed juice into a large mason jar, discarding the rinds in the compost bin. He set the jar of juice on the table next to the little bowl of flowers, making sure to cover the jar so no insects would help themselves.

When the doorbell rang, he felt a shiver of excitement run throughout his body. He was about to entertain the most beautiful woman he had met in years. *Deep breath, Brian. Try to calm down.*

Moments later, he reveled in the expression on her face when she saw the table that he had set.

"Brian, this is beautiful."

"You've been here before. Aren't you friends with the owner?"

"I mean the table. You didn't have to do this for me—" She cut herself off, blushed, looked down. "Not that you did it for me. How presumptuous. I—"

"I wanted to."

Claire smiled, and again he felt the deep connection that he'd felt when they were sitting on the hospital bed, and she was tasting his mole' enchiladas for the first time. Claire was so appreciative. He liked that about her. And it was surprising because when they had first met, she had been so prickly. He never would've guessed that every little gesture would mean so much to her. He felt his whole body relax; just knowing that he pleased her brought him a sense of peace. He barely even knew her, but he felt he had known her for a very long time.

"These are the crispiest fluffiest vegan waffles I have ever eaten. And there are no eggs in them? Really?"

"I swear to God, I did not cheat. It's this great egg replacer powder that Bob's makes."

"I've used that, but, honestly, I just gave up on waffles when I became a vegan. Brian Melodus, you've given me faith and hope in a brighter future for my breakfast menus!" She paused, blushed, giggled. "Wow. That was cheesy, huh?"

Her eyes were shining. He laughed. He wanted to kiss her. Would that be a bad idea? He tried to read her face. Did happy equate with 'I want you'? Not with Claire. She was skittish. He had to wait for just the right moment. He laid his open palm on the table between them. She placed her hand in his. As usual, her touch sent electricity coursing through his body. He was becoming addicted to the sensation.

An hour later, after they had lingered over breakfast and she had insisted on helping him clean the kitchen, they sped down the narrow bike trail. Following her may have been a bad idea, he realized. It was difficult to concentrate on the landscape, or even on the path in front of him when Claire's incredibly strong back was arching over the bicycle frame so gracefully. How could he focus on the trail, when Claire's calves were tensing and releasing with every pump of the bicycle pedals? If he wasn't careful, he'd run into her.

"It would have taken me forever to find this trail, Claire," he said, trying to bring himself back to earth.

"Really?"

"Google maps doesn't show any trails in the wildlife refuge."

"Maybe that's why it's always so peaceful! Let's keep it our little secret."

They slowed to a stop.

"This is the MacKenzie trail," Claire said. "My favorite trail. Wanna see something?"

He nodded. He knew exactly what he wanted to see, but she probably had other ideas.

"Do you believe in magic?"

"Uhh, I'm a scientist."

"I know. Me, too, but come here."

She laid her bike on its side in the understory and crooked her finger for him to follow her. A twinkle shone in her eye, and she suddenly seemed like a mischievous little girl. She pointed toward the seaside alder trees lining the east side of the path and tiptoed in that direction, then disappeared into the trees. He followed, and found himself in a magical opening — yes, even to his scientific mind magical was the appropriate description. The alder trees arced around them, forming a little hut lined with sedges and beach grasses. Claire sat on the sandy floor and patted the spot next to her. He joined her cross-legged on the sand.

"See?"

He nodded, entranced.

"Doesn't it make you feel…"

"Transported," he said, staring out at the beach beyond their little hideaway.

It was just a beach. He may have walked that very spot, may have gathered samples there, but from this vantage point, it looked like a setting from some childhood fairytale. He turned his attention back to Claire. Her face looked serene, light, joyful.

How would it feel to take her smooth cheek in his hand, to turn her face to his, to brush her lips with his? Magical.

This was the perfect moment. He wanted to hold her, could practically feel his arms vibrating from desire. His heart thudded in his chest.

"Are you okay?"

He cleared his throat. "Yeah. Why?"

"Your breathing sounds a little heavy."

Get a hold of yourself, Brian! For God's sake!

He took a deep, slow inhalation and released it slowly. "This place is…"

"Magical," they said together, then laughed.

He looked at the ground where her hand rested. Her other hand lay in her lap. *Take that hand, destabilize her. Take the other hand, and you're reaching into her lap. Not good.* He put his hand to his own heart, instead. "Thank you, Claire. I can't explain what it is about this place, but it's just very…"

"Moving," she said with him.

She smiled into his eyes. "I thought you'd like it."

Why are you holding back, Man? Look at her face. She's into you. KISS HER! But he couldn't. He could not kiss her. They hadn't been on a proper date, and he didn't want Claire to think he was some creep on the make. He couldn't bear it if she pulled away when he was starting to give himself to her.

"It's been quite a process restoring this refuge, huh," he asked. "Replanting the hardwoods, and rebuilding the dunes."

"Yeah," she said, a strange squeak in her voice. Was that look on her face disappointment?

His heart sank. Hardwoods. *Yeah. Right. I'd like to restore your dunes with my hardwood, Claire, but I can't quite muster up the courage to kiss you. You may be surprised to know I'm still single. Fuck.*

Chapter 25

Claire stood outside the office of Professor Melodus waiting for their meeting. *Professor Melodus.* Remembering the moment when they had met on the beach, when he was scolding her and she thought he was some sort of abusive creep, she never would have guessed him to be both a wildlife conservationist and a brilliant professor. Now, knowing that he shared her mission to save the magical species on her beloved beach…

"Claire, sorry to keep you waiting."

She turned. His hair was disheveled, face unshaven, making his blue eyes even more startling. His lips were fuller than she had realized. His neck was clean shaven, but a little tuft of hair peeked out from his undershirt. He rolled up the sleeves of his button down, revealing a small tattoo by his wrist — a scarab or something. What did it mean? Why hadn't she noticed it before?

"Claire?"

He was standing behind his desk and she was still standing outside his office, staring at him. How had he gotten over there? Had she followed him with her eyes as he moved into a different room? Heat arose in her cheeks. She dug into her backpack for nothing. There was nothing she needed to retrieve. She just wanted an excuse to look down. What was she going to pull out? *Oh, a notebook; that's plausible.*

"Nice office, *Professor.*"

He smiled and pointed toward the heavy wooden chair facing his. "Come on in! I'm excited about this next lecture and I'd like to review it with you in the context of the whole syllabus. It's really like putting a puzzle together, you know?"

She opened her mouth to speak when Brian's cell phone rang, a bird call. A red knot?

"Arthur. What's going on?"

Birds sewn from cloth hung above Brian's head. Paintings and abstract photographs lined the walls. Papier-mâché sculptures filled the space in the bookshelves not taken by books.

"What???"

An older man's voice filtered into the room. The words were unintelligible but the tone of his voice was tense. Claire moved to examine the artwork more closely.

"Are you sure?"

Despite the density of the materials, the sculptures had an airy, entrancing quality.

"Fuck!" Brian slammed his fist against the wall.

She jumped. Her breath caught in her throat. *Inhale. Exhale. Relax. You're safe. He's not yelling at you.*

She returned to the sculptures. Upon closer view, she realized they were not actually papier-mâché, or not the typical papier-mâché. They appeared to be made from scraps of paper — food wrappers, magazine pages, data reports. They were gorgeous. *I wonder where he got these. Etsy?*

"Of course, the harvest restrictions didn't make a difference. They've been violating them all along!"

She mouthed, "Should I come back?"

Brian met her eyes with his, pain evident in his gaze, "State's lifting harvest restrictions on horseshoe crabs."

She gasped, "My babies!"

"It's like a death knell."

She nodded, stunned, thinking of the fishermen she had encountered on the beach last month. Did the lawmakers understand what they were doing?

"Let's talk later, Boss, brainstorm or something... Yeah."

Brian shoved the cell phone into his pocket. "God damnit," he yelled.

She froze, unsure what to do. *He is not angry at me. He has a real reason to be angry. I feel angry, too.*

He took a deep breath and focused on her. "I don't know if I can think now. Fuck. I'm hungry." He rooted around in his desk, then looked at her. "You wanna get a bite? Getting upset makes me ravenous."

"Ummm, okay. I always have something in my bag. Would you like an apple?"

Brian sighed. "Thanks, but I need real food. Something substantial. How about the diner?"

She took a deep breath and exhaled slowly. "Sure. If you're okay. I mean, um…"

He looked at her face with a curious expression. "Are *you* okay? You're shaking."

Damn it. Why couldn't she control her nerves?

"You were yelling. It, I, uh… it makes me nervous."

"Oh, geez, Claire," he said looking into her eyes. "I'm sorry! I didn't mean to scare you! Oh, my God, I'm such an ass."

"I, uh…"

"Please let me buy you lunch. I promise, no more yelling."

"Okay?"

"I didn't. God. What an asshole. I, it's just so fucking…"

Brian stopped himself, closed his eyes and moved his hands in front of his body slowly with a deliberate yoga breath.

Mazzie had demonstrated that very technique. *You can control your energy, Claire*, she'd said.

Remembering the lesson, she thought: *Yes. I can.* She followed Brian's movements, copied his deliberate, slow breathing pattern, moved her hands in front of her body to steady her nerves. It was working.

"It's extremely frustrating," Brian said, his voice low, calm, controlled. "The horseshoe crab—"

She opened her eyes and looked into his. "I know," she said.

Pain creased his face. His eyes pled for forgiveness. Brian hadn't even done anything to hurt her. She reminded herself again that his anger wasn't directed at her. In fact, when she thought about it, she rather admired his righteous anger. He shared her passion for protecting wildlife. Now, the state was putting a threatened species in further danger. And for what?

148

Big business. Bait for the commercial fishing industry. Medical research that could be done another way. The situation was infuriating.

She reached across the desk and touched his arm. "Come on, let's go get you a solid meal."

Brian's face relaxed. "I'm in the mood for a veggie burger and fries with hot sauce. How about you?"

"That sounds perfect."

Chapter 26

Even as their meals were delivered and they rested across the table from each other in the vinyl booth seats, Brian still felt Claire's soothing touch on his arm.

"How are you?" he asked.

"Okay," Claire said.

"Really? You, um, you said… What happened earlier? My yelling made you nervous? Was it really — was I out of control?"

He watched Claire's face closely. Something flickered in her eyes. Fear? "I don't mean to bring up a painful subject," he said. "It's just, I'm not used to women, or anyone actually — I'm not used to people being afraid of me."

Her eyes widened. "Oh, no! It's not you, Brian!"

"I don't know what to do with it."

Claire started shaking again.

Damn it. What did I do?

Claire reached into her backpack and withdrew a small package wrapped in rumpled tissue paper. She held it in her hands for what seemed like a long time, just staring at it, then slid it across the table to him.

He looked at the package, looked into her face, noted the expectancy in her eyes, the trepidation. *What am I about to see?* He unfolded the tissue paper slowly until a photo fell out.

A woman, chin-length brown wavy hair, black eye, a gash on the side of her face, swollen nose (maybe broken), split lip, bruises on her left shoulder. *How could anyone do that to another human being?*

Tears sprang to his eyes as he recognized the woman. "My God! Claire, is this you?"

"It was. It's not anymore."

PTSD. That's what Mazzie had been talking about at the yoga studio that day. This was the cause. He wanted to take Claire into his arms, to protect her. He felt helpless. A wave of fury welled up inside him, and he knew the absolute worst thing to do in this moment would be to express it. *Claire already feels so vulnerable.* Rage. He breathed into the physical sensation of anger, felt the tension in his muscles, then exhaled slowly. He put one hand on his heart and reached across the table for her hand. She didn't take it. What was the right thing to say? What would Adrienne say?

"Claire, thank you for sharing this with me, for trusting me enough to be vulnerable in front of me."

Her eyes opened wide, as if she'd expected a different response. "I was three months pregnant with Teddy."

Brian shook his head sympathetically.

"Jim, my ex-husband, became convinced I was cheating on him, because I didn't want to have sex." She laughed. "What woman in her first trimester wants sex? I was vomiting all the time."

"Even if you had been cheating on the guy, there was no excuse for him to do that," he pointed to the picture.

Claire nodded. "I didn't deserve that."

"No one deserves that, Claire. I am so incredibly sorry that happened to you."

Chapter 27

As she and her family settled around the patio table, Claire heard Brian's voice in her head: *Thank you for sharing this with me.*

Brian had actually thanked her, had recognized the trust she had given him by letting him see that photo. No one else had responded that way. People had apologized and vented with her, even cried with her. Brian's response landed differently. It had made her feel she could open up to him.

"So, what's your big idea, Sweetheart?" her mom asked now, bringing her back to earth.

Claire brought out the reports. She felt a vague ache in her body, thinking about the closing of the gallery, the end of that community space. The ache turned into a sharp pain in her gut as she envisioned her parents selling the building and, with it, her apartment. *Good bye, central location and cheap rent.* She sighed. She understood the rationale for selling off a bad investment, but why did her dad, of all people, have to be so focused on profit?

But she had a solution: the environmental art show concept that had been percolating in her brain for over a month. If they sold enough work, they might break even on expenses and keep the gallery open another year. She'd done her research. True, her mother was not a big environmentalist, but she was always open to innovation. *Mom will love this: my passion for nature plus her passion for art — it's like a tribute to our relationship.* Even better, it would open a community discussion about environmental issues. *Everybody wins! Maybe.*

Brian replayed the conversation as he drove. Claire had called her parents after that final beating—the last of many. Frank had driven 1,000 miles to get his daughter and her things, to make sure she pressed charges. The 'ex' had gone to jail for a few years, then ignored his restraining order and come to find his son and "his woman." Claire had ended up in an ambulance. Teddy, not quite three at the time, had witnessed the brutal beating of his mother, had seen the blood and ridden in the ambulance with her. She had refused to let go of him. After that, the asshole had gone to prison, where he would be until Teddy was ten. *Thank God.* Brian's stomach churned just thinking of it.

Now, he turned off the road onto a long, wooded driveway paved with slate and grass. *Permeable. High end.* He pulled into the circular turnaround and took in the landscape—a mix of hybrid plants and native species. He felt relieved to be focusing on something else, something positive, a transitional landscaping design. He wondered how much of the yard design Claire had influenced. The home itself was spectacular. *Is this where she grew up? A two-story bungalow with cedar shake siding and large leaded windows? Geez.* Behind that lay a sprawling yard with a spectacular view of the ocean. The sun was lowering, casting an orange early evening glow on the water and bathing the house and its surroundings in warm light.

Claire's family home was nothing like his, and that was another reason to hold back on the romance. She was used to a lifestyle he could neither provide nor even begin to contribute to. He laughed to himself, remembering how realtors described his coastal southern Connecticut hometown. *Not fading, not industrial, not decrepit. No, among realtors, it's "a good value."* His parents could never have afforded anything like what he was staring at now. He considered the rundown Victorian in the center of town where three generations of his family had grown up. It must have been a gem when his grandfather was a boy. But for as long as Brian could remember, the beautiful Victorian woodwork and built-ins had been overshadowed by cracked plaster, peeling wallpaper, and a dank musty odor coming through the floorboards from the dirt basement below. For as long as he could remember, at least one side of the house had needed painting. And for forty years or more, his father had run Melodus Auto Body & Repair out of the cinderblock garage he had built next to the house. Brian's earliest memories included a front yard filled with cars in various stages of repair. The other day, his dad had told him that he was keeping busy with more repair work than he'd ever had, but Brian knew his father could not fix enough cars to fill the hole in his heart left by his ailing wife. And he knew exactly how that felt. He hated thinking of his dad alone in the house with only a cat for company. Jewel was a dear cat, but no replacement for his high school sweetheart. *Claire is no replacement for you, Adrienne.*

She doesn't have to be, Bri. She's someone new, with something different to offer. And you like that about her.

I'm sorry.

Adrienne's chiseled face appeared in his mind's eye. *Brian, the only thing to apologize for is the way you're not getting on with your life!*

Ugh. He took a deep breath, felt refreshed by the salt air, and refocused on the wide stone steps leading to the front door. "Wow," he said aloud, then tapped the doorbell. When the door swung open and Frank welcomed him inside, he saw an indoor space as beautiful as the outside. Clean and understated elegance, like the home and garden magazines were always pushing. The walls were filled with romantic, whimsical art prints and framed kid-art spanning decades.

Just as Claire started to ask whether her parents wanted to continue their discussion of the art show over dinner, the doorbell rang. Her father jumped up and jogged into the house. A moment later, he returned with Brian.

"Look who I found!" He winked at her.

"Hello, Brian!" Her mother gushed.

Why must she gush around him? It's not like he's the only man in town.

"Join us, won't you?" Her dad said. "Jane let's get our friend another place setting and an ear of corn. You like corn, right? Good."

Brian nodded, a deer-in-headlights expression on his face. "Did I get the wrong time? I came over to discuss the Partners Program."

"Oh, dear," Jane said, sounding innocent. "We must have double booked!"

Innocent. Claire snorted, then noticed Brian and her parents staring at her. Had she done that aloud? How embarrassing. She smiled at Brian, not wanting to appear rude or unwelcoming.

"Forgive my senile parents, Brian. They also requested Teddy and I join them for dinner to discuss art gallery business."

"No big deal; we can reschedule," he said, turning toward the front yard.

"Nonsense, Brian! We just happen to have extra veggie kabobs," her mother said.

"Oh, do you?" Claire asked, rolling her eyes.

"We always have extra." Jane shot her a warning look. "Don't we, Frank."

"Always! Be prepared; that's our motto. You never know who's coming to dinner!"

Jane giggled, "Who's Coming to Dinner? Oh, Frank!"

Brian looked utterly confused.

"They're referring to an old movie, called *Guess Who's Coming to Dinner.* Forgive their obscure references."

"Forgive my ignorance. I thought they were referring to Who's on First."

"What's on second," Frank piped up.

"Who's on third?" Jane squealed.

It was enough to make someone vomit, the way her parents flirted with him. Besides, they were misquoting the foolish bit. It wasn't Who's on first, What's on second. It was 'You throw the ball to first, then Who gets it.' Then there was something about someone named Naturally, and someone else named I Don't Know, and another player named Because. There was no one named What in the whole bit. Actually, maybe What was on second. Anyway, what did it matter? Why was she finding this so irritating? *Deep breath, Claire. This is not worth getting upset about.*

She looked at Brian. He was looking at her, smiling. She smiled back. He was so nice, so patient, so good natured. Jane laid a place setting at the empty seat next to Teddy.

Teddy patted the chair next to him. "Birdman, sit here."

"I don't want to impose."

"What does impose mean?"

"It means go somewhere you're not wanted," she answered, then hoped it didn't make it sound like she didn't want Brian there. They were friends now, and she would welcome his company. She would welcome more than his company. *Come off it, Claire. Just because he's a good, kind, attractive man, doesn't mean you should date.*

"I want Birdman here. Can he sit next to me?"

"If he'd like to."

Then again, he'd held her hand. But he hadn't kissed her, not even when she brought him to the magical Peter Pan hideaway on their bike ride. Anyway, it certainly wasn't his fault her parents were trying to play matchmaker.

Brian took the seat next to Teddy, but he kept looking at her. Why was he looking at her when he clearly was dating a bombshell? How many women did he need? She did not like it; maybe a tiny part of her liked it. When was the last time anyone had looked at her like that? He was easy on the eyes, and strong. She thought back to the moment when he carried her and Teddy from their apartment. His muscles had been taut, but he hadn't appeared to be straining. When he had held her in his arms, she had felt the warmth of his body, the bulge of his biceps through his work shirt. Then he had been so caring when Teddy was in the hospital. She sighed and stared into the ocean. It was not safe to trust someone who appeared to be so nice, who was so tough and could overpower her so easily. If she was going to date anyone ever again, she would be better off with someone frailer. *Really, Claire? That's what you want? A toothpick of a guy who'll never be able to help you with the heavy lifting of life? Seriously?*

Her ruminations ended abruptly when she noticed her mother showing Brian one of the family photo albums.

"We took these in Bali in April," Jane said.

Why, Claire wondered, did her mother think that Brian cared about their family vacations?

"I shot three below par on that course!" Frank boasted.

"He did!"

Her parents were both delusional.

A sharp pain bolted through Claire's foot and tears sprang to her eyes. "Teddy, that was my foot you just kicked."

"Sorry, Mama."

"So, gee, Brian. Play golf?" Her father asked.

"Once or twice."

Her mother thrust the photo album at Brian again.

"Oh, there we were in Argentina buying sculptures for the gallery."

"I did some research down there," Brian said.

"Really! What were you studying?" her mother asked.

"Mommy, can I have dessert?" Teddy asked, playing with his plate and fork.

"I'm sorry, Brian," Jane shot Teddy a *not now* look. "What were you studying?"

"The red knot migration to and from the North Tund—whoa!"

"Teddy! Oh, my goodness," Claire said, seeing the hamburger bits and blood her son had just flung all over their guest. It had been a particularly juicy hamburger, by the looks of Brian's shirt and face.

"I'm so sorry, Brian,"

"No worries."

"Teddy, this is why we do not wave our forks in the air when they have food on them. Remember?"

"I'm sorry, Mama."

"And what do you say to Brian?"

"I'm sorry, Birdman. It was a accident."

"It's okay, Buddy. Accidents happen."

157

She sighed and ran into the house for a washcloth, mortified. Of all people to dump animal parts on. *Disgusting.*

When she returned, Brian was standing with the hose in his hand, directing the spray at the shirt in his hand. There was a sight Claire had not expected to see — Brian, shirtless, his chest and shoulder muscles glowing in the golden summer evening sunlight. She cleared her throat, feeling inadequate with the limp washcloth in her hand. He looked up at her and smirked.

"You want a splash?"

She blushed, envisioning a playful water fight, clothing flying everywhere. She shook her head to clear her mind. *Clothing flying!* What was she thinking of? Her son had just sent blood all over the guy. Not only that, the guy was offering to help clean, this after listening to her parents drone on about their travels and golf scores and art buys.

"I want a splash! Splash me, splash me," Teddy yelled, running toward them.

"There will be no splashing today, Teddy," she said, trying to sound firm, rather than annoyed.

"Aww!"

Brian looked at her, as if asking permission.

"Alright. Fine."

Brian threw his wet shirt over the back of a chair, placed his thumb over the end of the hose and turned to spray Teddy. "Dun, dun, dun! En garde, Super Environmentalist. I stun you with my magic liquid."

Magic liquid. Claire giggled.

Teddy squealed in delight as the water doused him. "You'll never get me, Doctor Hose Head!"

"Ha. Ha. Ha," Brian said, putting on his fake French accent.

He's really into that fake French thing. French chef, French villain. I wonder if he'd like a French — Dear Lord, Claire. Get a hold of yourself. Maybe if he'd put on his shirt, that would be easier. Look at them playing. Teddy absolutely loves him. Birdman. Doctor Hose Head. So cute. And Brian's smiling from ear to ear. Those dimples. Mmm. Those dimples. Damn.

Suddenly it was quiet. Brian was staring at her, as if he was expecting something.

"Where's Teddy?" She asked.

"Bathroom break."

"Weird. I didn't see him leave."

"You seemed, uh, lost in thought."

She felt heat rise to her cheeks. Had she been staring at him? Worse, had he noticed her staring at him? She held the washcloth out to him. He wet it and wiped his chest and stomach clean. Just the right amount of hair encircled his bellybutton — an innie. She was finding it difficult to breathe.

"Glad you stayed for dinner?" She asked, then felt irritated at the breathiness in her voice.

He smiled at her — a genuine smile, a smile she could trust. It was one thing to smile at her when he was meeting her for coffee or delivering a pretend lecture, but in an awkward, unpleasant situation, to keep his cool… She had to believe that revealed something about his character.

They smiled at each other for several seconds. She liked the way his eyes softened when he smiled, the way his nose crinkled. He had full lips. And those dimples. Mm. Mm. She just wanted to—

"In Japan, this is considered a compliment," her dad said, breaking the mood.

"Not quite dear," her mom said, coming across the lawn with an unnecessary number of towels and handing one to Brian.

He wiped himself off and laughed. Was he laughing at Frank's stupid joke or at the idea that so many towels were necessary to dry off, or was he laughing at something else? Claire wasn't sure.

"It's all right," he said. "This is just a little hamburger juice. I work with wildlife. You can't get much grosser than studying bird excrement."

She wanted to tell Brian how impressed she was by his work, but her dad piped up, "So, you study bird shit, Brian?"

Truly, there would be no end to the embarrassment she was to endure.

"And other delightful excretions," he said with a wink.

"Have you always been this nice?" She asked.

"Nah, I used to be real ass...tute thinker, and kind of a jerk."

"Nice catch," she smirked. "So, what happened?"

He nodded. "My wife got sick. Pancreatic cancer. Then my mom got sick."

"Oh, Brian," she said, feeling as if her heart was literally reaching for his.

"Mom's alive, but basically lost. Dementia. They were my guiding stars."

"That makes some people bitter."

"I took care of Adrienne. We had thirteen weeks and four days after the diagnosis."

He looked toward the ocean, then back at Claire. His eyes were glassy.

"No one took better care of themselves, or of me. I grew up because of her. I learned to cook and do laundry and all those things a bachelor fudges and a young married guy with a demanding career skillfully ignores. I got way more attuned to her needs, more sensitive to her emotions. I don't even know why she put up with me before all that happened."

Claire didn't know what to say. What could she say, hearing that? It was tragic, and sweet. He was still in love with his wife.

"When did she pass?"

"Three years ago, last month. I learned about the job here on her birthday, moved in on the anniversary of her death. Tell me that isn't..."

"Synchronicity," she whispered.

Their eyes locked.

"Thanks for listening."

"That's what friends are for," she said, remembering how he'd said that to her when they had entered the emergency room with Teddy and she had been so scared.

It was silent. Why was it so silent? She peered around him. Her parents had disappeared.

"I should go," he said.

"What? Why?"

160

"Gettin' late, Lil' Miss."

She smirked. "You came for a reason. Didn't you want to talk to them about the Partners Program?"

"I did, but I get the sense they're not actually interested."

"Ha! You've got them pegged, but you know what, let's use their strategy against them." She winked. "We can play their game. They want to set us up? Let's let them think it's working, just long enough to get them signed on to the program."

Brian shook his head and laughed. "Aren't you the devious one!"

"I come by it honestly."

"I guess you do."

Claire took his hand and his heart leapt into his throat.

"Ready?" She asked.

He nodded. He was so grateful he wasn't one of those guys whose palms broke out all sweaty.

"Maybe this is too soon. They won't buy it."

"Sure, they will. They always see what they want to see. Just watch," she winked again.

He'd never suspected Claire was a winker. It was cute.

"Mom, Dad," she called as they neared the house.

She led him into the kitchen, where her mother was at a deep farmhouse-style sink rinsing dishes and loading them into the fanciest dishwasher he had ever seen. Teddy sat at a round ash wood table, coloring. Claire led him around the huge kitchen island to face Jane. Suddenly, their arms were swinging.

Boy, she's really playing this up.

"Mom, Dad, Brian has just been telling me more about the partners program. You really have to hear this."

"Oh, really," Jane said with a smirk. She was staring at their hands. "Do tell, Brian."

"I hand-washed your shirt, Brian, and threw it in the dryer," Frank said, walking in, then stopping short at the sight of Brian with his daughter. A broad smile crossed his face. "I hope you don't mind."

161

"Thank you, Sir," he said, moved by the show of kindness, surprised by the complete lack of machismo. His own father hadn't touched the laundry until there was no alternative.

"That's perfect," Claire said, sounding more enthusiastic than he'd ever heard her. "It gives us just enough time to hear Brian's pitch. Is anyone else in the mood for hot cocoa or wine?"

"Absolutely! Frank, where's that bottle of Sauternes? A little dessert wine and chocolate? Shall we? Brian's going to tell us all about the Partners Program."

"I'll just pop down to the wine cellar. Back in a jiffy. Get it? Pop. Jiffy? Like Jiffy Pop?"

"Oh," Claire laughed a little too heartily and yelled after her father. "Good one, Dad. Jiffy Pop. Good one! So, let's get started."

"First, I want to compliment you on the environmental measures you've already taken. Jane, who selected the pavers for the driveway?"

"I've always loved slate, Brian, but you know it was really Claire's idea," she said, setting out a box of Godiva and four wine glasses. "The grass between the stones is... it does... something, and the, you know, the, ahh, because we didn't use pavement, it's not as bad."

"Drainage, Mom. The grass promotes drainage. Pavement is made with fossil fuels — tar, which we should be using very, very sparingly. And because pavement is impermeable it prevents water seeping into the ground during a rainstorm. That's why, before you got the pavers, the driveway always used to flood. There was nowhere for the water to go."

"She is so knowledgeable, isn't she, Brian?"

He nodded, feeling his lips spread into a wide smile, "Indeed."

It appeared that Claire was incredibly knowledgeable. And, although at this point, she probably didn't need to, the knowledgeable Claire was still holding his hand.

Electricity coursed up and down his arm, flooding his body with warmth. Probably endorphins or oxytocin, the bonding hormones. The bonding hormones felt very, very good. He took a deep breath, and smiled when Frank entered with the bottle of wine.

"Let's talk about this Partners Program," Frank said in his booming voice. "We are big, big fans of partnership in this house, right, Janie?"

Chapter 28

The evening air felt warm and moist on Claire's bare shoulders, and she reveled in it. Downtown looked particularly good. Was she high from the night before, from helping Brian to get her parents to sign up for the Partners Program? Whatever it was, she noticed herself moving more lightly than usual down the sidewalk.

"It's old and new, you know? Gaiaosophy says we're all connected to the earth," she explained.

"OMG, Claire!" Mazzie shivered. "I just felt that all up and down my chakras!"

Claire looked at her friend. "Your chakras, huh?"

"Because meditation helps us feel that connection to Earth and all life! And with yoga —" She shivered again. "Balancing your energy through gentle exercise and meditation gives you what you need to complete your healing, find your center, and discern your path."

"You sound like you're testing sales pitches for the brochure."

"How did it sound?"

"Like you're ready for the big time."

Mazzie pulled keys from her pocket. "Are you sure?"

"How else will you get more students in the door if you don't let them know you're here?"

"You're right. I had my soft launch. I tested the waters. The energy is right. Now it's time to expand my connections and grow my business."

Claire smirked, not only because Mazzie was adorable, but also because her boyfriend was sneaking up behind her and

Mazzie had no clue. Greg Starret exuded the energy of the eternal bachelor. He hadn't changed since high school. The older heartthrob. Now, he owned the local boat-building shop and always smelled of freshly cut lumber, no matter how clean shaven and dressed up he was. Just as Mazzie stepped through the door, he wrapped his arms around her waist and kissed her neck.

"Hey, look, it's the most beautiful yoga instructor in the world!"

Mazzie pulled away, "Aww. That's sweet, but we're taking time apart, remember?"

"Honey, I—"

"Please, Greg. Not now."

Mazzie hadn't told Claire that she and Greg were taking time apart. Why? She felt her body tense in frustration. They were so cute together but… *Ugh*. *Constant drama*. She cleared her throat and walked past them into the studio.

"Honey, please," she heard him say through the open door.

"Greg, it's painful enough without you showing up randomly."

"But I miss you. We don't need to do this."

"Our priorities are not aligned."

He sighed.

This was exactly why Claire liked being single.

Chapter 29

T he next day, she still felt irritated with Mazzie for keeping her in the dark, even as she held the door to Book and Bean open for her friend.

"So, why are you and Greg taking a break?"

"It's just too much to get into now," Mazzie whispered.

Claire let out a slow breath. *Release the frustration. Breathe.* The smell of black bean soup and homemade bread wafted toward her. She followed Mazzie into the café and let her eyes adjust to the light. Across the room, Brian sat at a table with an older man with a long grey ponytail. They munched on sandwiches and stared at a laptop.

She felt heat rise to her cheeks and a broad smile spread across her face. Brian looked up and smiled, too. Her heart soared, until she saw what he was smiling at: the little blonde bombshell slipping past her and beelining to Brian and his friend.

The bombshell sat down and Brian and the old guy focused their attention on her. *He didn't even notice me.* She turned to the food counter where Mazzie stood placing her order. Suddenly, she craved an oatmeal chocolate chip cookie.

It had been a hard week, and Brian was exhausted. He was not used to doing field work in the early morning and then writing lectures late at night. He hated to think how much harder it would be when he actually started teaching. As he scarfed down his roasted veggie sandwich and soup, and Arthur pounded his grilled gruyere with tomato rosemary bisque, they reviewed the data on the laptop. The bell above the door jingled and he looked up just in time to see Claire walk in with Mazzie. Claire's dark hair framed her face and fell loosely over her chest. She was wearing a yellow sundress and sandals, and her toenails were painted in bright colors. *Cute.* He smiled, but then Tilly pushed past Claire and Mazzie and sat with him and Arthur. His heart sank a little. She was nice enough, and she was a decent intern, but as far as he was concerned, a little Tilly went a long way. For some reason, Claire was now scowling at him. *So mercurial.* Feeling self-conscious, he looked back at his laptop.

Satiated by soup, salad, a long chat with her BFF, and a big cookie, Claire hugged Mazzie good-bye and walked into the gallery. "Hello, people!"

"Hi, Mama," a muffled voice said from under the desk. "I'm making a surprise for you. Don't come in."

She smirked. "Okay, Little Love!"

Her mother walked in from the back room, rubbing her temples. "I sure will be glad to not deal with temperamental artists once I retire!"

"Why do you sound so resigned about it? I told you guys I have an idea to save the gallery."

"We never did get to that discussion, did we."

She raised her eyebrows pointedly. "You both were very busy orchestrating a surprise guest visit."

Her mother shrugged. "I can't be held responsible for who you father invites to the house."

"*Anyway*…"

"Anyway, I wonder if you can explain—"

"Mom, I really want to keep my home, so—"

"What is a native species of plants?"

"Plants that are indigenous to an area."

"Which means…"

"It means we'll have to save the gallery, so can you please take my idea a little more seriously?"

"What?"

167

"We have to save the gallery so I can afford a place to live."

"You can live with us for free."

Claire's stomach tightened.

"Come on, don't give me that look. We'd love to have you! Okay, I know it's not ideal, but living with us is better than being in some apartment in the city, isn't it?"

Thirty-three and living with my parents, like some spoiled, lazy—

"Do you know how many people crave that kind of support?"

Claire looked down, ashamed, frustrated with herself. She knew she should appreciate her privilege. Yet so often it felt like a trap. True, her parents had given up telling her what to do years ago. In fact, they were more supportive than she deserved. *That's not right, Claire. It's okay to have support, it's good. Mom's right; most people—*

"So, it's settled. You'll live with us if you need. Now, tell me."

Claire rolled her eyes. Apparently, her parents had not totally given up telling her what to do.

"Mom," she started.

"Tell me: what are plants that are indigenous to an area?"

"Indigenous plants have been in that area for all of recorded time."

"And that's supposed to be better?"

"Transplanted plants typically either wither or invade. Like an avocado tree would not do well in our climate, whereas—"

"Invade? How can a plant invade? Isn't that a little overly dramatic?"

"Gramma, it's simple," Teddy piped up from under the reception desk. "Some plants want to hog all the space, like the mean kids in the sandbox. If they're in their own place where they come from, then the wild aminals eat them so they can't grow too much. But if they come to a new place, the aminals don't eat their seeds 'cause it might make them sick, and the other plants don't know how to share with them, so they wrap their stems around them like a snake and squeeze until they die."

"Wow!" Jane said.

"That is very close to the truth," Claire whispered. "He kind of combined the activities of a number of invasive species, but I think you get the point, right?"

"I sure do. Thanks, Super Teacher!"

"Mama, can I have a Super Teacher cape?"

"Hmmm. I'm a little behind in my cape making right now, Love."

A thought fragment popped into her head. *Bittersweet: strangling Delaware's trees.* Claire grabbed a sticky note from the desk and jotted: *Delaware's changing landscape, new flowers on the side of the road, etc. Result of invasive species.* This was an idea she wanted to save and think about. Who knew how it might be useful?

"What are you thinking about, Dear?" Her mother touched her shoulder.

"Environmental anything is hot these days. Ha! No pun intended."

Her mother stared at her blankly.

"Get it? Global warming? A hot topic?"

Jane raised an eyebrow, apparently confused.

She sighed. *Brian would have gotten that joke.* "Anyway, Mom, I've been thinking about how we can combine my passion for ecology with our passion for art."

"Oooh," her mother put her hands on her cheeks. "Have you ever heard of ecological art? Or environmental art?"

"Like Patrick Dougherty?"

"Yes," Jane ran back to her office, yelling on the way. "I was just reading about an artist who made a drinking fountain for plants and people"

"Cool," she yelled back.

Her mother returned with the latest issue of *Art Weekly* and spread the pages so Claire could see.

"Interesting!"

"It's a copper wall planter with a porcelain drinking fountain at the end. Evidently, it's a statement about native species, which I didn't understand when I was reading this article, but now I do."

"Where is this guy? Never mind, don't tell me. He's probably too expensive."

"Maybe not. Besides, there's a whole movement of art that works with the environment. Of course, those pieces are typically outside."

"What about something like…" A picture formed in Claire's head of the art she had seen in Brian's office. "You know, Brian has a bunch of fun, like, playful stuff in his office. I don't know who the artist is. It seems like mostly the same person, but it could be a few different artists."

"Wanna call him and find out?"

Claire's heart fluttered, which annoyed her. Why was she smiling? Hadn't he just dissed her in Book & Bean?

"Oh, I see you do. You're blushing!"

Claire pulled out her phone and walked to the door. Yes, she would call. No, she would not allow her mother to look over her shoulder and listen to the conversation.

"This is Brian Melodus. You've reached my cell…" His voice sent shivers up her spine.

"Hey, Brian, it's Claire Dessalines. Listen, I noticed the art in your office and we're having a show of environmental art at the gallery. We'd love to include… No guarantees, of course, but can you connect me to the artist as soon as possible? Thanks! Sorry for the rush. We're just…" she sighed, "Doing things at the last minute, as usual. Anyway, I appreciate your help."

Later that night, once Teddy was asleep in his room, Claire sipped tea and read *Last Child in The Woods*. Why was Brian's voice narrating? Why couldn't she hear her own voice in her head? She sighed, both annoyed with herself and enjoying the beginning of the fantasy forming in her mind.

Chapter 30

C laire didn't normally go to the advanced yoga classes. She didn't feel like she had the physical strength or agility after only a couple years of practice, but Mazzie had assured her it was worth a try, that she was ready for it. Now with Teddy back in preschool, she had some time and in an adventurous mood. She set up her mat, grabbed a block and a strap from the props shelf, and returned to her mat to warm up. She started with some neck rolls, then inhaled and moved her shoulders up and back, and exhaled them down, and forward, up, back, down, and forward. She was getting into a nice rhythm, feeling relaxed, ready.

Then Brian walked in and lay his mat diagonally in front of her. Her heart leapt into her throat and she started coughing uncontrollably.

He turned, saw her, and smiled broadly. "Oh, hey, Claire!"

"Hey," she coughed, and waved, sensing heat rush to her cheeks. *Nice to see you without a shirt again — oh for God's sake, Claire, get a hold of yourself.*

Brian turned his attention to his own preparations and she tried to resettle her mind.

It's been a week, and I haven't heard from you. Not a peep. Not even about the art show. What's up? Didn't we share a moment on the bike trail? Was I the only one who felt something?

Moments later, Mazzie stepped to the front of the room and called the class to attention.

She was surprised that the class started similarly to the beginner class, with breathing, and what seemed like a long time warming up the joints. They did tree pose and warrior poses one and two. They did triangle pose. *Mazzie was right. I can totally handle this class. I know these poses.*

Just as she was feeling confident, Mazzie got tricky.

"Let's move from Tree into Flamingo now," Mazzie said in her soothing yoga teacher voice. "And as you do, notice the sensations that arise. Marichyasana improves focus, balance, and concentration."

Many of the students seemed to know what that was, as they just adjusted their position, sliding the foot from the outside of the knee to the hip crease on the opposite leg.

Claire snuck a peek at Brian. He was one of the students who just did the pose. She followed along. *That's easy enough,* she thought, until Mazzie spoke up.

"Nice, deep inhalation, exhale and fold, expelling all the breath, scooping out the belly, really engaging those core muscles. Right hand to the floor, left hand coming around your back to grab the toes of the foot you've folded over. Feel the stretch in your shoulders, arms, and wrists. Use your leg muscles. Where does the balance come from here? The core strength and the leg muscles. Good, Jonah! Nice, Brian."

Am I doing this right? It was bizarre.

"Mazzie?" she said, trying to sound relaxed.

Mazzie came over and ran her hand lightly up the length of Claire's spine. "Nice, Claire."

She pressed her hand gently into the top of Claire's head; to Claire's amazement, the touch made her lengthen her neck. *How is that possible?* Flamingo pose was giving her an amazing stretch in the hip area and to her surprise she was able to hold the balancing aspect of it. She didn't feel unstable in the pose at all.

"Beautiful job! Let's move into Eka Pada Galavasana."

Icky patty galavant? What? Okay, she's speaking Sanskrit now.

"Flying Pigeon pose," Mazzie continued. "Bring both hands to the floor, and lower your hips coming into a one-legged semi swat."

I can probably do this. Let's see, if I put my weight on my hands. Yup. I've got it. I'm balancing! Brian seemed to be in the one-legged squat with ease.

"Coming into the full expression of the pose, now, extending the leg behind you."

What? She looked at the other students. Everyone was struggling with it except for Brian who was poised perfectly on his hands with one leg tucked under his hip crease and the other leg shooting straight out behind him floating in the air. He looked, literally, like he was flying. *Holy shit; that's hot!* Brian's arm muscles bulged. His legs were taut. The muscles in his back rippled. She could see the breath moving through him even as he remained steady in the pose. He didn't even seem to be breaking a sweat. How was that possible?

"Do you need help, Hon?" Mazzie asked. Claire hadn't noticed her come to her side.

"Uh huh," she breathed.

Mazzie gently encouraged her to tip her weight forward onto her hands and lift the foot off the floor. "See, your weight is on your upper arms. Do you feel how that's where it should be?"

"Not really."

Mazzie demonstrated. Still in the half squat, Claire watched her friend then peeked at Brian. He was still holding the pose. Claire could barely hold Upward Boat for ten breaths. He had been holding this pose for a full minute, if not more. Then, following Mazzie's instructions, he lowered his knee to the floor, released the other foot, and finally rested in Child's pose with the other students. She felt slightly embarrassed that she, too, had taken Child's pose, even though she hadn't managed Flying Pigeon. *That's not what yoga's about, Claire. You know that. If Mazzie knew what you were thinking, she would say it's not a competition, it's about finding your edge.*

After a few breaths in Child's pose, Mazzie asked, "Ready for the other side?"

Claire stood, brought her hands together at her chest, raised her left foot up into the right hip crease and let her knee fall open to the side. Exhaling the breath out and tucking her belly toward her spine, she folded over the standing leg, placing her right hand by her right foot. She reached her left hand around her back and grabbed her left toes near the hip.

173

"Good," Mazzie exhaled. "Good job, Claire! That's right. Yes, Stacy. You've got it, Jonah. Very nice, Brian."

Claire resisted the urge to glance at him again. It was too distracting. This must be why Mazzie was always saying, "keep your eyes on your own mat." Following Mazzie's guidance, and imagining the rising fear drifting away like a cloud in the sky, she dropped her hips into a one-legged squat, bent her elbows, tilted her weight onto the back of her upper arms, and then allowed the right foot to come off the ground just a half an inch. *Am I doing it?*

"Mazzie," she called.

Mazzie returned to her side. "You're doing it, Claire! That's awesome!"

"Feels like I might fall on my face," she said through gritted teeth.

"Breathe. You're not falling. You're doing it. You're doing it. Just allow that leg to straighten." Mazzie gently pressed her flat hand into Claire's heel, which made Claire extend the leg. How had Mazzie done that? It was like she had pressed a magic button. Her leg was straight, and she was balancing on her hands.

"Am I doing it right?"

"Picture perfect!"

She let out a little cheer of joy, and the whole class laughed. She could not believe the sensation. She actually did feel like she was flying, like she was a bird soaring, or a superhero.

"That's it. Keep the breath steady. Let the breath support the pose," Mazzie said walking to another student.

Claire tried to keep her excitement under control, to return her attention to her breath even as she was feeling greater and greater ecstasy. She wished that Brian could see her doing this pose also. She wondered if he would feel the same excitement seeing her in Flying Pigeon pose as she had felt watching him do it. She knew it was ridiculous; she knew that Brian had to keep his eyes on his own mat so that he could maintain his practice. But she really wished he could see her. Wouldn't he be impressed? Would he be turned on by watching her the way she felt excited watching him?

By the time she was resting in Child's pose, Claire felt finished. She had experienced the advanced class, succeeded in trying an exciting new pose, and now she was ready for a nice long Savasana. Even in Child's pose, her muscles were shaking from exhaustion. Mazzie wasn't finished with them. *Forearm plank? Ugh.* Claire stretched her body into the pose, as instructed. *After this, we'll get to lie in Corpse Pose.*

Instead, Mazzie told them to ease their hips up and back into Dolphin Pose. Claire didn't feel particularly challenged by the pose, and she didn't love the balance of Dolphin. Stacking her shoulders over her elbows was uncomfortable. If she tilted her hips a bit more toward her hands, she would fall over. She didn't care if it was opening her shoulders. Why did they need to be open anyway? *Breathe, Claire. Inhale. Exhale. Let the pose be what it is.*

"Now, engage your core more deeply, tip your hips back another inch or so, and lift the legs for Pincha Mayurasana, Forearm Stand."

That's not happening. Exhausted, she returned to Child's pose and then peeked over at Brian. He executed the pose perfectly, as far as she could tell. His arm muscles bulged. Her breath started quickening. His strong jaw line was perfectly perpendicular to the floor as he looked down, while his legs were straight up in the air, toes pointing toward the ceiling. It looked impossible, yet he was doing it. His pecs flexed with the effort. His core was solidly engaged. The ripples in his abdominal muscles made her want to spend a little time alone in her bedroom. *Oh, my sweet lord,* she thought. She had never seen a porn film, and had absolutely no desire to, but watching Brian do yoga was the biggest visual turn on she had ever experienced. *I guess I should stop trying to deny I have a crush on him.* First, he had showered her son with the kind of fatherly attention he needed. Then, he had wowed her with his intellect and commitment to wildlife and environmental harmony. Then, he had melted her heart by cooking for them. Now this. Who needed erotica with Brian around? The tight yoga shorts hugged his ass and she could see the dimples in the cheeks as he flexed his glutes to maintain the pose for what, once again, seemed like an impossibly long time. While everyone else in class was coming out of the pose, Brian stood stable, even though he was starting to sweat. *Thank God, the man is human.* Exhausted both from her physical exertion and sexual fantasies, she rolled onto her back and let her arms drop by her sides in Savasana. She hoped that Mazzie would bring everyone else into the final resting pose momentarily so she didn't look like a complete idiot.

Chapter 31

Her parents had begged for another Teddy date. The question was: what would she do with the time? At moments like this, when she was offered a surprise reprieve from the demands of single motherhood, Claire frequently didn't know what to do with herself. There were so many options it was overwhelming. What if she chose wrong?

And then it occurred to her there was someone who had helped her out, asking nothing in return and she knew that person wanted to spend more time exploring the bicycle trails. True, he still hadn't called, but he was probably just busy. He had field work and he was preparing his class. Of course, the man could explore the trails solo, but things were more fun with a friend. And they really were friends now. She had cried in front of him. He had comforted her. He had listened and she had listened to him as well. They knew things about each other's lives and each other's pasts. When she allowed herself to stop thinking and just feel about Brian, she realized that what she felt was trust. She felt safe. With him, she felt she could relax and be herself.

True, he had sent some mixed signals — holding her hand, then showing up with the blonde bombshell everywhere. But they were in their thirties, not their teens. Holding hands wasn't that big of a deal. Maybe in Connecticut, where Brian was from, friends held hands all the time.

She texted him: Bicycle rider emoji. Question mark.

His response was immediate: Thumbs up emoji. "When?" "Now?"

Smiley face emoji. "Wait. What about (canoe emoji)?"

Thumbs up emoji. Thumbs up emoji. Smiley face emoji.
"See you at my place."

They met in his backyard thirty minutes later.

"Nice ride," she said, eyeing his bright orange canoe. She smirked; it looked a little girly actually.

Brian didn't look girly, though. His swim trunks revealed very masculine, sexy legs. And the way his muscles filled out the T-shirt was something she hoped to see many times again. Too bad they were just friends. He was something to behold. He threw her a life jacket and covered his gorgeous body with one. *At least I won't be tempted to gawk at him.*

They dragged the canoe to the salt marsh and slid it into the water, then climbed in one at a time. He insisted she go first and sit in the bow, despite her protests that she had grown up traveling the waterways.

"I'm as much at home in a boat as I am on a bike, Brian. I know how to steer."

"Cool," he said, holding the canoe steady for her as she stepped into it and got comfy in her seat in the front of the boat. *Totally unnecessary, but chivalrous.*

"Stay low," she cautioned as he climbed into the stern.

"Yes, Mommy," he said, smirking.

"Wise ass."

"Sorry, Mommy."

"If you think you're gonna call me Mommy this whole ride," she started and was interrupted by his raucous laughter.

"Jerk," she laughed.

"Aww," he feigned a wound to the chest, then handed her a wooden paddle.

They fell into an easy paddling rhythm and skimmed the vessel along the edges of the salt marsh. The quiet stirring of the water and the rhythmic movements soothed her. She hadn't even realized she was stressed until she felt the tension dissolve with every stroke.

"*Decodon verticallatus.*" Brian pointed to the edge of the marsh at the green leafy plants rising above the water. "Swamp loosestrife. See it?"

"It's hard to miss. What's your favorite marsh plant?"

"Salt grass."

"Mine too! But on the shore, it's Sea Myrtle."

"*Baccharis halmifolia*! You know that plant is named after the Greek God Bacchus?"

"God of libation and liberation," she said. "I wonder why. What is it about the clusters of snowy flowers that's reminiscent of liberation?"

"What does liberation mean to you?"

"Hmmm."

She thought about it. Soon, they were paddling in silence again. The earthy salty scent of the marsh filled her nostrils. The sun warmed her back. Her friend started humming quietly. Brian had a deep, soft singing voice that entranced her. She couldn't make out the tune, but felt as if she were melting into it. The sun beat down and reflected off the water, making her doubly hot. She loved the sensation.

At the end of the ride, they dragged the canoe out of the marsh and fell, sweaty and exhausted, onto the sand at Brian's place.

She took a long sip from her water bottle, until it was drained completely.

"Still thirsty?" He asked.

She nodded. She was having trouble catching her breath for some reason. She hoped her eyebrows weren't out of control again.

He rolled across the small stretch of sand to the house, jumped into a squat and turned the knob on the side of the house. The next thing she knew, he was standing above her with a hose in his hand, filling her water bottle.

She raised her eyebrow.

"What?" he said.

"Not a thing."

He flicked the hose at her, splashing her face with water.

"Hey!"

"Oops."

"Oops?" She got to her feet, and reached for the hose. "Let's see how you like it."

She wrestled the hose from him and aimed the spray at his face. He opened his mouth and gulped, then shook his head like a dog.

"You are so weird."

"Oh, really?"

He held his hand out for the hose, as if she would just give it to him. *Not a chance*, she thought, putting it behind her back, and inadvertently spaying her own head.

"Damn it!" she laughed.

He reached his arm around her and grabbed the hose. He was close. The heat of his body made her heart race. She couldn't have held onto the hose if she'd wanted to, and when he took it from her, she felt herself go weak in the knees.

"Whoa there, Claire," Brian said, catching her.

Heat rose to her cheeks. "I, I'm fine." She was embarrassed was what she was.

"You sure?" He asked, lowering his head to peer into her face. His breath smelled sweet, like almonds.

She opened her mouth to speak but no sound came out. And then she found his lips on hers, and tasted the sweetness in his mouth. Her whole body felt electrified. She didn't know what she was doing or how her hands wound up on his hips. She pressed her thumb into his hip, moved it along the ridge, lost in the taste of him and the sensation of his arms around her.

He pulled away. "Oh, ah... sorry. I, ahh..."

"Sorry?"

"I mean."

"Sorry?" Her voice went up a notch. *Sorry you kissed me?*

"I didn't ask."

"Ask what?"

"May I kiss you?'

Relieved, she laughed and pulled his face to meet hers.

"No," she spoke into his mouth. "It's my turn to kiss you."

She ran her tongue around the inside of his lips, bit the lower lip gently, found the tip of his tongue and sucked it. He released control, allowing his tongue to be pulled into her mouth. She inhaled deeply, holding his tongue in her mouth for two, three, four breaths. A soft moan escaped his throat. She ran her hands down his sides, back onto his hips, down his thighs, then pulled away and looked up into his face.

Brian was flushed. His eyes shone. He smiled at her and she felt herself smiling back.

"Now, you may kiss me," she said.

"I think I'd better not, actually," he panted.

She raised her eyebrow. "Oh?"

"I wanna take things slowly with you. Do this right. And right now, after that kiss, I might have a hard time stopping."

"Oh!" she sighed, leaned into him, and closed her eyes. *Safe*.

He held her for a moment and stroked her hair. "Is that okay?"

"That is very okay."

Chapter 32

An obnoxious fifties tune pumped from the jukebox in the corner of the diner. Claire couldn't help dancing in her seat. Mazzie beamed at her.

"It was just a little k-i-s-s-i-n-g," she said, hoping Teddy hadn't learned that rhyme in preschool. That was a first-grade rhyme, wasn't it? *Claire and Brian sitting in a tree.* Maybe even second grade. Not preschool. Definitely not preschool.

"Yeah, like tantric k-i-s-s-i-n-g," Mazzie joked.

Claire rolled her eyes and giggled. "Is it juvenile that I feel sort of… *proud* of this event?"

"Totally!" Mazzie laughed. "But so, what? You deserve it. This is the first EVENT in—what? Six years?"

"Four. No. Five! No, oh my God." She looked at Teddy, busy coloring villains on the placemat, and considered… He had turned five in April. It was June. She did the math in her head. "Almost exactly six years. Ugh!"

The waitress set plates of vegan burgers and fries and soy strawberry milkshakes on the table in front of them.

"My only question to you, Sistah, is: how was it?"

Claire smiled broadly.

"Oooh la la!"

"Oooh la la," she sighed, content and giddy. "I hope for more events—oh, my goodness, it's him."

Her heart went into ecstatic spasms seeing Brian enter the diner.

"Hey! Brian!" Mazzie waved with both hands.

Embarrassing. "Cool it, Frack."

"What?" She kept waving, which drew Teddy's attention from his coloring, and, seeing his new hero standing by the hostess table, he zipped under the table and toward the man before Claire could say a peep.

None of that was horrible. But why was that blonde bombshell walking in with him? *What the hell?*

Brian held the door open for Tilly and followed her into the diner for their mid-internship celebration. Fun, vibrant atmosphere, a delicious meal. Just the right way to say, "keep up the good work." Who knew? If she continued performing as well as she had in the first few weeks, maybe she'd end up being a permanent colleague. Right now, though, he'd settle for a great finish to her summer internship.

"Bird Man!"

Teddy emerged out of the crowd, running toward him. He wore a new cape, black and white with the letters S.P. Salt and Pepper? No, that made no sense. *Think birds.* Suddenly, the mystery was solved and Teddy was hugging his legs.

"Hey! Where did you come from?" He felt his mouth spread into a wide smile as he knelt down to greet his little friend. "It's Super Penguin, right?"

Teddy pointed toward the booth where Mazzie waved and Claire hid behind a menu.

"I'm gonna get a Bird Man costume. Right, Mama?" he yelled over the din.

Claire responded from behind her menu, "Teddy, come back here, please."

Why was she hiding behind her menu?

"It's gonna be yellow with a cape and feathers, and the letters on the front: B.M."

Brian stifled a laugh and looked at Tilly. Tilly scowled at Teddy. Apparently, she was not a kid person.

"I think you should just go with the letter, B, buddy."

"Teddy, leave Brian alone. He's with someone."

"No. B for Bird. M for man."

"Aha."

Claire put her menu down and shot Teddy an intense look.

Hmm. Claire the disciplinarian. An image of Claire holding handcuffs flashed through his mind. *Jesus, Brian. Not here. Not now!*

"Teddy!" Claire called from her stool.

"It has to be B.M."

Claire slipped out of the booth and came toward them. "Sorry," she mouthed, as she dragged Teddy away. She seemed nervous, but why?

"It's gonna be B.M. Right Mommy?"

"Right now, that seems appropriate."

The hostess, whose hair was now an alarming shade of school bus yellow, led Brian and Tilly to a booth. Was it his imagination, or was the hostess eyeing Tilly?

Finally settled and looking at menus, Brian turned his attention to his intern. She was pretty, in that pin-up kind of way. A bust as perky as her nose, straight blonde hair, minimal makeup. He imagined she made a lot of women jealous. "So, how are you feeling about the internship? Do you have any personal goals or anything for the remainder of your time in the program?"

"Excited. I want—"

Could that have been what was going on with Claire? Was she jealous of his summer intern? *That's ridiculous. What could Claire possibly have to be jealous about?* Obviously, she was acting strange for some other reason having nothing to do with him. After all, he had helped her through a rough time and they had bonded. He'd finally gotten up the courage to kiss her, and it had been spectacular. The passion… She had felt something. He could tell she'd felt something, but now she seemed to be avoiding him. No, she wasn't. She was just shepherding her kid. He had said he wanted to take things slowly. With Claire, he knew that was absolutely the right thing to say.

"—and sampling. Using data to—"

"I'm sorry, Tilly. I got distracted for a minute. Could you repeat what you just said, please?"

Watching Brian and his date move further into the diner, Teddy slumped over the table.

"I wish Bird Man stayed and ate with us."

Claire sighed, corralled the crayons on the table and flipped Teddy's placemat over. What was Brian doing out with this bombshell person, anyway? *Not that anything serious is happening between us, but…* He had been so solicitous lately, so friendly, so… *following us home in his jeep. Asking me to text him when I got home to make sure we were safe. Who does that? Kissing me! And that kiss. So hot. So tantalizing. So erotic and titillating and… And he said he wanted to do this right.* Was this his idea of doing it right? Seeing someone else? He didn't seem like a player.

Mazzie looked on sympathetically. "They do *not* look like a happy couple."

"The only happy couple I know are my parents."

"Besides me and Greg, they're the only happy couple I know, too. Where are they, anyway? I thought you were inviting them."

"It's Friday."

"Right," Mazzie grimaced. "Remember that time?"

Claire shuddered. "I can't tell you how many times I've tried to burn it from my memory."

"On the kitchen island," they squealed together.

Chapter 33

Monday night, Brian took Claire, Teddy, and his imaginary students to the beach to practice taking water samples, then brought "them" back to the lab at school. While demonstrating how to extract different elements from a water sample, he looked up to make sure Claire was following him. Their eyes met and he lost his breath for just a second. But there was a coolness in her eyes now.

Later, he introduced E.O. Wilson's wonderfully descriptive and important conceptual acronym regarding threats to wildlife:

H - habitat loss
I - invasive species
P - pollution
P - population explosion
O - over harvesting

As he wrote the letters and their brief meanings on the board, he saw that both Claire and Teddy were spellbound. He felt larger than life, sharing this important concept with two generations at once. Yet when he smiled at her, she looked away.

She was so blown away by Brian's teaching, by his brilliance, she wanted to cheer. His every word inspired her. And the way he had moved around the lab and was now moving in the classroom, engaging imaginary students in discussion, and including her in the conversation invigorated her.

What's he doing with that blonde anyway? Isn't she too young for him? Wasn't he into me? What happened? She sighed aloud, then blushed and looked at Teddy, hoping maybe Brian would think Teddy had made the sound. Teddy was coloring silently in the chair next to her. Brian looked at her and smiled.

Her breath caught in her throat. Feeling angry tears well in her eyes, she looked away. The last thing she wanted him to see was her crying over him. It wasn't like they'd made promises to one another. It was just that she hadn't let anyone get close since Jim, and she thought she'd finally met someone she could trust.

Tuesday morning, he took water samples. There was nothing new or different about this particular morning. Just routine data collection, but for some annoying and beautiful reason, he kept seeing Claire's face in the ripples at the shore.

That afternoon, while he and Tilly conducted their field work, a group of drunk teenagers trespassed onto the beach's restricted area. *Again? Shit.* It was like clockwork; at the end of every school year, and at specific points throughout the summer, some group of high school kids would show up drunk on the beach. It didn't matter where. Brian had observed this pattern in Texas, in Maine, and in Oregon, and now he was seeing it in Delaware. He shooed them off the beach with warnings about arrest (and this group of kids actually listened). As he shooed the kids away, he remembered the first time he saw Claire and Teddy on the beach, how he'd made a point to alert her to the impending beach closing. Of course, she hadn't listened; in fact, she had brought her son back to that spot the very next day. But then, she was on a mission; she wasn't just some idiot kid coming to the beach to get wasted and get laid. *Sex on the beach with Claire...*

Before he knew it, Brian's mind was off on a tangent that had nothing to do with shorebirds or harvest restrictions.

"Geez Louise, Brian! Pull yourself together!"

"Everything okay over there, Boss?" Tilly asked.

"Yup!" He jogged in place to snap his mind into gear, then grabbed his clipboard and recorded the details of the teen interruption on the beach.

Brian drove through the pre-dawn mist, cutting the headlights just before he entered the protected wildlife area. He hadn't felt this tense since the stakeout when they had caught the poachers in Texas.

"Just in case," he said to Tilly, who was nursing a cup of coffee.

"Just in case what?"

She was so innocent.

"In case the poachers are already here," he said. "We don't want to announce our arrival."

"Oh," she whispered, like the secrecy was a big revelation.

He parked the Rover, grabbed his gear and got out. "One way or another, with more data or with evidence, we're gonna get these creeps."

"Right! Because…?"

"If we don't, they'll just keep harvesting the horseshoe crabs illegally and overfishing them, and their population will decline, and there will be less food for the Red Knots to fuel up for their long journey to the Arctic."

"Got it!" Tilly said, then took out the camera.

"I'm just going to take a look at this, make sure it's all set up for us," he said, taking the camera from her. *Is she always this spacey? Maybe she just isn't a morning person.* He was sure they had discussed the Red Knot/Horseshoe crab conundrum.

He looked at the lens. Fifty-millimeter: perfect. He double checked the F-stop setting: one-point-eight. "Okay, we're all set." *She may be spacey, but she did set up the camera correctly.*

They walked to the beach observation area and erected the tripod. Tilly attached a video camera to the tripod, focused on the shoreline and started recording. He followed her to the shore, handed her the still camera, pulled out an audio recorder and his notebook. They waited, but not long.

A light flashed across the shore just in front of them, and a little red boat dropped anchor a few yards from the shoreline.

Hands shaking, he pressed a speed dial button on his phone. "Environmental Police" lit up the screen. He covered the light and whispered, "Brian Melodus from DFW here. I'm calling to report illegal harvesting of horseshoe crabs."

Tilly snapped photos of the boat. Brian hoped, trusted, knew… he was sure that Tilly must be zooming in on the ID number and the equipment. Of course, she was. Tilly was an intern, a sharp intern, almost a professional. He was just nervous. Would this be their only shot?

"Yeah, I know the restrictions were lifted," he whispered, "but that doesn't take effect until after mating season ends… Thanks." He shoved the phone into his pocket.

Two fishermen emerged from the boat with buckets and started harvesting crabs. He could hear the shutter in Tilly's camera clicking in rapid fire. He turned on the audio recorder, and took notes.

Fifteen minutes later, Environmental Police officers arrived just as the boat was leaving. Brian tried to keep his breathing easy. He had felt frustrated by so many of his encounters with the EPs, but after all these years, he had learned to get convincing evidence. Now, he showed them his notes, played the audio recording, and Tilly showed them the photos. The EPs reviewed the video footage together, and then asked Brian and Tilly to email the evidence ASAP.

"Thank God that video footage turned out, huh?" Tilly said, as they packed the equipment into the truck.

"Thank God is right."

"And the photos and the audio…"

"I think we got 'em this time. I really think we got 'em." His muscles relaxed.

"This is super exciting!" Tilly practically squealed.

"A judge would have to be blind, deaf, and dumb to ignore that evidence, if it goes to trial."

"Why wouldn't it?"

She was so young. He sighed, thinking of the numerous cases where the EPs failed to gather and present the proper evidence.

"EP's do their job right they'll scare those fishermen into revealing their buyer."

"That'd be a big, big case. Right?"

Brian nodded, lost in thought.

Sitting in his office, Brian stared at the phone number on his contact list until the digits almost didn't make sense anymore. It was not a big deal to call her. He had a perfectly legitimate reason to call her. In fact, she had given him that perfectly legitimate reason. All he was doing, if he could muster up the courage, was returning Claire's phone call. Anyway, he'd called her before. In fact, he'd kissed her before. A delicious, hot, sexy kiss. A wet kiss in the hot sun. A salty kiss. A barn raising... *oh for God's sake.*

Why was he so nervous about calling her now? He had no idea. *Brian, just pull yourself together and dial.* He inhaled sharply, let it out slowly, and tapped the digits on the screen.

"This is Claire. you've reached my cell. Leave a message."

"Hey, ah. I'm returning your call about the artwork. This is Brian, by the way. Brian Melodus. Haha. You know who I am. At least I think you do. You should. Oh, shit, I didn't mean it that way. What a bozo."

He sighed and clicked End Call. *That could not have gone worse.* Maybe if he'd let one rip in the middle of the call it would have been worse. Other than that, he had blown it from start to finish, like a zit-covered kid. He knocked his forehead with his palm. "Brian! Come on, man!"

Chapter 34

The amount of paperwork that needed filing just to have an art show seemed endless. How could there possibly be so many documents for such a tiny gallery? Claire was not in the mood for spreadsheets and calculations today, not in the mood for art. She was in the mood for chocolate and wine and…

The door chimed and Brian entered with a large box. "Oh, hey, Claire! What are you doing here?"

"That's a silly question," she responded. "What are *you* doing here?"

"Birdman!" Teddy yelled from under the reception desk.

"Hey, Super Invisible Man. Who's your sidekick?"

"Crab Woman!"

"You mean Crab*by* Woman?"

Claire shoved her notebook at Brian. "What do you think?"

Brian reviewed her notes. "I can't read your writing."

"The idea is about education and art."

"Okay," he looked at her expectantly. "Tell me more."

"Well, you got my message, so you know we're thinking of an art show"

"Yes, and—"

"And I'm thinking about the educational opportunities."

"Such as—"

"Something with kids. That environmental superhero corps you mentioned."

"Interesting! And—"

"Right now, that's all I got. It's just brewing in my head."

"Can't wait 'til it's fully percolated."

She giggled. He smirked, revealing those deep dimples. She sighed. *Aloud? Did I just sigh aloud and give him the dreamy look? Shit! Cough, Claire.* She coughed as forcefully as she could to cover up the embarrassing display of emotion. Clearly, the kissing had been a one-time thing, a fluke. He wasn't interested in her, not romantically, anyway. He hadn't even called her since then, except to talk about class and the art show. He was a jerk and she deserved better. Just because he was hot and they had a lot in common and he was nice to her son and sympathetic and helpful… that meant nothing. They'd had a momentary lapse in judgement, nothing more.

"Speaking of the art show: you asked me to bring my artwork."

"What? No, I didn't."

"Uh… you called me like two weeks ago and asked about the art hanging in my office. You said your mother was interested in art with an environmental theme."

Claire laughed, "Brian, I said I wanted you to connect me with the artist so he or she could come in with slides and meet my mom."

"Yup, and—"

"Sorry to waste your time."

"I can bring slides if you want, but I just thought it'd be easier to bring the work."

"But we need the artist."

"I *am* the artist."

"What?"

"I am the artist. Me. It's mine. I do this to blow off steam."

"Make art?"

Brian nodded. "Is your mom around?"

Claire nodded, speechless, excited, annoyed. She texted her mother: "New artist here to meet you with art."

Jane hurried into the room. "Oh! Hi, Brian. Claire, where's the artist?"

"You're looking at him," Claire said, both proud and annoyed.

"Shall I?" Brian gestured to the large box of artwork.

"Of course!"

Without a word, Brian reached into the box, removed a fabric sculpture and held it aloft. Jane nodded. He withdrew more fabric sculptures, then laid a series of framed photographs against the wall, and finally removed some sculptures made from trash. Jane spent a few minutes assessing each piece.

Brian pulled Claire away from the art and handed her a manila envelope. "You didn't respond to my email about your resume, that fellowship from ARM Foundation. The info's inside," he whispered.

"Oh, I, you know, between the job search and helping my mom out and Teddy recuperating…"

"Huh. I thought this would be a great fit for you."

Claire sighed and returned the envelope unopened. "I don't think I have a shot at getting a major fellowship like this."

"Why would you say that?" He asked, touching her arm, sending a charge through her entire body. The expression on his face — softness, concern — made her weak.

She pulled up the fellowship info page on her phone and cleared her throat. "One: it's only for students attending universities in communities under-represented in the environmental movement. Okay, I guess Delaware counts. And I am interested in pursuing a leadership position within the environmental field. That's two. But, three: it says applicants must be graduate students at universities physically located within the Foundation's areas of focus: Washington, Oregon, Idaho, western Montana, southern Alaska, New Hampshire and Connecticut. Last: the Foundation encourages applications from a broad diversity of students, with a particular emphasis on *students of color* and others who have overcome significant hardships."

His eyes roamed her face. "Haven't you overcome significant hardship?"

"I guess so, but I'm not in one of the focus areas."

"Trust me; you should apply anyway. There's always wiggle room."

She raised her eyebrows at him.

"Maybe they won't get any outstanding applicants from their focus areas."

"You think I'm outstanding?"

"You're my best student!"

"That would be so flattering if you had any other students, and if I didn't already have my degree in the subject."

"Brian!" Jane called from the other end of the gallery, "This is something!"

"Thank you! I've got more in my Rover. Shall I bring it in?"

"Absolutely."

He turned back to Claire and said more intensely, "You've got something special, Claire. Don't let it go to waste."

Something special. A new energy flowed through Claire. *I've got something special.* And the concern on Brian's face, the warmth of his touch. *Something special.*

Brian left and returned a moment later with another large box, which he set on the reception desk. Then he ran back to the door and held it open. The blonde bombshell entered with a large canvas.

"What would I do without you, Tilly?"

"I've really rocked your world, haven't I?" the bombshell said.

Brian smirked. Claire exhaled slowly, irritated. *Tilly. Rocked his world.* Claire turned to the canvas, reminding herself this was a meeting about the art, nothing more; the art and the fellowship from the ARM Foundation because Claire had, as it turned out, something special to offer the field of wildlife biology and restoration ecology.

"Claire. Tilly. Have you met officially?" Brian asked.

"No," Claire said, scowling.

"Claire, Tilly is interning with us this summer. Tilly, Claire is a dear friend and someone you should get to know if you want to see a superhero in action."

Tilly stuck out her hand enthusiastically. "Great to meet you, Claire!"

"Well, that, hands down, is the most flattering introduction I have ever received." *Even though he introduced me as his 'dear friend,'*

194

not someone he's dating… Sigh... Think business, Claire. "How's the internship going, Tilly?"

"So far, so good. Right, Boss?" She beamed at Brian. It was nauseating.

"She's doing a great job," Brian said.

"And I'm learning so much from him," Tilly gushed.

"I'm sure," Claire said. "So, let's see this painting!"

She rescued it from Tilly's arms, noting its heft (Ten pounds? Fifteen?), and set it on the floor against the wall. The painting was good — beautiful, in fact. Claire had spotted it in his office, quickly determined it to be potentially important, but hadn't thought more deeply about it. Now, seeing the gentle striations of color, the undulating waves of light throughout the abstract work, Claire found herself transfixed. She could have stared at it for hours. "What do you think, Mom?"

"You have great instincts, Dear."

Claire smiled at the compliment. Two compliments in the space of a few minutes. Who needed wine and chocolate after all?

"And Brian," Jane continued, "You may be the voice of your generation."

Brian strutted around the gallery, playful, grinning. "The voice of my generation, Tilly. Hear that?"

"Oh, I get the feeling we won't hear the end of that."

Chapter 35

Claire was still thinking about the art show as she rode into the beach parking lot, took Teddy out of the bike trailer and started strolling the unrestricted area of the beach. Teddy twirled around, showing off his new Crab Boy cape while Claire paused to peer through her spotting scope. Through the lens, she saw a path of mini candy bar wrappers littering the sand behind a family of four. Two little girls in matching pink and purple outfits, not much older than Teddy it seemed, collected feathers and brought them to their parents, who walked ahead of them. The dad finished a candy bar, dropped the wrapper, and reached over to tickle the girls.

Claire tucked her scope in her pocket, ran to pick up the candy wrappers, and called to the family. "Excuse me! You dropped something."

They stopped. Claire and Teddy rushed to them. Claire extended the candy wrappers to the dad. "Hi," she sputtered, out of breath. "You dropped these."

The parents looked surprised. The father scowled but took the wrappers.

Claire smiled, "I know you wouldn't want any birds to choke on these."

"It's so small," he snorted. "They can't choke on a little candy wrapper."

"Their throats are small, too," Claire explained, then turned to the girls, "Hey! Nice feathers."

"We collect them for good luck," the little girl in pink said, wiggling a loose tooth with her tongue.

"Those are Oyster Catcher feathers. Here," Claire said, pulling a red knot feather from her pocket. "This is one of my favorites. This bird comes to this beach each year for just a few weeks. Without the food it gets here it couldn't survive."

"Seriously," the mom said. "This place is that important?"

"Mm. Hm," Claire said, handing the feather to the little girl in purple. "Why don't you keep this safe? Okay?"

Teddy gasped, "Mama, that's mines."

"Yours is at home, Honey. And we'll find more."

"Okay," he said.

"What kind of bird is this feather from?" the girl wearing purple asked.

Teddy puffed up his chest. "That's from a red knot, right, Mama?"

"That's right! It's got a great story. If you Google it, you'll find stuff."

"And, Mama, what about *Moonbird*?" Teddy yelled, hopping from one foot to the other.

"Good thinking, Hon," Claire said. "Do you guys like to read?"

"Yeah!" the girls said in unison.

"Awesome! Check out the book *Moonbird* from the library. They have a few copies. It's a beautiful story."

"Thanks," the dad said, putting his arms around his family.

Claire nodded at them and led Teddy away.

When they arrived at home, an image flashed through her mind. As she locked the bike under the stairs, a surge of excitement flowed through Claire's muscles, making her giddy. Giggling, she helped Teddy out of the trailer.

"What's funny, Mama?"

"It's so simple."

"What's simple?"

"Information plus understanding equals knowledge. Information plus compassion equals respect. Knowledge plus respect equals right action! Saving the shorebirds and our baby crabs is as simple as adding up numbers."

"What?"

"Education! We have to… I knew it before, but now I've got how."

"What are you talking about, Mommy?" Teddy sighed exaggeratedly, shaking his head.

"I just figured out how to do it! A festival! A big, old fashioned street fair to save our little friends."

"Mama?"

"Yes?"

"You're really not making any sense."

She ruffled his hair and led him upstairs.

Chapter 36

Claire sang along with the kid music streaming from the living room, half-listening to Teddy coerce Fallon into playing superhero, half-fantasizing about the festival she envisioned. There was nothing like a Sunday morning. With the gallery closed and no preschool, she could totally relax. Fallon made a strange sound in the other room.

"Teddy," she warned. "Are you sharing with your friend?"

"Mama," he whined.

"Friends share," she said, whipping the chia mixture into a froth, or trying to. She had yet to make delicious vegan French toast, and she was really hoping this would work. *Some things just can't be replaced*, she thought.

A knock on the door followed by Mazzie's quick entrance and tearful hug jolted Claire out of her reverie.

"What happened?" Claire asked.

Mazzie sniffled.

"It's that bum, Greg, again, isn't it?"

"He's not a bum, just… an introvert."

"Oh, Honey. I hate to say it, but he's not good for you."

"No," Mazzie pulled away from Claire and reached for the teakettle and a mug. "My therapist said I just have to accept Greg's need to withdraw sometimes. It's not personal."

"Accept his need to withdraw? What if he wants to start seeing other women? Is that okay, too? Do you just roll over and take it?"

"That's a bit of a stretch, isn't it, Claire?"

Mazzie poured her tea water, retrieved a bag of chamomile from the cupboard, and dunked it in and out of the mug. Silence.

Nothing, Claire thought, *says pissed like silence.*

Finally, taking a spoonful of honey and alternating it between the tea and her mouth, Mazzie looked at Claire again. "That's not what we're talking about. We're talking about how to make my relationship work. And it's working."

"Okay?"

She pulled a letter from her purse, waved it at Claire and smiled, "My man, who never writes even emails, my man wrote me a love letter."

"Great! So why are you crying?"

Mazzie held the letter to her heart, then returned it to her purse. "I just miss him. He went camping without me, and… You have to give a little to get a little, Claire, but I guess you wouldn't know that."

"Excuse me? You come in here crying, telling me he needs time away, then suddenly jump all over me when I call a spade a spade." Her voice was rising.

Mazzie groaned. "You don't get it, obviously. I just want a fairy tale romance like your parents. There's nothing wrong with that."

"Except that it doesn't exist. You and I both know my parents are total freaks."

I wanted a love like that too, once, Claire thought, then remembered the flame under the skillet. "Oh, shit. The French toast."

She melted some coconut oil in the pan, bathed a piece of bread in the chia mixture, and laid it on the hot oil.

"I talked to my therapist about them, too, how perfect their love affair is, how I—"

Claire shook her head and sang along with the kid music. "Yellow is the color of the sun. Green is the color of the leaves on trees in spring, and blue is the color of the daytime sky."

"You're ignoring me now?"

Claire flipped the experimental slice of French toast. "I don't need to hear about my parents' perfect love affair."

"You know what?" Mazzie hissed. "I'm sorry things didn't work out with you and Jim, but that doesn't mean every romance is doomed."

"I think I can recognize an unhealthy relationship when I see one."

"Really? How about Jim?"

Claire glared at Mazzie, "My child is in the next room."

"Teddy? Come say 'Hi' to Aunt Mazzie."

They listened and waited. Mazzie smiled. "He's not listening. He can't hear us."

Claire laughed caustically, then whispered, "What about Jim? Why throw that in my face now?" She pulled the French toast from the pan, took a bite. *Not bad.*

"You used to call me all the time complaining about him—"

"Lower your voice," Claire whispered hoarsely.

Mazzie continued in a hoarse whisper, "About how controlling he was, but what did it take for you to leave?"

"What does this have to do with you and Greg?"

Mazzie sighed, "Nothing. I just, you know, I supported you through that hell. I wish you could support me in creating the love and life I want."

Claire turned off the stove. The surge of anger that flooded her was not good. It needed a place to go. She shook her arms to exorcise it. Her backpack was hanging on the hook by the door, where it always hung. Inside it, was the photo. She grabbed her bag, pulled out the package of red and black tissue paper, unwrapped the photo and handed it to Mazzie.

"Do you remember this photo?"

"I could never forget it."

"He didn't like me to spend time with other people," she whispered, glaring at Mazzie. "He was always jealous and irrational. I thought when we got married, he would learn to trust me, see reality. I kept giving him second chances, trying to make it work. This time, I knew he'd only get worse."

"Claire, I… that's not what is happening with Greg."

"Isn't it? He's up; he's down. You're high; your low." She nodded. "Growing up with my fairy tale father—" her voice broke, but she could feel the muscles in her face tense like stone. "How could I ever imagine someone would do what Jim did?"

Mazzie stood very still, like she wasn't sure what to do. "Why didn't you call me?"

"And tell you I had failed? That I felt worthless and didn't know how to rescue myself?"

"And you had your dad."

"Exactly. The eternal knight in shining armor drove the thousand miles to get me and the thousand miles back, with me retching and promising myself I would never become that again." She pointed to the photo, then wrapped it in the tissue paper again and placed it back in the zippered pocket in her bag. "Whatever you think you know about relationships, whatever your therapist said sounds nice and sweet, but I can tell you from experience, you have to be careful. And sometimes, it's just not worth it."

"You know what, Claire?"

"You want to spend every other night crying over your man and his ever-changing winds, be my guest. I have enough on my plate; I don't need a man to confuse me."

"Brian?"

"I have to keep myself together for my son. That is my priority. Not figuring out whether it's safe to trust some guy."

"This isn't about you, but—" Mazzie pointed to the bag, "I didn't do that to you. I've only loved and supported you. All this time I thought you were here in front of me, but you were still stuck in Boulder."

"Denver."

"Denver, with Jim. You have not healed, Claire, and if you don't find a way to move on, you're going to push everyone and everything you care about away. You'll be alone and miserable, and Jim will have won."

Claire opened the door. "I think we're done here."

Mazzie put the mug on the counter and glared at Claire as she stormed out.

Claire held the door handle so Mazzie couldn't slam it like she normally did in arguments. *No need to alarm Teddy.* She stood on the landing, watched Mazzie leave and then, staring off into the distance, raised her arms above her head, inhaled deeply, and exhaled into a forward fold. Claire laughed at the irony; if Mazzie wasn't so furious with her, she'd be proud of her for relieving her tension this way, with a deep breath and a little yoga.

Claire went back to the stove, ignited the flame under the skillet and made two more pieces of French toast.

"Hey Superheroes," she called. "Who's ready for French toast?"

As Teddy and Fallon ran in and followed Claire's gesture to the sink to wash their hands, her thoughts returned to her idea for the shorebird festival. Shorebirds and horseshoe crabs. *How can I engage both kids and adults in a unique day of learning? What will draw a crowd and make a difference?* She wondered who she needed to contact first, what she needed to research to make it happen. It seemed like a real opportunity to create the future she wanted.

She thought about calling Brian. He would have great ideas. But no. Claire wanted — needed — to do this on her own.

Besides, she didn't want any confusion about what was happening between them romantically —*which is nothing* — to cloud the project, especially in the planning stage. She could find other resources to help. What about her parents? If she could rescue the Gallery with the art show and convince her dad it was a wise investment to keep the building, could she use the gallery as festival headquarters?

She dialed her mother.

Thirty minutes later, they had a plan. They would announce the festival at the environmental art show, and take donations at the show to be used as start-up funds for the festival. That would give people a double reason to buy the art: they'd save the gallery both for art's sake and for the environment. The gallery, which would be renamed from ArtGal to something more community and eco based, would become a space to hold discussions about environmental issues all year long, not just during the festival. In fact, they could use those discussions as fundraisers for the festival. Energy coursed through Claire's body as she reveled in what she and her mother were creating together.

Her mom would convert the store room into a second office for Claire. With a launchpad and an office space, Claire would hire some volunteers and have a place to store any materials they amassed. It also gave them a respectable mailing address to use if anyone wanted to send donations. But they had gotten ahead of themselves. Claire still needed to figure out what kind of activities to include.

She decided to call Veronica Meery. Just because the woman hadn't hired her didn't mean she wouldn't give her advice. In fact, she had said quite clearly that she wanted to help Claire.

Chapter 37

Three days later, Claire and Teddy rode from the beach straight to campus. Her heart was pounding, and, though she hated to admit it to herself, it was not because of the bike ride. She was excited to see Brian, eager to share her vision for the festival with him. Her idea was good; it had the potential to make a difference. Not only that, but she had brought the whole presentation to the office supply store and had it professionally bound. That was sure to impress him, not that she cared what he thought of her personally.

Of course, I don't care what he thinks of me. Apparently, he doesn't think of me romantically. Fine. This is business. He's a colleague. I respect his work, and he could probably give me ideas for fundraising.

His office door was wide open. He was running his thick fingers through his hair, staring at the laptop on his desk. She really liked his fingers. She knocked. Brian looked up.

Was she imagining it, or had his face started to glow when he saw her?

"Hi," he said.

Teddy jumped in from behind the door, pantomiming.

"Hey, Super Silent Man!"

Claire placed the dossier on Brian's desk.

He nodded approval. "You didn't have to go to all this trouble."

She laughed, too loudly she realized, then tried to shrug her embarrassment away. "In the corporate world," she started, then thought better of it. "Anyway, I hope you enjoy my proposal."

"I'll take a look and send notes."

The hairs on the back of her neck rose. "Send notes?"

"Feedback. Corrections. I mean, you just graduated, with unusual circumstances to boot. No one would expect you—"

"No one would expect me to what?"

"Have a full grasp of the—"

She stared at him, dumbfounded. He was so insulting. He had been so sweet; now he'd turned around and was insulting her. *Why is he tapping the side of his head? Is he suggesting I'm stupid?* Of course, he was, and she had expected it. She'd been through it before.

"—happy to look at it for you."

"Thanks, Professor. Come on, Teddy." She grabbed her son's hand and dragged him out.

"But, Mommy!"

"No buts. We've got... stuff!"

She slammed the door.

Chapter 38

Brian stared at the space left empty in Claire's absence. What had just happened? Claire had walked in. Teddy had jumped out. Brian had said Hi. Claire had been smiling. She had given him her fellowship application, at last. He had said sympathetic things to show he understood how hard it was being a single mom. Claire had stormed out. What had gone wrong? He shook his head, picked up the dossier and flipped through it.

This was not a fellowship application. This was a business plan. Each page was rife with information: diagrams, research, photographs, calculations, spreadsheets. Claire had created a full-blown business proposal for a festival to raise awareness about the plight of shorebirds and horseshoe crabs on the Delaware Bay. Not only that, but it was an idea that could be replicated in other parts of the country, heck — other parts of the world — focusing on different threatened species. Brian was blown away. Never had he imagined that anyone would come up with something so wonderful, so life affirming, so aligned with the way he actually felt about the environment and all life. It was like he was seeing his personal values presented in the pages of Claire's project. He wanted to pick her up and kiss her. Of course, she wasn't there now. She had stormed out for reasons he still couldn't comprehend. But if she were there —

And she wasn't enrolled in a graduate program because she was trying to save money. Had she filled out the application for the ARM Foundation Fellowship yet? Could he fill it out for her? What program had accepted her? Frank would know.

He texted him, "What graduate program did Claire get into?"

"MA/Ph.D. at Delaware Ecological Institute."

"And she's not going?"

"Tuition + 5-year-old = $$$$$. Headstrong; won't let us help. Has to do it herself," then "Why?"

"NVM"

"?"

"I'll explain in person."

He picked up the office phone and dialed, tapping his pen on his desk with his other hand. When his brother-in-law answered, his voice sounding more nasal than usual, Brian took a deep breath and made a concerted effort to speak at a normal pace. "Nick, do you have an applicant named Claire Dessalines?"

Nick asked him to hold while he flipped through the applications on his desk. "No, but we are very close to making our funding decisions for this cohort. Why?"

"I have someone for you. She's just an exceptional thinker, and we're in danger of losing her."

"Losing her?" Nick asked.

"The field of wildlife rehabilitation could lose her if she doesn't get funding. Major funding. She deferred her MA/Ph.D. admission so she can try to earn money to pay for it."

Nick reminded him that it would be highly irregular and unfair to consider an applicant whose materials arrived late.

"Don't you have that discretionary fund, though? I mean, it's your call, of course. But I'd schedule an interview with her if I were you. She belongs in this field. She's passionate and brilliant and hardworking. We'd do well to have Claire on our team, Man. And you can make it happen."

"You really know how to lay it on."

"Nick, your sister would approve of this." *Your sister DOES approve of this. She's the one who keeps pushing me to pay attention to Claire. Not that I can tell you that. You'd think I was insane.* "In some ways, she's quite a bit like Adrienne."

There was silence on the other end of the line. Then the sound of Nick clearing his throat. "What is it about her, Brian?"

"The passion, the creativity. She just dropped a proposal in my hands that — well, I can't even tell you. It just blew me away. She could revolutionize the field of wildlife rehabilitation through public support. She's…. And you know she's struggling to find a job so she can pay for school, while raising a little kid on her own. She should be focusing on two things: her kid and her career, not some half-ass job that doesn't even cover the cost of her tuition."

"Too bad you won't be here to make her case to the rest of the board next month."

Brian took a deep breath, flipped through the pages of his calendar, circled the date of the next board meeting. "Maybe I will."

"I'd love to see you, Brother."

"Me, too. In the meantime, though, I'm going to FedEx you a copy of this proposal."

Chapter 39

T he hinges on the door squeaked. *When did that start?* Brian walked down the narrow aisle, noting the ever-present musty odor, then laughed as he rapped on the entrance to Arthur's office.

"You're duct taping your window together now?"

"Such is the state of affairs for Flora and Fauna Service, my friend." Arthur said without looking up.

Brian had come to realize it was Arthur's catch phrase. *Such is the state of affairs for Flora and Fauna...*

Arthur tore the duct tape from the roll, rubbed the end of the tape onto the window screen and sat in his duct-taped office chair, flashing Brian a sardonic smile. Arthur looked tired and older than his fifty-seven years. He looked ready to retire. Brian hoped Arthur was nowhere near retiring; that would be a disaster.

"And this state of affairs is not helped by the data coming from the Delaware Bay shorebird observation station."

"I know." Brian took a seat in the ripped upholstered chair.

"How can we prove, even to ourselves, that the climate smart landscaping adaptations we've made also benefit these shorebirds if there are no birds?"

"I know."

"I'm not saying I blame you. I know how it goes out in the field. But Native Species Restoration needs funding, and it could use your talent. I'd rather put you there."

"I know, and *thank you*, but listen. I've got a way to boost public education, get local business involved, and pique state's interest, which would, as you know, lead to more funding."

Arthur leaned forward; his eyes open wide.

"A shorebird and horseshoe crab festival."

Arthur groaned and leaned back.

"No, no. Hear me out. The festival is funded initially by local business sponsorships and maybe a grant."

"Come on! You know how many festivals there are?"

"But this is for the kids, and parents will wanna bring them to give them something to do. And for the parents it's like a fun conference — not just lectures, but also wine and cheese socials, performances, and workshops while the kids are engaged in yoga and art and cooperative games, all focusing on—"

"Since when do you know anything about kids?"

"This is my friend's idea. She's a mom… a brilliant, motivated single mom who has all the passion you lost twenty years ago!"

"Give her time," he said, dryly.

"When this festival succeeds, it'll prove the public cares about our cause, which gives us leverage to go for more state funding, make the governor look good in the eyes of voters who care, *and* boost the local economy."

"So, get me a plan and bring her with it."

Brian leapt from the seat, slapped the proposal on Arthur's desk, saluted his boss and left.

Chapter 40

Arriving home, Claire spotted the banner in the art gallery window announcing the environmental art show: "Eco-Cultcha." It looked good. She thought of the work she had put into conceiving and planning the show with her mom over the last several weeks and felt a pleasant warmth in her stomach. If she could create sponsor request flyers for the festival that looked as good as the art show materials, she'd probably get a lot of support. She hoped she would. She'd gotten no response from Brian yet.

Why hasn't he called? Should I call him? No, Claire. He hasn't called because he doesn't take your work seriously. He was so confusing, so hot and cold. He had seemed so supportive, but when she'd handed him the proposal… Insulting.

"Hello, men of my life," she called as she opened the door.

"Mommy," Teddy sang, flying down the hall to greet her.

She lifted her little boy into the air, kissed his soft, pudgy cheeks. He would be going to kindergarten soon, a thought that both pained and thrilled her.

"Darling," her dad said pushing himself off the floor where a pile of books, toys and crayons surrounded him. He sounded like a man who had just spent a full day with a highly energetic little boy: exhausted. "I promised your mother I'd make something special for dinner tonight."

"Wow. It's not even Friday."

"I may be old, but I've still got it, Kiddo."

"Oh, God, sorry I brought that up," she said, kissing him on the cheek. "Thanks so much, Dad."

"Of course! Sorry about the mess, but we had fun, right Teddy?"

Teddy nodded vigorously.

"Sionara!"

As Frank left, Claire looked at the mess on the floor, thought about cleaning it up, and changed her mind. "Teddy, can you help me?"

Teddy nodded.

"Can you bring my folder from my bed and your crayons? We are going to make some posters and flyers."

Teddy leapt from her arms and ran to his room, arms in front of him like he was flying, cape flapping behind him. *How am I going to tell him he has to wear normal clothes to kindergarten?* Would it be a real problem? Perhaps her father would be able to get Teddy excited about clothes shopping. *Well, if I can help solve an environmental problem, I guess I can figure out how to help my son come to terms with dressing like a normal kid.*

Teddy returned with the supplies, just as Claire finished wiping the table. She dried it, opened her folder and reassessed the half-finished brochure design.

"Can you draw a horseshoe crab, Honey?"

"Of course!"

"Awesome. Can you draw it on this big blank piece of paper?"

"Yeah," he said, like it was no big deal.

"Yeah?"

"Yeah!" He yelled, throwing his arms into the air.

"Yeah, yeah, yeah!"

Teddy climbed onto his booster seat and settled in to drawing. He was adorable; his skinny little fingers, the focus in his eyes. He looked up to see if she was watching. She smiled and ruffled his hair, then turned her eyes to the design she needed to finish. This is where her training in the financial industry would come in handy. Marketing. Sales. She recalled the refrain her colleagues in that world had often repeated: *Who's your audience? What do you want them to know? Why should they care? What do you want them to do? What misperceptions do you need to overcome about the product?* In this case, the product was the festival. Who was the audience?

She made a quick sketch on her notepad: children, adults, families treated as individuals. Kids treated as kids; adults treated as adults. Sure, it was fun to watch your child enjoy an age-appropriate magic show. It was also mind-numbing to sit through several such performances. The adults needed more. She was giving them more. She wanted them to know that. They would care because they didn't want to go to another boring, annoying festival where the only real adult activities were eating and drinking. What did she want them to do?

She drew groups of adults in circles — a charette — she wanted them to dialogue about these environmental issues, to think about more than recycling. She wanted them to learn, try their hand at turning a compost pile, attend talks and then bring that knowledge into their lives. She wanted them to make posters about the importance of harvest restrictions that they could take to their own communities.

She drew hands signing papers. She wanted festival attendees to write letters to the governor and local lawmakers. This wasn't just going to be a weekend of entertainment; she was going to engage people in grassroots activism, while their kids did yoga, planted seeds, and played cooperative games.

A pleasant warmth flowed through her body as she envisioned the event, the people, and the experience.

Chapter 41

Early August was one of Brian's favorite times of year. The hot days and cool nights, the farm stands filled with freshly harvested produce, the prevalence of shooting stars at night. Of course, he knew they were meteors, nothing magical about them. Still, he felt a childlike sense of wonder and awe whenever he saw one streak across the sky.

Walking down sunny Main Street with nothing on his agenda for the afternoon, he felt an unusual sense of freedom. Maybe he would drop into the cafe for an iced chai. Maybe he would go to a yo… nope, the café suddenly looked like the most attractive option, since Claire had just entered it. She was wearing a knee length skirt and a business kind of blouse. She carried a stack of papers. Her legs made his brain feel foggy. Yes, an iced chai would be perfect. He crossed the street toward the café. As he closed the distance, he saw her through the window. Claire was giving an animated presentation to the owner, showing him something on a brochure. Ahh. Was she selling him on the festival? Had she started work on this already? He really needed to book that meeting with Arthur.

Brian ducked into the bookstore as Claire emerged from the cafe and skipped, actually *skipped*, down the sidewalk toward Mazzie's Yoga. She would be passing the bookstore in one, two, and…

"Oh, hey, Claire! Fancy meeting you here," he said, emerging as casually as possible from the bookstore.

"Uh, hi." She seemed a little tense.

"I hear you got a fellowship from the ARM Foundation. Congrats!"

"Yeah," she said, her shoulders relaxing. "I'm still on cloud nine! I already started registering for classes!"

"Glad I was able to help."

"What?"

"I figured you could use a leg up, so I called over and put in a good word for you."

"Wow. That was really…"

Brian looked at the pavement. He wanted to at least appear modest, even though he knew she would be thrilled.

"Presumptuous. What made you think I'd need your help?"

Ouch.

"Are you always so condescending," she asked. "Or is it just with me?"

Is she joking? He looked at her face. Her dark brown eyes seared into him, and he felt burned. "Mmm. Hmm. Well, Claire, you… have a nice day."

He turned and walked in the opposite direction, neither knowing, nor caring where he was going. He had seen that conversation going so much differently in his mind. What had just happened? He had gone out on a limb for her, yet she seemed to have nothing but disdain for him. Could it be that Claire genuinely did not like him? He had believed they were developing a deep friendship — more than that, a budding romance — finding so many areas of real connection.

Then why are you walking away, Brian? Don't be an ass.

What?

Turn around and go after her. Find out what's wrong.

He sighed and turned around. She wasn't on the sidewalk anymore, but he knew where she was. He strode to the bookstore, suddenly feeling a deep sense of purpose. She would be making her pitch, he knew. That was just fine. He had time to wait for her.

When he reached the door, however, he discovered her standing on the other side of it, arms by her sides. Something about the way she held herself seemed… *dejected?* He pulled the

216

door open and she didn't move. He looked at her profile; it was as if she was lost. "Claire?"

"Hmmm?"

She didn't move, just stared into the bookstore. Nothing seemed unusual inside.

"What's going on?"

She took a deep breath and exhaled heavily with a sigh.

"Are you okay?" He put his hand on her shoulder as lightly as possible. "You, uh, seem upset. Wanna go somewhere and talk for a minute?"

"Why?"

"Because it seems like maybe… because I want… because… Why not?"

She turned toward him and he could see sadness in her face.

"Come on. Let's walk to the common, get some fresh air." He opened the door and gently guided her outside, his hand on her upper back.

"Did I offend you in some way?" he asked, leading her down the sidewalk.

"Didn't you think I could do it on my own?"

"Do what on your own?"

"Get that fellowship. Why did you have to help?"

The call of the downy woodpecker filled the air. They crossed the street and sat on a bench under the woodpecker's oak tree.

"Why wouldn't I help? Isn't that what friends do?"

"I could have done it myself." She examined his face and he felt his cheeks flush.

"Except you missed the deadline."

"But they called me and invited me to apply."

He smiled. "Because I called them, and I went to their board meeting and spoke on your behalf."

"Why? Why would you do that?"

He sighed and smiled at her, "Because I could, and because, Silly, you're worth it."

A tear rolled down her face.

"I thought this would make you happy," he said, wondering what the hell to do now. Why on earth was she crying?

"It does," she sniffed. "I just wish you hadn't helped."

"But then you wouldn't have the fellowship," he said, wiping her tears with his thumb.

She glared at him, then narrowed her eyes.

Damn. She's pissed.

"You're pretty hot when you're mad, you know."

She flared her nostrils and stormed away.

Chapter 42

C laire heaved open the door to Mazzie's Yoga and huffed, "Ugh! He is such a creep!"

"Om," a chorus chanted.

Why is it so dark, she wondered, before noticing the slivers of light streaking across the floor from the edges of light-blocking drapes. As Claire's eyes adjusted to the dark, she saw about twenty people meditating in the candlelit room. Mazzie looked up from her position on the floor and shook her head. Claire flushed and sank to the floor, assuming a half lotus position. Apparently, she was early; that was something new. This was the day they had said they'd meet for iced tea, wasn't it? The day Claire was to deliver her brochure and proposal to Mazzie?

Her mind raced while the chanting continued around her. She closed her eyes and tried to get comfortable, but her leg was twitching, and now her elbow itched. She felt bloated. She should have peed before coming in, but she was not going to be even more rude by getting up and leaving. This was miserable. This was not how meditation was supposed to be. She and Mazzie were so different; it was a wonder they were friends. She was terrible at meditation and yoga; Mazzie was building her whole life around it. Sometimes, Claire was sure Mazzie was judging her, disappointed in her, just wanting her to be more like a real yoga person. There was a word for that. It wasn't called yoga person; it was called… yogana. No…yogini? Yes.

And Brian… of all people to run into. He always started out so friendly, and for a fleeting moment she would think she could trust him, but then he'd attack. "I'll throw some ideas your way," as if she didn't have ideas. "I put in a good word for you," as if she needed his stamp of approval to get funding from the ARM Foundation. She had been valedictorian of her graduating class, for God's sake. She'd never needed anyone's help with academics.

So why was she so behind in her career? Why was it that her old college classmates had established careers and she was just graduating? Maybe it was focus. Maybe it was raising a kid alone. Maybe it was…

"Namaste," Mazzie said, bowing at the waist.

"Namaste," the class repeated, bowing toward Mazzie.

Mazzie turned on the lights as people put their yoga mats and props away. She handed Claire a swiffer, "Would you mind?"

"It's the least I can do after barging in on your class like that."

By the time Claire finished cleaning the floors, the students were gone and she and Mazzie had the space to themselves. Claire recounted her interaction with Brian on the sidewalk.

Mazzie took the swiffer from her and put it away. "You do know, all men are not Jim."

"I know that. It's just—"

"At some point, you need to learn to trust again."

"But, Brian…"

"Helped you get a fellowship? That's really nice."

"Abusers start by being helpful, then they take control. Remember Jim helped me get that promotion?"

"There's a difference between being controlling and reliable."

Claire shuddered, remembering the way Jim had looked so sweetly at her as he said cruel things, the way he would gently remind her that without him, she'd be nothing. It was getting hard to breathe. "Suddenly, he had me cut off from everyone. Everything was him and me, us and no one else."

She tried to suck in air, to inhale deeply through her nose and mouth at the same time. The room was spinning. She felt nauseous. "I was trapped, and he—"

Mazzie came fast at Claire, took her hands, and looked into her eyes. She inhaled slowly. Mazzie's eyes were calm and soothing.

Claire felt the breath coming now, the room expanding to its real spaciousness. Everything was still and quiet again, save for the birdsongs coming through the windows. "Oh, my God, Maz, you're right. I go there without even thinking about it. I go right back there and I get stuck."

Mazzie exhaled and nodded.

Claire followed Mazzie's lead. "I'm sorry, Maz."

"I'm sorry, too. I'm sorry that happened to you, Honey."

They released each other's hands.

"Let's go to the beach, huh?" Mazzie suggested.

"Good idea."

Meditating on the sand, with the ocean's gentle breeze and the sound of the waves lapping against the shore, was much easier than on the hard wood of the yoga studio floor. Claire sat next to Mazzie, chanting "Om," until she no longer heard Mazzie chanting next to her. After a period of time that seemed to go on forever, she felt Mazzie's hand on hers and she opened her eyes.

"Thanks, Maz."

Mazzie hugged her. "What kind of friend would I be if I didn't help you move forward?"

They took a deep breath together and released it slowly, smiling at each other. She retrieved a brochure from her bag and put it in Mazzie's lap. Mazzie examined it, rose and wandered around the beach with it, gesturing and nodding. She turned back to Claire and let out a happy squeal.

"You like it?"

"Like it? This is positive energy, Woman! This… This is how you know you're on your path, because it's like… the flow is just… you know? My chakras are like… Wow!"

"Yeah?"

"Yeah! We're gonna do something to make this town and this shore and this earth stronger. How awesome is that?"

Chapter 43

It seemed like everything was coming together, with the response to her idea for the festival and the crowd pressing in to Art Gal. "Eco-cultcha," looked phenomenal. After accepting Brian's work, Jane had selected a few other artists to be part of the exhibit. *Spread the risk*, her mother had been repeating to herself and Claire for the last month-and-a-half since they had come up with the idea.

All the art flowed together well. The playlist was perfect for the event: a blend of ethereal lounge music, and earthy drum pieces. The only problem was the caterers were arriving now, instead of at 5 pm, as Claire had instructed. She had wanted the food laid out way before patrons began arriving. *Nothing I can do now but let it go.* She watched them lay out the food on a table at the back of the room.

Jane added artful decorations to the table. "Mmm. Doesn't this look delicious."

It looked a little too delicious to Claire. She went to the back office, retrieved a few plastic zipper bags and returned to the table.

"What are you doing?"

Claire took a spoon and swept the caviar off the plates and into the plastic bags.

"What is this? What are you doing?"

Claire continued to remove the caviar from the plates.

"Claire! That caviar is a garnish!"

"These are fish eggs."

"Exactly! Very. Expensive. Delicious fish eggs."

Claire closed the bags full of caviar. Her mother reached for them, but Claire held them aloft.

"Didn't we agree the whole theme of this show is harmony with nature?"

"What could be more harmonious than people gratefully eating..."

"We have a population of shorebirds that is dying out due to starvation because we keep 'gratefully eating' THEIR food," Claire said, using air quotes to emphasize her point.

Her mother responded with a blank stare. "They eat caviar?"

Claire smiled and carried the bags to Brian, who was standing by one of his photos, looking unsure of what to do.

"Oh, fish eggs," he said, looking at the bag.

"For that lab experiment you're planning."

"That's surprisingly nice of you."

"Surprisingly?"

"I mean, considering how much you hate me."

"I don't hate you."

Brian looked at his feet and seemed oddly vulnerable, "Thanks, but after our last few interactions, I finally get that you are just not into me."

"I'm not into you? You're the one seeing someone else."

"What gave you that idea?"

"Oh, please." She hated it when guys were coy; it was a sure sign they were hiding something.

He raised an eyebrow at her.

"Tilly? You think I don't see what's going on?"

"She's my intern. You know that."

"Intern," Claire snorted. "Right."

"She is. What's your problem?"

"I don't have a problem."

"Then ease up," he said. "Look, if you don't want to date me, that's fine, but I've done nothing but try to help you. In fact, I talked to my boss at Flora and Fauna about your festival."

Warning bells rang in Claire's head. She had been working so hard on that project. Why would Brian bring it to his boss without even asking her first? Her whole body tensed. "You're stealing my work now?"

He frowned at her. "Now, why would you say something like that? You know, I try to be nice to you, and you… every time… it's like… If you didn't want me to share it, why—"

"You didn't even ask," she hissed.

"So, you assume I'm trying to claim it?" He said, his voice steely. "Why did you give it to me, if I wasn't supposed to share it?"

Brian glared at her; his face hard. He had never been angry with her before now. Now, he was obviously furious. At her. And she felt — what was that feeling? She took a moment to identify the sensations in her body. There was the tightness in her muscles that came with frustration, the pounding heartbeat she typically felt when she was angry, but there was something else. As she looked at him and acknowledged his anger, she realized something significant was missing. *Brian is really pissed at me. And I do NOT feel afraid, not even a little bit. In fact, I feel totally safe. Huh.*

She looked into his cold eyes, inhaled deeply and exhaled the words, "You're right. I overreacted."

"It's not even that," he said. "It's… look, you barely know me. I have been trying to change that, you know? I'm totally into you, but it's like you look at me and don't see me."

Claire looked down, ashamed, frustrated with herself. She knew better, and after her conversations with Mazzie, she knew how to…. *Wait. What did he just say?*

"You're totally into me?" she asked.

"Duh! Didn't my cooking, my helping you, and that kiss get the message across?"

"But afterward, you—"

She smiled, suddenly feeling shy, flustered, and excited like she had in high school when Jon Marsh first reached for her hand. She looked into Brian's eyes for a moment, until Teddy, a.k.a. 'Super Artist' ran up to him and hugged his legs.

"Birdman, I've been waiting for you!"

"Hey, Super… Artist?"

"I protected the gallery with my supersonic tongue when Mama and Gramma hung everything."

"No supersonic tongue tonight, though, Sweetie, remember? You're Super Artist, not Super Frog, and you've got paint on your cape. Show Brian."

Teddy spun around, a blur of color, then ran off. She winked at Brian then followed her son. Had she just left the man hanging? She looked back at him. Brian stood still, watching her, an odd expression on his face.

Brian watched Claire follow Teddy across the room to the surreal nature film projected on the wall above the food table. They wended their way through a sea of people. He marveled at how deftly Claire maneuvered her son and kept the boy in check.

Another ethereal lounge song played. The music was getting on his nerves, but he moved with it anyway, hoping no one would notice his lame attempt at dancing.

An elderly woman approached with a middle-aged woman, maybe an aging model, wearing a large fur. *Here is someone else who's missing the point,* he thought. *What is that? Seal?* Thinking about it made him feel ill. *Poor baby.* It wasn't even cold out, yet here was this woman wearing a pelt from an intelligent and beautiful creature. He shuddered. On the other hand, these two women presented a perfect opportunity for education. If one or both of them bought a piece, then they would show it off to all their friends and they would be starting conversations about wildlife rehabilitation all over the region, at every fancy dinner party or club gathering.

"What do you think of the work?" He asked the women.

"Oh, it's quite stunning," said the woman in the pelt. "Are you one of the artists?"

"Be careful, Teddy," Claire warned, as he threaded himself around her legs and Jane's legs. She was trying to focus on the conversation Jane was having with the two other artists whose work was displayed, but between Teddy, the film, the music, and replaying Brian's words in her mind, she was having a little trouble keeping up.

"Sweetheart, you met Zhena. Yes?" her mother asked, gesturing to a voluptuous redhead dressed in varying shades of purple.

She nodded. "You did the film. I love it."

Zhena shoved an h'ors d'ouvre into her delicate mouth and smiled. "Thanks."

Claire wanted to laugh; she had always thought of artists as having so much class.

"And Sage is from New Haven, near where *Brian* grew up," her mother enthused, placing heavy emphasis on Brian's name.

"I discovered Sage at Oceanside Art Colony, Mom. Remember?"

"Of course! But did you realize she's from New Haven, *Connecticut*?"

"How was your residency, Sage?" Claire asked, ignoring her mother's pointed stare.

"Amazing! I got more done in those three months. The Delaware Bay is just so inspiring," Sage said, in a gentle, yet commanding voice that made Claire feel instant admiration for the woman.

"She created the reclaimed trash art, Dear."

"I know. *Washed Up in the Delaware* is brilliant, Sage," Claire said.

Sage released a happy sigh. "Thanks! If you love this project, wait 'til you see the new series of augmented photos I started."

"Augmented photos?"

Sage leaned in conspiratorially, "I've started augmenting large format photos with refuse and found objects I've collected from—"

Claire tried to listen. She loved Sage's work and wanted to hear what was probably a fascinating story. But at the moment there were too many distractions.

First, Mazzie and Greg entered arm in arm and Mazzie waved, displaying a big diamond ring. Then Tilly, looking like a total knockout, entered and made a beeline for Brian. And he hugged her.

What happened to, "I'm totally into you?" Claire never would have pegged Brian for a player; he seemed far too nerdy, which she adored, but that was beside the point. What was he doing flirting with her and then hugging the cartoon barbie/intern who was at least ten years younger than him?

"Claire?" Her mother's touch on her arm brought Claire back to the conversation.

"Trash is everywhere, really," Sage said.

"It sure is," Claire agreed, looking back at Tilly.

Sage launched into a lengthy description of her dumpster diving activities.

Claire nodded as if she was listening. Really, she was trying to listen. Sage was saying something about hand sanitizer. But across the room, Brian and Tilly were engaged in an animated conversation. If only she could read lips.

"During soft shell season, the fishermen leave all sorts of refuse," Sage continued.

"Wow," Claire said.

"Can I steal this lovely young lady away from you for a moment?" Frank wrapped his arm around Claire's shoulders and steered her to the food table, then whispered, "You looked a little lost."

"Oh, it's nothing. You know…"

"It's hard to focus on mere business when you're in the middle of falling in love."

"Falling in love! What are you talking about, Dad?"

"I see the way you look at him; the way he looks at you."

"Who?"

"Come off it, Claire. I'm your father."

She sighed and returned her gaze to the man of the hour, as he lifted her son into his arms to get a better view of a painting.

"So, he helped you get a fellowship, huh?"

"As if I couldn't do it on my own!"

"You're an independent woman," her father affirmed.

"Thank you!"

"The last thing you need is some guy trying to be supportive of your dreams."

"Yeah! Wait. What?"

"I mean," her father looked into her eyes. "You don't want a relationship like Mazzie's and Greg's or, gag, your mother's and mine."

"Yeah, it's great he finally proposed and everything, but I'm just worried she's going to disappear."

"And you'll lose your best friend?"

"Come on, Dad. I didn't mean that. I just meant…"

Frank raised his eyebrows. "She's always been there for you, and as long as they've been together, he's never gotten in the way. You, on the other hand, have shut out many people who love you in your quest to find someone to confirm that you are just as stupid and incapable as you think you are."

"I… I'm not stupid and incapable."

"Now, Jim was perfect for you. He let you know on a daily basis you were worth nothing without him. If you had stayed with him, you could still have that kind of relationship, and the added bonus would be he'd be showing Teddy the right way for a strong man to treat a woman."

Claire watched Teddy remove his Super Artist cape and tie it around Brian's neck. She sighed. "Brian was just being nice to me, Dad. He's with someone else."

"Really?"

She scanned the room, then pointed out Tilly. "Over there."

Frank gestured toward Brian, who was totally engrossed in Teddy. "Doesn't seem like it."

"Oh, geez." She left her father's side to gather her son.

"Sweetheart, Brian is working now. Let's go chill out in Gramma's office."

"Aww. Do I have to?"

"Just for a little while."

Brian waved at Teddy as Claire led him away. Sadness washed over him. *That little boy is extraordinary, so much more fun to talk to than most of the adults in the room.* He scanned the gallery for someone to help him feel less awkward. He saw the hefty hostess from the diner sneak up on Tilly, slide her arms around her waist, and kiss the back of her neck. Tilly turned around and kissed her passionately. They were such an odd couple, but both so grateful to Brian for introducing them to each other.

Chapter 44

B y the time they arrived at the diner, Claire was a little tipsy. Champagne always went straight to her head.

Vinnie greeted them in his usual boisterous manner, and they slid into a booth.

"Congratulations, Sweetheart," he said, kissing Jane's cheek. "I hear you're postponing retirement. People been coming in all night talking about your environmental show and the new community space. What's it called?"

"Why, thank you, Vin," Jane beamed. "We're calling it Eco-Cultcha! It was all Claire's idea."

"The kid's turned us both into hippie freaks and, Vin, it's profitable," Frank said with a wink.

"I might start painting again, too," Jane said. "Maybe a series on native plant species. Ooh! Or invasive plants! What do you think, Claire?"

"I love it!"

"You don't paint, Gramma!"

"Actually," her dad said, "Gramma's paintings won some awards back in— Join us!" He interrupted himself and waved in the direction of the door.

Claire turned and saw Brian coming to their table. She gasped, then glared at her father. Brian loped over and slid into the booth next to her.

"What are we talking about?" Brian whispered in Claire's ear.

His breath was warm and sent shivers down her body. *Control your chakras, Claire*, she imagined Mazzie saying. She inhaled deeply and let it out slowly.

"Our new business endeavor," she whispered back, wondering if her breath in his ear affected him the same way.

Brian flashed a thumbs up at Jane.

Claire looked at her mother. "How come I never knew about your art awards?"

Jane shrugged. "I don't paint for the awards, Dear. Anyway, it was just more practical to represent other artists than to try to sell my work."

"And you did a wonderful job, Darling. You are an excellent businesswoman with a great eye for art."

Jane leaned into her husband, an expression on her face that Claire had seen many times before but had never been able to identify. Now, she recognized it, the feeling of trust, of knowing the person you were with believed in you and had your back. She had experienced a glimpse of that feeling the first time she met Brian in the bookstore, and he said she had a lot to offer the field of wildlife ecology, and again in the gallery when he'd said she had something special. *What would it be like to feel that all the time? To be with someone that supportive?*

Jane sniffled and smiled at them. "When do you and Teddy start school?"

"Right after the juvenile crabs molt."

"Aha," her mother said, wearing an expression of total confusion.

"End of August, Mom."

"I have some good news," Brian said, sitting up taller and turning to face Claire. "My boss wants to meet you. Monday."

"What?"

"To discuss your festival and see if we can pull it together."

Claire's jaw dropped. "Thanks, but I really can…"

Jane groaned, and Claire looked over in time to see her mother rolling her eyes.

"I can do…"

She felt a kick under the table and looked up to see her father glaring at her.

"I can do this…"

She felt another kick under the table.

"Myself," she finished, although now she was somewhat confused about the whole idea. She had planned to do it herself. She believed that she could do it herself. Why was everyone so insistent on her having help?

"Claire," Brian said. "This is a huge undertaking. No one can do this kind of thing alone, not without huge money."

"I've already gotten five local sponsors donating supplies and food and a couple thousand bucks."

"Of course, you did," Brian said, as if it was no big deal.

Claire nodded, proud.

"Teddy, did you know your mom is a real live superhero?"

"Yeah," Teddy said. "Crab Woman."

Frank coughed and shot her a pointed look.

"So, Crab Woman, how many more sponsors do you think you could get with Flora and Fauna behind you?"

Frank nudged her under the table. She looked at her dad, who looked ready to kill her, then at Teddy, who stared hopefully at her, and her mom, whose eyes were wide in anticipation.

"Umm…. Well…" She peeked at Brian's smiling face and smiled back, suddenly sheepish.

After her parents drove away with Teddy for a special sleepover, Claire led Brian down the block near the diner. She was eager to discuss what she envisioned in detail. Of course, he had read her proposal, but reading about the idea was not as powerful as seeing the presentation of it in the real location. Twenty minutes later, they stood on the sidewalk by Book & Bean, and she spread her arms out, as if drawing a scene in mid-air.

She described her vision: two small stages at either end of the town common, one with demonstrations of various wildlife-friendly activities and the other with performing arts. A series of lectures and grassroots engagement events at the library. Workshops in tents around the green. It would be colorful, despite the muted tones of horseshoe crabs and red knots.

Children would be playing and singing. Adults would be congregating and brainstorming.

"So, it would look like that."

"I see it! I see it!" Brian said.

She smiled up at him, and then he put his hand on her back, just above her waistline. It was more than a friendly gesture.

She caught her breath. "Wait!"

He pulled his hand away. "Sorry."

"So, *what's* going on with you and Tilly?"

He sighed. "Tilly? She's my intern. What's left to say?"

"You hugged her tonight. You show up everywhere with her."

"She's my INTERN," he insisted, irritation in his voice. "We work together ALL the time."

"But you hugged her."

Brian turned to her, put his hands on her shoulders, and lowered his head so he could see her eye to eye. "She's from L.A," he enunciated. "Everyone hugs everyone there, apparently."

"Mmmhmmm."

"She's also GAY."

"What?"

"Claire, Tilly is madly in love with your friend from the diner."

"Bel?"

"The one who keeps changing her hair color."

"Really!" She said, shocked. Since when was Bel gay?

"They're madly in love with each other," Brian said.

"Huh!" she giggled, then turned serious. "But you—"

"But I what?"

"Haven't called in, like, a month." She hated that her voice was rising. It sounded like she was whining.

He sighed. "I've been inundated at work, took a trip to Massachusetts to make a case for YOU to get that fellowship, been trying to do my part to promote the art show, reading the festival proposal of yours, and, quite frankly, kinda freaked out by your ever-changing moods."

"My ever-changing moods?"

"One time I see you, you smile. The next time, you scowl. Then, you won't look at me at all. I don't know how to read you, and—"

"It's that bad, huh?"

"Sure feels like it."

"Well, you kept showing up with Tilly, and I thought you were some sort of player, and—"

"Player?" He laughed and turned to face her. "Me? Claire, you're the first woman I've even considered dating since my wife died!"

"Really?"

"Three years and four months ago!"

"Oh," she said softly, then looked at the ground, embarrassed.

"Claire?"

"Yes?" She raised her eyes to meet his.

"Would you go out with me?"

"You mean, like, on a date?"

"On an actual date. Maybe to a movie or a nice restaurant. There's gotta be some vegan-friendly place in the city, right?"

She nodded.

"Think your parents will watch the superhero tomorrow night?"

"I can ask. There's a place called Green Tara I've wanted to try forever."

Brian smiled and kissed her cheek. "Now, let's get ready for our meeting with my boss."

He returned his hand to her back, and this time she didn't fight it but reveled in the warmth and tingling filling her body as they continued down the street, and she animatedly described the festival. Her heart was pounding so furiously, she was sure he could hear its drum beat, and yet for the first time in years, she felt completely safe.

Chapter 45

C laire could not believe she was actually in the office of Delaware Flora and Fauna Service, speaking with the guy who ran the operation. Not only was she speaking with Arthur, but he was actually listening to her, and so was Brian. They hovered over a large map and watched her place index cards with pictures of storefronts and data on it. They were hovering and listening. She was basking in the glow of the experience, even reveling in the musty odor and overabundance of duct tape.

Arthur interrupted her reverie. "How would this benefit the bookstore or the yoga studio?"

"Book and Bean are excited about boosting sales of nature and tourist books. Mazzie wants to increase the exposure of her business, so she's doing a kids' class called Yoga Birds and Yoga Crabs just for the festival."

Brian nudged Arthur, and the two men exchanged a look. *That seems like a good sign.*

"Let's say these local businesses can't provide enough capital," Arthur said.

"Then we can reach out to the whole county, even the state board of tourism. This could be huge, like Newport Folk Festival or Clearwater."

Arthur whistled. "This is quite a vision, young lady."

Brian cleared his throat and glared at Arthur.

"Ah, I'm sorry. I mean, Claire. How would you feel about partnering with Delaware Flora and Fauna?"

In the parking lot outside Flora and Fauna, he and Claire looked at each other and giggled. She did a little victory dance, then threw her arms around him.

"Thank you! Thank you so much," Claire said, then kissed his cheek and looked for a response.

He looked into her eyes and wrapped his arms around her waist.

"Thank you."

"For what?"

"Are you kidding? Your insight and hard work and the fact that you were willing to share it with Flora and Fauna. This could really make a difference. You could really make a difference, Claire."

She smiled, searched his eyes, took a deep breath, and kissed him on the mouth quickly. His lips were soft. She pulled away to examine his face. He smiled, pulled her just a bit closer, and kissed her. His lips lingered on hers. Warmth spread from her mouth throughout her entire body. She giggled and melted into his arms, allowing her lips to part and his tongue to enter her mouth, entwine with his. His breath was warm and pleasant, and in some way that made no sense to Claire, he tasted like high school. Claire inhaled deeply. She loved his scent. It wasn't perfume-y, like cologne or after-shave, but fresh and clean and raw.

Why did I push him away for so long? She exhaled, letting the thought go, and allowed her hand to caress his back, to feel the long, taut muscles through the fabric of his button-down.

"Do you two have dinner plans tonight?" he asked.

"Us two?"

"Can I take you and Teddy to dinner?"

"Ummm."

"Maybe a kid movie after or a mini-golf excursion?"

She smiled. "If you think you can handle the pressure of playing against Super Golfer!"

"And how about lunch? Can I make you lunch?"

"When?"

"Now."

"Lunch? Now? Don't you have work to do?"

"Everyone needs to stop for lunch. Let's celebrate. I've got some fizzy water and fresh OJ, and — do you like veggie burritos?"

"Who doesn't?"

"I've got peppers and onions, and potatoes, tofu, avocado… I make a mean guacamole."

"Cilantro or oregano?"

"Both plus a hint of garlic."

"As long as you let me help," she said, remembering the mushy texture of the enchiladas.

Brian strode to the passenger side of his vehicle and opened the door for her. "Madame Superhero?"

She climbed inside and turned to face him. She wanted to kiss him again. Instead, she put her hand over his heart and smiled. "You are the superhero. You are helping me make all my dreams come true."

That was cheezy, she thought immediately. *Why did I say that? What's wrong with me? I'm going to scare him away. Oh, my —*

Suddenly, she felt his hand on her heart and his mouth on hers. She smiled and felt him smile too.

"That may be the most beautiful thing anyone has ever said to me, Claire."

"Oh," she sighed into his mouth, finding his tongue again, feeling Brian's heart racing under her palm.

"You are so beautiful, Claire."

She slid her hand from his chest to his neck and caressed his strong jaw for just a moment. "Let's go."

He pressed his hand into her chest gently, then pulled away and slowly closed the car door.

Chapter 46

B y the time they arrived at his house, her body wanted more than just kissing.

"You hungry?" he asked as he took her hand and led her into the foyer.

"Mmm. Not especially," she said, playing with his fingers.

She paused and looked around. "I recognize that hanging sculpture from your show. It looks great there."

He smiled, pulled her to him, and kissed her neck.

"Mmm," she offered, running her finger along the outside of his ear.

"Mmm," he replied, sliding the palm of his hand from her hip to her underarm. His hand was so close to her breast. It hadn't been caressed in so long. Feeling him move his fingertips underneath it, she gasped, then had a fleeting anxious thought. *Oh no. What bra am I wearing?* But as he slipped his hand away from her breast, around her back and undid her bra, she released the concern. Suddenly, her shirt and bra were up around her neck, and his tongue was playing with her nipple. The warmth of his tongue, the gentle caress of his hand sent shivers throughout her body.

"Are you cold?" he asked, moving her against the wall.

"No, I. I. Ahhh. Oh, my God, Brian."

"Am I moving too fast for you?"

"No."

She gasped. She should say yes, shouldn't she? Why? She wasn't sixteen. Didn't she trust him? Isn't that why she had agreed to "lunch" anyway? Didn't she want him? Wetness dripped down her leg. She had never been so aroused.

"Claire? Honey?" He brought his face to hers, concerned. "Are you okay?"

She nodded. "Take me."

He kissed her firmly on the mouth, pressed his hands into her thighs over her skirt, then slipped them underneath the fabric. He ran his hands up the outside of each thigh, then up the back, grabbed her behind, then finally slid one hand up the inside of her thigh just far enough to feel how much she wanted him. He moved his hand higher, played with her panty line, placed his flat palm on the outside of her panties. Her lips quivered. He gently slid her panties off, then brought two fingers to her lips, gently spread them apart, inserted another finger inside her. They both gasped.

"I want your skin on mine," she whispered.

He pulled away from her and slipped his shirt over his head. There were the abs she had been dreaming about ever since she first set eyes on them.

"Take off your pants, Brian."

He reached for the button on his cargo pants, undid the zipper and pulled them off. He stood naked before her, erect. He had the most beautiful cock she had ever seen. The others she had accepted as a kind of a means to an end, but this one she wanted. She pulled her bra and skirt off.

He beamed at her, "You're stunning."

"So are you."

Before she could even take another breath, she was in his arms, her legs wrapped around his waist, her mouth sucking on his neck, and he was ascending the stairs.

Then they were on the bed, and he was poised over her, the condom in place.

"Are you ready, Claire?"

She kissed him, took him in her hands, and guided him to the opening, where she rubbed the tip in circles, put her hands on his hips, and pressed herself toward him. They both moaned, as he filled her for the first time, a perfect fit. She held him there for a moment, kissed him, and let him move inside her at his own pace. They rocked with each other gently at first, moaning and kissing and caressing, then faster and faster, the breath coming faster, the cries louder, until the energy coursed up the length of her spine and out the top of her head and they shuddered in climax. She could feel it wasn't over yet. Waves of energy and emotion flowed through her in a way she had never experienced. Her whole body felt electrified. And he was still hard, pulsing, and thrusting.

"Did you come?" she asked.

"Uh, huh, and I'm going to again."

Again, he thrust into her, shuddering, crying out. And as he came, she climaxed again as well, riding the wave of coursing energy, her back arching beneath him.

She sank back into the soft bed linens, spent and more relaxed than she had been years.

He kissed her and panted, "That was mind-blowing."

She wrapped her arms and legs around him, holding him close. "Truly."

"Can we do that again soon?"

She giggled, "I'd like to."

He held her close and rolled onto his back, pulling her on top of him, still inside her.

"You are amazing, Claire. You know that?"

"Thank you."

"I'm not just talking about in bed. I mean, you are an amazing woman."

She let her head rest on his chest. "And you are an amazing man."

"You're beautiful, you're brilliant, you're kind. You're a great mom. You're funny and creative, and you even cook. Well, you say you do. You haven't cooked for me yet."

"Why don't you let me make you lunch, then?"

"We'll do it together. How about that?"

"Deal." She kissed him again. "I love the way you taste."

"I love the way you taste. All of you."

"You haven't tasted all of me yet."

His eyes went wide. "Not yet. I will, though."

"I'll hold you to that."

He kissed her. "I can't wait."

She giggled.

"This is where the real magic happens," he said, leading her into the kitchen and pulling things from the fridge.

"And there I was under the impression we just made magic in another part of the house."

"Baby," he turned from the fridge, wrapped his arms around her bare waist, and whispered into her ear, "That wasn't magic; that was earthshaking, groundbreaking, mountain-moving divine ecstasy."

"Oh." Claire leaned into him for a moment, and he reveled in the feel of her weight against him. "Well, then… Show me the magic."

"As you wish," he said, watching her find her way around the kitchen like she already lived there. He loved seeing Claire take charge of things. She washed her hands, found a cutting board near the stove and a knife. He handed her a red bell pepper and an onion. They worked in silent synchronicity as if they had been cooking together all their lives.

"Brian," Claire said. "Is there anything you can't do? Anything you're not good at?"

"I've heard I'm pretty bad at cleaning."

She looked around, nodded. "Hmmm. Anything else you're keeping from me? Because you seem kind of almost perfect."

"Actually, I have been keeping a secret from you, and I don't know how to break it to you."

Her shoulders tensed visibly. He lit the stove, warmed the olive oil in the skillet and added salt, cumin, oregano, then went to Claire and massaged her shoulders.

"I'm hoping this won't be a deal-breaker," he said, turning her around to face him. He looked into her eyes. "Claire, I really love cars."

"Huh?"

"I mean, it's a thing. I'm like, seriously into cars. It's something I share with my dad, and I just — the smell of motor oil, the sound of a finely tuned engine. That Land Rover out there is almost like family to me."

"You're serious."

He shrugged. "Growing up, you know, we didn't discern between eco-friendly and not; that wasn't even a category. But since the emergence of biodiesel and electric cars and hybrids, and… well, there's all this new technology coming up. Claire, they're making roads that recharge electric cars now!"

He could feel his blood pumping, the excitement building as he shared the news with her.

Claire looked stunned. "You're into cars."

He nodded.

"I'd love to share it with you. I mean, I know you hate them, but they're not all bad. My Rover runs on the refuse from Vin's Diner, actually. Oh, God, please say this isn't a deal-breaker."

She looked into his eyes. He had expected to see disappointment, maybe even anger. Instead, what he perceived was amusement.

"So, you're kinda somewhat like a normal guy… except you're nice."

"Ummm… yeah?"

"And you're not out there driving ATVs or anything?"

"God, no."

"And you actually are adorable when you talk about—"

She wrinkled her nose. "What's that smell?"

He sniffed. "Oh, shit! The spices."

He dashed to the stove where the cumin and oregano were burnt in the cast iron skillet.

"I guess we'll have to start again," he smiled, sheepish.

Chapter 47

It was funny how much could change in a short time. Two weeks earlier, Claire was helping her mother run an environment-themed art show. She had thought she was going to singlehandedly create a large festival, and she had already gathered some support. Two weeks ago, Claire was single and pushing away the man she had been attracted to since they met.

Now, Claire sat by the outdoor fireplace in her parents' backyard. While her father and the man she was dating built a fire, Claire and her mother whittled sticks into skewers for roasting marshmallows. Teddy was, of course, flying around in a superhero costume.

"You're going to a car show, like as an activity?" her father asked.

"An eco-friendly car show, Dad."

"Wow. This must really be love!"

"No pressure, though, Brian," she said, rolling her eyes. "Hey, Super Grampa, think you could get your grandson to take that fire hazard off his back?"

Frank looked at Teddy's cape, rushed to him, tickled him, and swooped him into the air. "Oh, no! The marshmallows are in danger!""

"Teddy and Grampa to the rescue!" Teddy yelled.

Claire's dad flew her son into the house. Two down; one to go. Claire shot her mother a pointed look.

Taking the hint, Jane headed for the house, too. "Don't forget the graham crackers, superheroes."

Claire rummaged through her bag, pulled out the black and red tissue paper package with the photo inside, and brought it to the fire. She unwrapped it, put the tissue paper in the fire, stared at the picture for a few seconds. Brian put his chin on her shoulder.

"How you feeling?"

"Ready to put my past behind me."

"I'm so proud of you," he whispered in her ear, then caressed her cheek.

"I'm proud of me, too," she whispered in his ear. "And I appreciate you, Brian, so much."

She turned back to the fire, dropped the photo into the flames and watched it wither into ash.

As Brian put his arm around her waist and kissed the top of her head, she sighed happily. She didn't need to lean into him, but she wanted to. Allowing herself to rest against his body, she felt his sturdiness supporting her. To Claire's delight, Brian leaned into her, as well. In the distance, she saw the full moon starting to rise.

The End

Thank You

Thank you for reading *For the Birds*. If you enjoyed this book, please take a moment to write a review on the website where you purchased it. If you purchased it at a bookstore or borrowed it from your library, please be sure to let your bookseller or librarian know what you thought of it.

To learn more about the science behind the book and for discussion prompts, please see the Book Club Resources section at the back of this book.

Acknowledgements

This book is what it is thanks to the support I received from numerous people. Laura Chasen provided editorial assistance. Chris Buelow, of Massachusetts Flora and Fauna's Natural Heritage & Endangered Species Program, inspired the idea for this book and offered feedback. Linda Puth, lecturer at Yale's Department of Ecology and Evolutionary Biology, shared her course syllabus, which I used as the model for Brian's course syllabus. Bethany J. Miller, John Hauser, and Suzanne Decker are the rockstar beta readers who provided feedback on numerous drafts of the manuscript. My peeps in the Greater New Haven Writers' Group provided helpful notes on the first several chapters of the manuscript in its early stages. Anthony DeCarlo shared info about photography in pre-dawn light. Pattibelle Hastings invited me to work in her backyard garden when I needed to be in nature. My brilliant cousin Sue researched Delaware laws and sentencing for domestic abuse cases.

My amazing and dedicated Patreon subscribers — Mira Bartok, Nate Bixby, Susanni Douville, Genevieve Fraser, Tom & Charlene Fraser, Fernando Hendler, Doris Kelly, Robert Krause, and Susan McCaslin — provide consistent financial support and encouragement as I build my career.

About the Author

A digital nomad, Tara L. Roí currently resides in New England, where she writes novels about her two obsessions: love and climate change. Before turning to fiction, she worked as a journalist and covered numerous environmental issues, including climate change, agriculture, landmine and UXO pollution, and electronic waste management. The author also published a historical novel and a nonfiction book about climate change, using her real name.

For the Birds is the first of many romances that will be published under the pen name Tara L. Roí.

To learn more about the author, and be the first to find out about new and forthcoming books, events, and giveaways, sign up for Tara's newsletter at bit.ly/TaraLRoiEnews.

Book Club Resources

To learn more about the science behind the book, visit www.TaraLRoi.com

Discussion Questions:
1. What was your immediate reaction to *For the Birds*?
2. What makes the setting unique or important?
3. What themes did you detect in the novel?
4. What was your favorite quote or passage?
5. Did the story feel realistic to you?
6. Did the book's pace seem too fast/ too slow/ just right?
7. Which characters did you like best? Why?
8. Which characters did you like least? Why?
9. If you could read this story from another character's perspective, which would you choose?
10. Were you surprised to learn how much of the science in this book is actually based on fact?
11. What about this story surprised you?
12. This novel addresses a number of social and political issues, including domestic violence, environmental degradation, the value of art, and the realities of single parenting. How did it feel to read about these issues in a romance novel?
13. Which parts of the book stood out to you?
14. What did you think about the ending?
15. Would you read another book by Tara L. Roi? Why or why not?

About Bee Books

Bee Books publishes love stories and both fiction and nonfiction titles that address environmental issues or feature people who live in the margins of society. Learn more at BeeBooks.org.

Free Offer from Bee Books

If you loved *For the Birds* and you care about the impact of climate change on your life and future generations, you'll love Bee Books' eBooklet. *For Romantic Environmentalists* features *The Promise of Purple Berries in Spring*, a short story by Tara L. Roí, and *Tips for Climate-Smart Living*, a handy guide by Rebekah L. Fraser, author of *The Farmer's Guide to Climate Disruption*.

This booklet is free to you, when you sign up for Tara's email list at bit.ly/TaraLRoiEnews.